A HOLLOW DEATH

Is Justice more important than the law?

COLLEEN DUMAINE

ALSO BY THE AUTHOR

Beyond Goyder's Line – a tale of murder, mystery and love.
'A clever whodunnit...' – Readers' Favorite.

. . . . .

**To find out more about this book
or to contact the author, please visit:
www.vividpublishing.com.au/ahollowdeath**

Published by Vivid Publishing
A division of Fontaine Publishing Group
P.O. Box 948, Fremantle
Western Australia 6959
www.vividpublishing.com.au

Our printers ensures each of its paper suppliers to be environmentally responsible
as well, and not use papers sourced from endangered old growth forests, forests of
exceptional conservation value, or the Amazon Basin.

 A catalogue record for this
book is available from the
National Library of Australia

For my mother, my three sisters and my four granddaughters
– strong, loving, spirited females all.

'It follows that it is an arbitrary and unjust Government which compels its support from those whose will in relation to it is never consulted. That as women assist in maintaining the Government they have a right to say how they should be governed and by whom they shall be governed, in other words—to the vote.'

Mary Lee, Letter to women,
(from the S.A. Register, 14 April 1890, page 5)

ADELAIDE, 1894

Off the beaten track, this neck of the woods rarely hosts leather boots trampling its soils. Deep within the bushland, escarpments drop into stony gullies and narrow tracks thread through the scrub. During the autumn months, a southerly wind can flare up at dusk, chilling the air. The man slumped on his side is clad in a light cotton shirt and trousers, scant clothing for the cold night ahead. He awakens, a vague dream of flying over tree canopies still lingering. His right arm is wedged between the ground and the side of his head. Now the buoyancy of flight has waned his head is reeling. Taking in a deep breath, he wiggles his fingers. With his left hand he touches the crusty skin on his forehead and scratches off the congealed blood. The exposed gash bleeds. He presses his fingers over the wound, holds them firmly in place. The scent of damp eucalyptus leaves and heady bush flowers fills his nostrils. Resident magpies warble in the trees. Twilight shadows spread across the track. Pain rips through his body as he tries to sit up. Steeling himself, he rolls onto his stomach. A cold breeze gushes down the track, the towering eucalypts sway and creak. Try as he may, he cannot move his legs. Lying prone, he puts weight onto his hands and lifts his torso at least twenty inches off the ground. He heaves himself forward on his elbows, inches at a time. Later, in the buff glow of a full moon, he comes to a clearing and rests briefly before turning into it. Whirring, ticking, drumming insects fill the night, a boobook owl is calling.

THURSDAY, 9TH AUGUST 1894

Faith Ellsworth's late husband had once fancied himself a promising artist, however these days his atelier is used as an office for the Bethany Investigation Agency. Refurbished with two oak desks, comfortable chairs and deep shelves, only two of his paintings still adorn the walls. The sunny seascape is uplifting, but his self-portrait hangs from the picture rail for one reason only: it was his dying wish it remain there forever and a day. The gaunt man's eyes seem to watch every corner of the room, his skin the colour of citrus pith glows in the dark and his thin lips are eternally fixed in a down-turned smile. Why he wished to embody the ravages of illness on canvas is a mystery, as if death could be duped into doing away with the portrait and not the artist. Beth's desk is positioned away from the wall on which the painting hangs; her bookkeeping accounts are demoralising enough: fifteen pounds, five shillings and sixpence in the black. She is wondering how they'll pay their mounting debts when the frosted glass door bursts open. Wearing a royal blue ankle-length dressing gown, Faith enters carrying the mail. 'Three things,' she says, thumb and two fingers held aloft, as if Beth is incapable of counting to three, 'Mr Burkett's mastiff has escaped again. The poor man is beside himself, he'd like us to find Carl as soon as possible. Besides our fees there's a reward advertised in the *Observer*, twenty pounds, my word that man is loaded.'

'Carl pays most of our bills,' says Beth, recalling her last encounter with the dog. Missing for several days, he'd been courting a bronzed female mastiff he'd met at a dog show and followed home the same day. By the time Beth tracked him down he wasn't going to budge without a snarling struggle. Her most forceful contralto voice did little to master the hefty dog. Thankfully, his desire for sustenance prevailed over his carnal yearnings and a handful of biscuits distracted him long enough to attach a leash to his collar.

'Secondly,' says Faith, now holding up two fingers, 'Mrs Hillcrest wants to know whether you've found Cupcake.'

'We might boast a ninety percent success rate, but little Cupcake is a member of the ten percent club,' Beth says, tempted to raise her ten fingers.

'Poor Mrs Hillcrest, Cupcake is her closest companion.'

'I'll call in later this morning to give her the bad news. Don't suppose you'd do it?'

'No chance, she'll howl like a baby and set me off.'

'What's the other thing?'

'I've saved the best 'til last – a two-legged assignment. Mrs Lydia Emerson's husband has disappeared without a word. She'd like us to find him.'

'Sounds like Casanova's been up to his old tricks again. How long has he been missing?'

'Four months. You'd know that if you read the papers.'

Beth rolls her eyes. 'How many times have I heard that?'

'An investigator worth her salt would keep abreast of the news.'

'I wonder why Lydia has waited so long to contact us.'

'She probably thought he'd return home eventually. The police found no evidence of foul play; they maintain he chose to leave. Mrs Emerson begs to differ. She'd like you to call in tomorrow morning around ten.' Faith turns to leave the room and remembers to tell Beth there's a letter from Skipp inside the house. 'I received one as well; my little brother's an accomplished wordsmith these days, who'd have thought?'

'There's nothing little about Papa.'

'He's an amazing baker and an incorrigible sweet tooth, no wonder he's a bit paunchy.'

'He still enjoys a drop of tea with his sugar.' Beth grins.

'Talking of food, Sam's enjoying a hearty breakfast with Harry, come and join us.'

'I'll cast an eye over Mrs Emerson's file while Sam is happily occupied. I won't be long.'

The door slams without shattering its glass panels and Beth is left wondering why her auntie always leaves a room as if fleeing a blazing inferno.

Standing at the files, Beth runs her index finger along the folders and stops at the letter 'E'. She grasps Lydia Emerson's file and plonks it on her desk. Written almost a year ago, the final report comprises several pages. Beth recalls following Eric Emerson every night for two weeks before catching sight of him in the company of an attractive young brunette. One particular night is vivid in her memory: the couple had gone out to dinner, entered a classy hotel and emerged arm-in-arm several hours later. Waiting outside in the comfort of a hansom cab, Beth, envious, watched them embrace one another in a warm hug. When the couple parted company in separate cabs, she instructed her driver to follow the young woman. Subsequent information gathering revealed her name to be Anna Hopping, twenty-one years old at the time, married to Angus Hopping, a sailor. Informing against the amorous couple was a pity, but ultimately Beth's loyalty was to Lydia who was shelling out a tidy sum and expecting results. Eric Emerson's infidelity exposed, he promised Lydia never to lay eyes on Anna again. And now, aged thirty-three years he has absconded, perhaps with another woman, perhaps with Anna. The mouth-watering aroma of toast and bacon wafting from the kitchen steals her attention. The folders can wait.

Outside, she stops briefly to dust her bicycle seat with the underside of her sleeve. Propped up against the wall and protected from the elements by a lean-to attached to the main house, the bicycle is in impeccable condition. A gift from an appreciative client, it is Beth's favoured mode of transport. Having had plenty of practice riding around the Botanical Gardens she considers herself a competent cyclist, but getting her skirts caught around the pedals is a pesky nuisance. A recently purchased bicycling costume: fastened to the legs just below the knees and worn with stockings, has overcome this problem. To date she hasn't had rocks or rotten fruit thrown at her like so many women who dare to wear practical clothing in public. Bloomers do cause inquisitive heads to turn, but the convenience and freedom of a bicycle far outweighs the occasional snooty grimace on the faces of those who oppose progress.

~

Rule number one: never leave home without carrying an adjustable dog collar, a pair of leather gloves, a leash, and most importantly Harry's irresistible dog biscuits. The canine penchant for the chase can be perilous for cycling enthusiasts, more than once Beth has had to peddle frantically to evade snarling jaws. Whether escaping dangerous situations or simply riding for pleasure, the speed always gives her a breathtaking rush of power she cannot find in any other preoccupations. Cycling along Kensington Road on a bracing winter's day would normally be an exhilarating thrill, but today she is dreading her imminent meeting with Mrs Hillcrest. How on earth will she tell an elderly woman her best friend has not and cannot be found? There'll be a flood of tears.

Serendipity strikes as she is cruising along. Having worked with dogs for several years, she believes she has developed the canine's keen sense of hearing, at least the ability to recognise their individual barking tones. And now, putting her dog ears to the test, she listens intently to the high-pitched yapping coming from a cottage belonging to Andrew Hall's mother. A small pooch is in trouble.

Having slowed down to a standstill, she dismounts and leans her bicycle against the fence. A short-legged dog with a long blue coat is whimpering. Kneeling, Beth is able to see the name etched on the dog's leather collar, it confirms her suspicions. 'You know me, don't you Cupcake? I've come to take you home.' To pat Cupcake's moist nose she pokes her index-finger between the slim timber palings, but reminiscent of the little Dutch boy in Mary Mapes' novel, her finger is stuck fast. 'Stupid,' she chastises herself for wasting precious time. She slathers her reddening finger with spit before yanking it free, the splinters she'd dig out later. The dog lets out a horrible wailing yelp.

The perimeter fence is at least five feet high. The gate is closed and padlocked. The dog would probably be moved or sold within days as a pet or for breeding purposes. There won't be a second chance. Feeling agile in her cycling apparel she scrambles over the fence, but just as her boots hit the ground a huge dog emerges from the house, baring his teeth. The thought of those jaws clamped to her calf muscles drives her hand into her blazer pocket for a handful of dog biscuits. She lobs them into the air and the dog springs a good yard off the ground to snap one before scrambling for the rest. The muscular beast distracted, Beth grabs Cupcake and drops her over the fence into her bicycle basket and tells her to stay put. The urgency sends Beth flying over the fence with astonishing athletic dexterity. At the same time, a stout, pudgy middle-aged man makes for the fence, bellowing threats of thrashings and murder, his arms waving in the air, his fists clenched. Unable to clamber over the fence, he curses wildly. 'I'll get you, I know who you are!' he shouts. A wiry, more athletic man dashes out of the house. Just as Beth is riding off, he takes a running start to leap over the boundary fence. She peddles faster and faster, willing her wheels to outpace her pursuer's long legs. Edging closer, his boots hammer the cobbled path. Pushing her legs so hard she can barely breathe, sweat rolling down her face and stinging her eyes, her clammy palms are almost slipping off the handlebars. She keeps going, harder and harder.

When her own heavy breathing is the only sound thumping in her ears, she takes a quick glance back. The man is gone but she keeps peddling, only slowing down when she comes to Mrs Hillcrest's mansion, a mile down the road. The gate wide open, she swerves in and follows a wide path leading to the front porch where she dismounts and props her bike against the railings. 'You're home, my furry little friend. You can stop shaking now,' she says, patting the dog. Cupcake is gently set down at a porcelain bowl labelled with her name, and without spilling a drop she scoops up the fresh water. Beth rings the doorbell several times. The familiar sound triggers unbridled yowling and Beth wonders how a small dog could produce such an ear-splitting pitch. The door opens the length of the security chain. Instantly recognizing her caller, Mrs Hillcrest's trembling fingers release the chain and the door springs open. 'Cupcake,' her crackly voice calls.

The dog is spinning in circles chasing her own tail and bucking like a horse. Laughing and weeping at once, Mrs Hillcrest crouches down to pick up her beloved bundle of fur. Cradled in her arms, Cupcake burrows into her woolly shawl and whimpers. 'Thank heavens she looks well.' Cupcake responds by lifting her head to lick comfort into her mistress's wrinkly neck.

'She's over the moon seeing you again, Mrs Hillcrest.'

'I could jump over the moon myself. Where did you find her?'

'Mrs Hall's yard, I'll report her son to the constabulary if you like.' Having trespassed Mrs Hall's property, Beth is unsure where she stands before the law, she crosses her fingers hoping Mrs Hillcrest won't pursue the matter any further.

'I dare not report that callous dog snatcher, he'd take it out on me or my little girl. Cupcake is safe, that's all that matters. I can't thank you enough for bringing her home.'

'You're welcome, Mrs Hillcrest. I'd suggest you keep her indoors for several days in case Andrew Hall tries to get her back.'

'My son and his family are moving in tomorrow, they'll look

after me. Wait there, I'll fetch your fee before you go.'

Taking an alternative route home to avoid Andrew Hall's fury, Beth is obliged to peddle an extra half hour. Once home, she dismounts and wheels her bicycle to its resting place under the lean-to. She chuckles as she listens to the vegetable patch choir, each singer competing to be heard rather than singing in harmony. She follows her ears to the garden.

'You take the high road and I'll take the low road,

And I'll be in Scotland afore ye,

For me and my true love will never meet again,' sings Beth, joining the hubbub and laughing wildly.

'On the bonny, bonny banks of Loch Lomond.'

'Mama, look what I pulled up!' Sam shouts, holding up a bunch of carrots. 'Uncle Harry said I'm a good helper.'

'Of course you are, my darling boy.'

'We'll be dining on home grown carrots, potatoes and cabbage this evening,' says Faith, wiping her hands on her apron.

'I found Cupcake. Mrs Hillcrest gave me ten pounds.' Beth hands over the hard-earned cash.

Faith slips the note in her apron pocket. 'Wonderful, I won't have to hock my best silver.'

'You've already hocked it, Aunt Faith.'

'Except for the tea setting, that's not going anywhere.'

'Fingers crossed.'

'Where did you find the fleecy little bundle?'

'I'll tell you all about it over a cup of tea.'

'We're just about done here.'

'I'll take the veggies inside.'

Swinging a handful of carrots by the leafy green tops, Sam follows his mama inside for lunch.

~

Sprawled on a long reclining chair beneath the leaf-bare jacaranda tree, Beth closes her eyes and tilts her face towards the gentle afternoon sun. Four-year-old Samuel is playing beside her. Having saved Papa's letter for this relaxed moment she unfolds it. A scent of cinnamon, vanilla and nutmeg drifts from the creased pages. Thumbprints stamped on the margins tell a story, Papa has put pen to paper immediately after a hard day's work. Touched by nostalgia, images of the bakery pass through her mind so palpable she smells the mouth-watering aroma of hot bread. Scanning the letter, she dries her tears; already the saline beads have distorted several words, the smudged ink resembling pressed flowers.

My darling daughter Beth,
I hope my letter finds you happy and well. Sorry I haven't written in weeks but another mine has opened and we're flat out baking bread to feed the rising population.
We're all going well here, I told you about the floods last month, well now we're dealing with the aftermath. The squelchy mud is starting to dry up and most people are still repairing the damage to their homes. Shame you're too busy to visit, we got green grass for the first time in years and the creek is brimming with fresh water. The best part is we hear frogs croaking at night. Local kids go swimming most days despite the water being bloody cold. I've seen them come out red-skinned and squawking like galahs as they run home to warm up by the fire. I don't know how long the green scenery will last but it's a welcome change from red dust. The downside is the wet has borne bush flies, thousands of them, so there's no chin wagging when outdoors!
Alicia says hello, she's kept busy with her two lively sons and with another child on the way she's lucky she's got Florence to help. I get invited to dinner once a week.

It turns out Alicia's a good cook. Lewis is still coming up with new ideas and recipes – he must dream them up in his sleep. He's introduced confectionery to the business, boiled lollies, fruit drops and toffees. Lewis the lolly-maker! The local folks love them and the lollies keep good if wrapped up proper. Lemon drops are his biggest sellers. He's doing most of the heavy work these days as my back's acting up.

Merle Appleyard took a bad fall while celebrating her wedding anniversary last week. She helped herself to a few too many tipples. When the band played Strauss she sashayed onto the dance floor and started spinning around. The other dancers returned to their seats when the music stopped, but she was still spinning. In the end, she collapsed like a dunny in a sand storm. Luckily, a nurse was amongst the guests.

I know you're busy in the investigation agency, but when you need a break come and see us. I wouldn't mind seeing my grandson again before he grows up a stranger. I'm planning a holiday in Adelaide in December; it's about time I celebrated Christmas with my dear family.

Say g'day to the little lad for me.

Your loving Papa.

PS Has my sister received my letter? I'll never hear the end of it if she hasn't.

Farina now magically transformed into a green oasis; Beth would love to see that before a dry spell reinstates Farina's parched splendour of yellow and tangerine. She longs to visit Papa and the friends and acquaintances she'd met many years ago. Since returning home from Afghanistan she has only seen him once, just days after Samuel's birth. Papa cried when he held his first and only grandchild. Everyone was crying as the swaddled baby was passed from one to the other, all in awe of new life. Beth remembers being on board the steamship which had almost been swallowed up by the swirling Indian Ocean, hundreds of nautical miles from Port Adelaide. To stay calm, she'd focussed on protecting the child she was carrying, the child moving within her, kicking her sides, the little friend she would soon meet and hold in her arms. There was a lingering stench of vomit well after the storm had abated. Initially, the giddy passengers and crew were too ill and sapped of energy to take heed of the mayhem around them. Certain Beth would return home, Faith chose to ignore the rumours of a shipwreck which were floating around Port Adelaide like bad air. Staying in the Seaview Inn, Faith passed hours seated on a balcony looking out to sea, anticipating the late running ship would bring her niece home. When the ailing steamer appeared on the misty horizon she hurried to the port and joined the cheering crowd as the ship docked. One of the last passengers to disembark, Beth stumbled onto South Australian soil, her sea legs slowly adapting to a motionless land. Heavy with child, she collapsed into Faith's arms. Dehydrated, half-starved, she was carried to a waiting coach and taken home. A midwife was summoned, within hours she gave birth to a healthy son. Wearied by the rough sea voyage, the usually robust Beth was fighting for her life. With her family rallying around her she soon recovered and Samuel grew stronger every day.

'Sam, come to Mama, we'll read Grandpa Skipp's letter.'

Having used a mound of sand, sticks, wooden blocks and toys, he and his imaginary friends have created an entire village. He parks his train carriages under an intricate bridge supported by stone pillars. Clapping the dirt from his hands, he goes to his mother and climbs onto her lap. Beth brushes the sand from his clothes. Reading the letter slowly, she stops every so often to respond to Sam's queries.

'Did Papa live in Grandpa's house in Farina?'

'No, he lived with his cameleer friends near the railway station.

He was often away transporting food and goods to faraway places.'

'Did you go with him?'

'No, I had to stay home and work in the bakery. But I knew how to ride a camel, your papa taught me, the camel's name was Bibi and she loved carrots.'

'Were you scared, Mama?'

'At first I was, until I learned how to ride properly.'

'Can you buy me a camel?'

'I'll get you a bicycle when you're a little older.'

'Is Grandpa my papa now?'

'No, but he loves you like a son.'

'Read it again, Mama.'

Reading through the letter draws her father closer to her; she sees him so clearly seated at the kitchen table, bowed over the paper, his large hand pushing the pen across the page, flecks of dough glued to the base of his fingernails, the smell of wood-fire and fresh bread on his person.

'Are you sad, Mama?'

'No, little bear, I'm happy to hear from Grandpa Skipp.' Beth tousles his curly hair, which seems more red than black in the morning sun.

'Can we visit Grandpa?'

'He's coming to visit us this Christmas and he can't wait to see you.'

Sam slides down from his mother's lap and resumes his imaginative game. His train springs to life as he tootles and honks and guides the carriages along rickety tracks. Aunt Faith would say he's away with the fairies. Prone to flights of fancy herself, when she first met Arif she would plan overland journeys across central Australia and visualise the landscapes as clearly as if she had been there many times before. The colours always enhanced, the fatigue never considered, the climatic discomforts, the remoteness, she'd get used to as long as Arif was beside her. She would milk his resilience, his sense of adventure, and he hers. Together unbreakable or so she thought until his father fell ill. Leaving her behind, he travelled home to Afghanistan promising to return within a year. Two years later, he asked her to join him in Afghanistan; her overland adventure realised in another country, in another world.

'I'm thirsty, Mama.'

'Running the railway is very thirsty work, Station Master Sam. Stay put. I'll get us a cool drink.'

When she returns, holding two glasses of orange juice, Sam is gone. She places the drinks on the garden table and listens intently for his voice, for he is rarely quiet. Whilst calling out his name she races around the yard hoping he is playing hide-and-seek. Then she spots him near the front gate chatting with a man dressed in a black suit. As she draws near, she tries to identify the man, but he looks away and strides down the road, his hands in his pockets, a young man's swagger.

'Please don't talk to strangers, Sam.'

'Sorry. He gave me this.' He holds aloft a brown paper bag. 'What's inside, Mama?'

Beth grasps the bag and pulls out the contents. 'It's a kite.'

'Can I play with it?'

'It's not windy enough today.' Beth gives him a hug. 'Did he know your name?'

'He called me 'boy'. I told him my name is Samuel Durrani.'

'Did he tell you his name?'

He shakes his head. The man didn't provide a name, nor could Samuel describe him, except for the fact he was very tall and had dark eyes like Uncle Harry, but this man's hair is thick and black, not white. When pressed for more details he says the man has a big nose like Uncle Harry, and Beth stifles a chuckle. A brief thought floats through her head, the two men could be related, but Harry has never married and he has often communicated regretfully he has no living relatives.

'If a stranger ever calls you again, come and get me first.'

'What if you're not home?'

Beth throws the same question back to her son, asks him to tell her what he'd do.

'Call Auntie Faith and Uncle Harry?'

'Clever boy, now promise me you'll call an adult next time.'

Sam's cherubic face breaks into a wide smile. 'Promise, Mama.'

'Come and get a drink.'

FRIDAY, 10TH AUGUST

The scent of pipe tobacco and almond oil shaving soap still lingers in the air but Lydia is not ready to have the room cleaned, not yet. She was rarely permitted to enter the hallowed study when it belonged to her father. An academic at Adelaide University, he passed most of his time in his study, thick textbooks and fat cigars his preferred company. Besides an occasional pat on the head, his lonely daughter was rarely the object of his frugal affections. Little wonder Lydia's mother chose to live by the sea in her Port Adelaide summer residence. When Lydia's father died Eric took over the study and the room became less cloistered, although a closed door always signified 'no entry'. Once, seeing the door wide open, she entered expecting to find Eric busy at his desk or sprawled on his daybed, instead she was greeted by a terse note on a large sheet of paper: *Home soon darling, gone out on business.* Wondering why he'd be conducting business at six o'clock in the evening, it occurred to her that his business dealings were increasingly being managed after hours, at times well into the night. For the first time in their marriage she searched his study for signs of a secret life. She noticed a trace of purple behind a pile of grey files beneath his desk and crouched down to take a closer look. The files frantically cast aside revealed a quilted box which she placed on the desk. Her heart thumping, she debated whether she should look inside. Curiosity got the better of her. Inside were two silk gowns, one red, and the other violet.

Halter necked designs. Not her style at all. At first she'd believed he'd purchased them for her as Eric was in the habit of pampering her with special gifts, usually jewellery or flowers. Holding the gowns aloft revealed they were several sizes larger than her slight figure. He'd overestimated her dimensions; not surprising given they hadn't had intimate relations in weeks. The gowns were revealing and showy. Lydia preferred pale colours, bottle green an adventure, but never violet or red. Hoping she was imagining Eric's infidelity, Lydia engaged Bethany's Investigation Services to confirm her folly. When Bethany's detailed report was delivered to her she fell ill and was bedridden for days. Eric cared for her. When she recovered and felt strong enough to confront him, he admitted he'd been seeing another woman for several months. Contrite, he begged her to forgive him and promised he'd never see Anna again. What a gullible fool she'd been to believe his sobbing lies. Now Eric is gone. At times, she misses his company, especially in the evenings when they would dine together. She has always considered him her best friend and confidant. Recently, her grief has turned to anger and she is adamant she will not shed another tear for the man she loved, still loves. She wants him found, she wants peace.

Despite a brisk breeze, Beth has taken her bicycle out for the three mile ride to Lydia's home on Greenhill Road. Cool air caresses her skin as she cruises along, the exercise enlivening all her senses. Arriving at the appointed hour, she halts her bicycle out front of Lydia's grand two storey home and slides off the seat. Standing idle for a brief moment, she recalls her last visit to confirm Lydia's worst fears. She unclicks the front gate, leaves it wide open behind her and continues along the garden path. Noticing a trampled bed of jonquils she tells herself to take a closer look on leaving. On the front porch, she leans her bicycle against the elaborate wrought-iron balustrading before ringing the brass bell. The clanging echoes through the house. Lydia appears at the door, welcomes Beth inside and leads her down the hallway to the parlour. Beth checks her clothing for bicycle grease before sinking into the plush cushions of the white sofa.

'I used to enjoy cycling but I'd never be daring enough to get around in bloomers,' Lydia smiles. 'Pity, they look so comfortable.'

'I've had my skirts caught around the pedals too many times. Once, I ended up on the ground unable to free myself. A kind stranger came to my assistance, but my bicycle was damaged and my skirts were torn to shreds. I decided I'd never ride in full skirts again.'

'Men certainly have the upper hand when it comes to comfortable clothing. Constrained by voluminous petticoats with more layers than a cabbage is a tedious burden to bear,' Lydia chuckles.

'When we get the vote we'll have more control over our lives, including what we choose to wear.'

'That's what Eric believes. For all his shortcomings, he's a supporter of women's rights.' Lydia brings her clapped hands to her chin as if in prayer. 'He left me four months ago, without so much as a word.'

'I'm sorry for your troubles, Mrs Emerson.'

'The constabulary believe he left of his own accord. I beg to differ; I think he's in danger, that's why I'd like to employ your services.'

'With respect, Mrs Emerson, why have you waited so long to contact me?'

Lydia takes a while to answer, her dark blue eyes reflecting intense emotions. 'Something happened recently that rattled me.'

It's as if Lydia has a lump in her throat and is waiting for it to melt. Beth notices she is thinner than the last time they'd met. She holds her silence and waits.

'I recently saw him in town. I was sitting in the Café de Paris in Rundle Street. Eric stepped inside, I couldn't believe my eyes. I stood up and approached him. I called his name. When our eyes met he turned on his heels. I followed him down the street. He turned his head, saw me and hurried on. He looked unkempt and nervy, like a hunted animal. I think he's in trouble.'

'If I find him and he wishes to keep his whereabouts secret, what then?'

'I'd respect his wishes. I can't force him to return home, I'm aware of that. I simply want to know why he left and if he's safe. Will you accept the commission, Mrs Durrani?'

Missing pets and cuckolded spouses being her usual domain, missing persons is unchartered territory. Beth's mind falls on her mounting debts; the recent dog-catching fee is a drop in the ocean of unpaid invoices. 'I'll do my best to find him, Mrs Emerson.'

'I'm sure you will. Are your fees the same as last year?'

'They are unchanged.'

Lydia hands Beth an envelope containing an advance payment. 'Please be assured that all expenses incurred during the investigation will be reimbursed.'

Beth places the envelope in her vest pocket. 'As you know, our fees include a weekly progress report.'

'Excellent. Do you mind if we address each other on first name basis, as well as using Eric's first name in our conversations?'

'Not at all, Lydia,' says Beth, taking a scribble pad and pencil out of her drawstring bag and posing her first question. 'Besides your most recent sighting, when was the last time you saw Eric?'

'Saturday, 31st of March, the day I left for my mother's home in Port Adelaide.'

'Did he seem troubled, distracted perhaps?'

'Eric was in good humour the day we said our goodbyes. When I returned the following Sunday, he was gone.'

'That would be Sunday, 8th of April,' says Beth, taking note. 'What time did you enter the house?'

'Around three in the afternoon, I remember looking at the hall clock. I expected Eric to be home so I bellowed his name several times, but as there was no answer I began looking for him, my first port of call was his study, but the door was locked. Eric often works in the garden on Sundays so I looked outside as well. Then I thought he might have gone for a stroll or a bushwalk. He enjoys that sort of thing.'

'Was he expecting you home on that day?'

'Yes, he knew I'd be home mid-afternoon on Sunday.'

'Does Eric normally lock his study?'

'Not really, if he doesn't want to be disturbed he simply closes the door.'

'Do you possess a spare key to the study?'

'No, for as long as I can remember we've only ever had one key.'

'What did you do next?'

'I went upstairs, unpacked my bag and took a nap. When I woke up about an hour later, I descended the staircase. I called for Eric, thinking he must be home by now. I knocked hard on his study door, but there was no answer. Then I went outside and walked through the rose garden leading to his study window. I looked in and he wasn't anywhere to be seen.' Lydia pauses to recollect the details. 'I moved back inside the house berating myself for over-reacting, and imbibed a tonic to settle my nerves. As we always eat out on Sunday evenings I changed and made myself presentable for dinner and waited, but he didn't come home.'

'That must have been difficult.'

'Very, I've never felt as lonely as that night.' Lydia takes a moment to breathe deeply. 'When our cook, Charlotte Bechard, turned up for work on Monday, she informed me she hadn't seen him since Saturday when she'd served him lunch in his study and was given Irene's cab fare.'

'Irene?'

'Irene Howard, our elderly cleaner. Prone to memory lapse and confusion, she often got her days mixed up, thinking it was Monday she turned up for work on Saturday, her day off. Apparently, Eric told her not to worry, she could work Saturday and take Monday off. She agreed to the change of roster and worked all morning, but by early afternoon she was feeling out of sorts. Eric gave Charlotte Irene's cab fare and asked her to walk the dear lady to the little shopping village up the road.'

'May I speak to Irene?'

'That won't be possible, she recently passed away.'

'Oh, that's unfortunate.'

'Yes, I miss her, she was very trustworthy.'

'When did you contact the constabulary?'

'Monday morning. They showed up during the afternoon, tramped all over the house, jotted down a few notes and found nothing unusual. Using a skeleton key, they unlocked Eric's study and looked around. They commented on the mess and determined it was an organised mess and not the result of foul play. They came to the conclusion Eric would probably contact me before too long and galumphed off.'

'May I speak to Charlotte later?'

'You can speak to her now,' says Lydia, smiling as Charlotte enters the room pushing a rattling tea trolley.

Beth greets the dark-haired cook who sets the tray of tea and cake on the side table.

'Please try my gateau,' says Charlotte, a light spray of crumbs on her chemise.   Beth takes a generous bite, swishes it around her mouth, the flavours bursting on her tastebuds. 'Mm, delicious, let me guess: coconut, eggs, flour, butter, sugar, vanilla and something else.' Holding the portion of cake to her nose she closes her eyes. 'I detect a hint of ginger.'

'*Bien.*' Charlotte smiles.

'I used to make cakes for Papa's bakery. I loved experimenting with different flavours.'

They indulge in an easy conversation, exchanging cake and dessert recipes before Charlotte leaves the room.

'Charlotte's been with us for seven years now. A French immigrant, she's a genius in the kitchen. Do you speak French, Mrs Durrani?'

'*Un peu.*' Beth chuckles. '*Et vous?*'

'I'm not a gifted linguist. One of these days I'll travel to France, I've always wanted to but Eric has never been interested in travel.'

After tea, Beth is led to Eric's study. She surveys the spacious room; shambolic is the first word that comes to mind. 'An intruder?' she asks with raised eyebrows.

'Very droll, Beth.' Lydia smiles. 'I've seen it worse than this.'

A large desk occupies the centre of the room on which there are several overflowing ashtrays, a pipe, a blotter pad, pens and pencils and a pile of folders. More files are stacked on the floor than within the deep shelves lining the walls. Volumes of leather-bound law books are displayed in the shelves. Finished in velvet aquamarine-blue upholstery, a mahogany daybed stretches along the right-hand side of the room. There's a cosy alcove with a large bay window that overlooks a rose garden, it is furnished with a small table and a cushioned chair tucked under it.

'Is this exactly as you found the room?'

'Yes, only the lunch table has been cleared.'

'Do you mind asking Charlotte to set the table exactly as she'd found it following Eric's disappearance.'

Lydia agrees and leaves the room to call for Charlotte's assistance. In her absence, Beth sits at Eric's leather-topped desk, complete with inkwell and stationery. She tries the drawer on the left-hand side, which is brimming with paper, and is unable to tug it open. The drawer on the right-hand side is more amenable as it contains only one item: a pocketknife. On its face is an engraving: To my dear son Eric, from your proud father, 1882. She flicks it open; the metal blade is about four or five inches long, and the handle is made of solid gold. With a drawer set aside uniquely for its stowage, the knife must be very dear to him. She wonders why he left such a sentimental object behind. On hearing approaching voices she quickly returns the knife to its rightful place and closes the drawer.

Lydia and Charlotte enter the room carrying trays of luncheon ware. They set the table exactly as they'd found it – a mutual consensus as to the placements and lunch menu: a saucepan of beef stew, the silver serving spoon lodged upright in the stiff sauce, a bowl of rice, condiments, an empty wine glass, a spatter of red wine in its base, lip smears on its rim. On the plate: a chewed gristle of meat, grains of rice sopping up the gravy dregs, a sprig of cauliflower. His cutlery was placed neatly across the plate.

'Eric had the presence of mind to place his cutlery neatly side-by-side on his plate.'

'As long as I've known Eric and despite my remonstrations he has never followed that mannerly convention.'

'The chaotic study doesn't tally with such a neat, finicky habit. Why on that day did he obey cutlery etiquette? Did you mention that anomaly to the police?'

'No, at the time I didn't think it was important. In any case, the police had already decided he'd eaten his lunch and left of his own volition. There was no sign of a scuffle or theft. I insisted they make further enquiries as Eric would never stay away for two nights without telling me. Days later, they informed me Eric had withdrawn his savings and closed his bank accounts two weeks prior to his disappearance, that's what clinched it, case closed.'

'Did he pack a bag of clothing?'

'He may have taken a change of clothes. I have no idea how many suits he has in his wardrobe.'

Beth takes notes, wonders if she'd be able to decipher her scribbly writing later on. Turning her attention to Charlotte, she asks her to describe a typical day's work.

'I commence at ten o'clock, clean the kitchen, prepare lunch. Each afternoon, I do shopping for fresh food, clean lunch dishes, bake bread, cakes or biscuits, cook dinner and leave at six o'clock.'

'What about the day Mr Emerson disappeared, was it any different?' Beth asks, observing the tall square-shouldered woman, her solid build bestowing an air of strength and competence rather than lumbering burliness.

'Yes, different. Poor Irene came to work on her day off. She cleaned the 'ouse, in the morning but later in the day she did not feel so good. Before going 'ome she drank some brandy to quell the dizziness. Mr Emerson gave me two shillings to put Irene in a cab. We walked to town together. I put her in a cab and did some shopping. When I returned to the 'ouse, Mr Emerson was in 'is study, the door was closed.'

'Does Mr Emerson usually have lunch in his study?'

'Every so often.'

'Was his door closed when you left the house that evening?'

'Yes, I wanted to collect his lunch dishes and serve 'is dinner, but he did not answer when I knocked. I put a note under 'is door informing 'im his dinner was in the kitchen.'

'Did the police take the note?'

'I think so.'

'So when you left the house you believed he was still in his study?'

Charlotte nods. '*Mais oui*.'

'Has he ever ignored your knocking on the door before?'

'When busy or sleeping, yes.'

'Do you live close by?'

'I live three doors up the road in Madame Zambetti's lodging 'ouse.'

Beth gives Charlotte her card and asks her to contact her should she remember anything that might help. Charlotte tucks the card into her apron pocket and leaves the room to go about her business.

'Who'd want to harm or harass Eric?'

'As you know, he'd ended his affair with Anna Hopping, perhaps she was angry about it, or worse, her husband found out?'

'Anyone else?'

'No, Eric is well-liked, he's generous and amusing.'

'Have you asked your neighbours if they saw anything suspicious?'

'The house on my right belongs to an investor, he rarely stays there. As for the neighbours on my left, they're in England visiting their daughter. It's crown land across the road.'

'Has Eric been unwell lately?'

'He suffers from insomnia. The economy's downturn meant several of his wealthiest clients lost a fortune. He wasn't getting any new contracts.'

'We're living in hard times, Lydia.' Beth remembers the Bank of Adelaide crash two years back when Faith lost all her savings. Teary for days, Faith was more concerned about Samuel's future than her own predicament. Her solicitor assured her she'd keep her two-storey bluestone home as she owned it outright. At least she'd have a roof over her head provided she could manage the spiralling council rates and household bills. Some people lost everything.

'Can you give me the names and addresses of anyone who might help?'

'Vincent Stirling is Eric's business colleague and good friend. I've advised him of my intention to engage your services. He'll assist you in any way he can. Do you still have Anna Hopping's address?'

Beth nods.

'Mr Stirling informed me Mr Hopping is away at sea, any time soon could be prudent to interview Anna Hopping.'

'How would Mr Stirling know that?'

'Mrs Hopping recently visited his office as he is now representing her. He has taken on most of Eric's client lists.'

'Do you have any other hired help?'

'Eric employed an odd-job man for several years,' Lydia pauses to recall his name. 'Nolan Lloyd, I've heard on the grapevine he's in hospital.'

'And Irene Howard's address please.'

'Very well, you could try chatting with her sister but she's very disobliging, to put it mildly.' Lydia moves to Eric's desk and lists their details on a sheet of paper and passes it to Beth.

'Just summing up my notes: On the day Eric left you were staying with your mother in Port Adelaide. Irene Howard was present in the house as she came to work thinking it was Monday. Charlotte Bechard was present; she works here every day until six o'clock except for Sunday, her day off. During the afternoon, when the two women left the house, Eric was still at home. Charlotte put Irene in a cab, did some shopping and returned to prepare Eric's dinner. When she tried to collect his dishes he did not respond to her door knocking, so she assumed he was busy or sleeping on his daybed. Before leaving, she slipped a note under his door informing him his dinner was in the kitchen. Eric was last seen on Saturday, 7th of April when he gave Charlotte Irene's cab fare.'

'A succinct summary, Beth,' says Lydia, in the manner of an impressed school mistress.

'Did the odd-job man, Mr Nolan Lloyd, resign because of illness?'

'Eric let him go, said he was incompetent. In retrospect, the poor man was probably ill.'

'I noticed there's a flattened flower bed out front. Did the police comment on that?'

'It was probably those burly men who trampled all over it, there were several of them.'

'Do you mind if I take a closer look on my way out?'

'Not at all.'

Outside, Beth stops near the trampled area, lays her bicycle on its side and treads carefully amongst the flowering yellow jonquils. Crouching, raking her fingers through the greenery, she inhales their sweet, almost overpowering fragrance. A small lizard takes her attention. As it zips away she notices something small and round amongst the leaves. She grasps the dark-tinted button, about half an inch in diameter. Holding it in her open palm, she observes it's made of metal, perhaps brass with a raised anchor design, a rope style border and a loop on the back. She remembers many years ago she would often visit the Port Adelaide docks with Papa, he had told her an anchor is a symbol of hope and good tidings. Her first thought is to hand it over to Lydia, if anyone needs good news it's Lydia. Instead, she holds onto it for the moment, she might be able to garner some luck out of it first.

~

Harry attends his rifle club meetings most Friday afternoons. Regarded as one of the best marksmen in Adelaide, he boasts an average hit of 85/100 targets at most matches and he intends upholding his reputation at the tournament scheduled early next year. On his way to the shooting range, he drops Beth off in King William Street and arranges to collect her around five near the post office.

Strolling through the heart of Adelaide, Beth's eyes sweep in all the views: the imposing Italianate post office, the Town Hall and the Supreme Court with its façade of sandstone and thick columns. Vincent Stirling's legal practice is located in Pirie Street, just a short walk from the Town Hall. Near the entrance, attached to the wall is a brass plate with names stamped in the metal: *Stirling and Emerson Solicitors*. The door is unlocked. Moving into the building, she inhales the soothing combination of beeswax furniture polish and coffee. An opulent interior greets her eyes: a patterned oriental rug running along the timber floor, clean white walls. A young woman in a tweed suit is seated at her desk opening and sorting mail. Beth introduces herself and is directed to Vincent Stirling's office. She is taken aback by the man who leaps to his feet and offers his hand in greeting; she had expected an elderly gentleman. Early to mid-thirties, of medium height, with a shaven face and a tanned complexion, a man who enjoys the outdoors, she speculates. The large window behind him lightens up the room; a lofty eucalypt throws dappled sunshine over his tidy desk.

'I've been looking forward to meeting you,' he says, gesturing Beth to a seat. 'I've never met a lady detective before.'

'I don't think I'm the first, certainly not the last.'

'Let's hope not,' he gives a practised smile, revealing his perfect white teeth. 'Lydia has informed me you'd take on the case. I assured her I'd assist in any way possible.'

'Thank you, that's most appreciated.' Beth takes out her notebook and pencil from her drawstring bag, and sits poised to begin an interview. An uncomfortable silence creeps by.

'Fire away, Mrs Durrani.'

'Can you tell me about your relationship with Mr Eric Emerson?'

'For the most part he's been a good friend and work colleague over the years. He would've told me if he intended leaving Lydia, he knows I've never judged him.'

'So you know about his affair with Mrs Anna Hopping?'

'Yes, I do.'

'Has he contacted you?'

'No. I don't know where he is, or for that matter how he is.'

'What do you think happened to him?'

He smiles. 'If I knew that I'd have told Lydia.'

Conceding the point, Beth suggests he might venture an educated guess.

'I know what didn't happen to him. He hasn't run off with Mrs Hopping, she's still living with her husband. She recently visited my office to discuss keeping her house deeds secure in our safe. Perhaps Mrs Hopping's husband found out about the affair. Apparently he's a violent chap. Eric once told me about his concerns for Mrs Hopping's welfare.'

A thought crosses Beth's mind, why would Eric go into hiding to protect himself, yet allow Anna to continue living with a violent man? It just doesn't pass the gallantry test.

'How long have you been working with Eric?'

'We started out as partners about seven years ago. More recently,

I took over the business and purchased Eric's share of the company. Eric continued working here as an employee until mid-March, and that was the last time I saw him.'

'Perhaps he was planning to disappear then?'

'It's possible.' Rubbing his chin he remembers the awkward weeks following the sale, Eric had become nervy. 'He didn't tell Lydia about the sale,' he adds as an afterthought.

'Does she know about it now?'

'Yes, the constabulary has informed her of Eric's financial history.'

'Was he a competent lawyer?'

'Eric's contribution and interest in the business was dwindling.' Vincent pauses, casting his mind back to the thorny moments in their working relationship. 'He was providing his clients with reckless advice, some of whom abandoned ship.'

'And no doubt you were the lifeboat?' Beth gazes at him, but his self-satisfied face seems inherently fixed, as does the twinkling amusement in his shiny dark eyes.

'In a manner of speaking, yes.'

'Do you know of anyone besides Mr Hopping who'd want to cause Eric harm?'

Shaking his head, he describes Eric as a cheerful, personable chap. Well liked.

'What about his clients, did he get on the wrong side of any of them?'

'Like I said, his disgruntled clients took their business elsewhere.'

There's a pause in their conversation as the clerk enters the room and places some paperwork on his in-tray. Vincent nods a thank you, her shoes clack on the timber floor as she leaves the room, her swift gait giving her an air of competence.

'Tell me more about Eric?'

'Where to start?' He leans on his elbow, his eyes looking upwards as he mentally sums up Eric's most obvious traits. 'He's an avid reader and loves the theatre. He's amusing and quick-witted, he'd had an affair, but he genuinely loves Lydia. He enjoys bushwalking and spending time in his rose garden.'

'If you don't mind, I'd like to go over his client lists.'

'Miss Verity Clegg will help you with that. Highly confidential client information is kept under lock and key, only I have access to those files. I'll show you Eric's office.'

Before they leave the room he gazes warily at Beth. 'Have you conducted many missing-persons cases?'

'Our Agency specialises in missing individuals.'

'Murder?'

'No, I haven't murdered anyone to date,' she quips.

He grins and rephrases his question, 'Have you ever conducted a murder case?'

'No, I haven't.'

'Let's hope beginner's luck rules the day.'

'Do you think Eric was murdered?'

'He vanished without a word to anyone four months ago; surely we can't discount foul play.'

'Lydia recently spotted him entering the Café de Paris in Rundle Street. She told me he looked bedraggled and hunted.'

Vincent shrugs his shoulders and dons a dubious expression. 'If that's the case why hasn't he contacted me?'

'Has he ever sought advice from you?'

'Yes, on occasions he'd ask for advice, business and personal.'

'Does he have any other close friends besides you and Mrs Hopping?'

'He'd socialise over a drink with associates, but I can't think of any other close friends. If you find Eric I'd appreciate it if you'd ask him to contact me.'

'I'll do that, Mr Stirling. May I see his office now?'

'Of course, please follow me.' Vincent leads the way to Eric's office. 'He often works in his study at home,' Vincent says, opening the door to a poky, dimly lit room. He draws the curtains and opens the slash window. The view consists of a towering brick wall overlain by plumbing pipes. Most of the office space is taken up by a large desk and vertical file drawers on which nameplates indicate each client's name and address. A violet-scented fragrance overrides the wafting mustiness when the clerk enters the room. Verity is about twenty-five with round spectacles sitting on her pert nose. Flashing a ready smile, she presents as a dedicated employee. Before returning to his sun-filled office, Vincent asks Verity to assist Beth when required.

'You should find what you're looking for. Mr Stirling asked me to tidy the room following Mr Emerson's disappearance.'

'Tell me about Mr Emerson?'

She responds without the slightest hesitation, 'Despite losing quite a few clients he was generally a cheerful sort.' Her voice descends into a whisper. 'His pride took a beating when he became Mr Stirling's employee.'

'Did they argue?'

'No, they've always been good friends.'

'I suppose I'd better start going through these files.'

'I recommend you start here,' says Verity, her hand tapping the oak file cabinet nearest the desk, 'these files go back five years at the most.'

'What do you think happened to Mr Emerson?'

'The policemen asked me the same question. I told them it was totally out of character for Mr Emerson to leave without telling anyone. They couldn't get out of here soon enough, they pulled out a drawer or two, flicked through a few sheets of paper and off they went. I hope you find him, poor Mrs Emerson must be beside herself with worry. Anyway, call me if you need anything, I'll bring you a cup of coffee and a nibble shortly.'

'Thank you, Miss Clegg, you've been very helpful.'

Beth spends the afternoon scanning Eric's client lists and

accounts: small business people, those who employed him to create or scrutinise contracts, wills, and conveyancing. Anna Hopping is on the list, she pays a nominal fee to have her house deeds kept on the premises. At least six larger companies have recently transferred their affairs to Mr Stirling's client list.

By late afternoon, she concludes that most of the contracts appear above board, with one exception, a furniture company called O'Halloran Furnishings. First commercial transaction in 1891 and more recently in February this year, they appear to have paid vast sums of money to Eric's business account for promotional services. Amongst the bills and receipts she finds a bundle of leaflets advertising their business:

O'HALLORAN'S FURNISHINGS
PARLOUR, OFFICE, BEDROOMS
SUPERIOR QUALITY
FURNITURE RENTAL
PURCHASE OUTRIGHT OR HIRE PURCHASE
MAKE AN APPOINTMENT
FULLY INSURED

Beth is wondering why the words 'fully insured' are circled and superimposed with a large question mark when Vincent Stirling enters the room enquiring about her progress.

'You said you keep confidential client information under lock and key, do you have anything on Mr Stanley O'Halloran?'

'No, I'm afraid I don't.'

'I'm going to see him Monday morning.'

'He's a very unpleasant fellow; you'd be advised to communicate with him by mail.'

She is about to ask him to elaborate when the pesky cuckoo clock announces five o'clock, time to pack up and hurry to the post office where Harry would be waiting for her in his wagon. Before leaving, she asks Vincent if she could call in again in a week or so, to which he invites her to call in whenever necessary.

SATURDAY, 11TH AUGUST

An unfamiliar thump comes from Anna Hopping's front yard followed by shrieking cries. Tired, bruised and sore, she rises from her chair, leaving her cup of tea behind to see what the commotion is about. Outside, the centre pole holding up the clothes line has collapsed and a tangle of washing lies heaped on the ground. Her daughter is sobbing and Audrey is on the verge of tears.

'Sophie got the fright of her life, lucky the pole didn't fall on her,' says Audrey.

Anna picks up her wailing three-year-old and hugs her tightly.

'Sorry, luv, I didn't see her tugging at the washing, she's a force to be reckoned with that one. Pity, the washing's almost dry.'

'Never mind, Ma, we might be able to shake the dirt off,' says Anna, letting go of Sophie who has made a swift recovery.

'If Angus notices dirt on his uniform he'll fly off the handle,' says Audrey, pushing back a lock of grey hair from her forehead.

'Don't worry; we'll clean 'em up good as new.'

The soiled washing removed from the line, they hoist the pole from the ground and stand it up firmly under the line. Anna puts aside the laundry needing a second rinse.

'A woman's work is never done.' Audrey heaves a deep sigh.

'There'll be more of it when this little one comes,' says Anna, patting her stomach.

'I'm no stranger to hard work but the bruises on your neck are ...'

'I'm all right, just tired.'

'If Angus ever hurts you again, I swear I'll report him to the police,' Audrey murmurs.

Anna squares her shoulders and feigns a commanding voice. 'It's a private family matter, madam, go home, be a good wife and stop wasting our precious time, we're run off our feet tackling real crime.'

They laugh out loud and continue parodying police inaction because laughing is better than crying.

A row of neat, identical timber cottages crowd both sides of the road. A medley of door and window frame colours differentiates the homes. Several terracotta pots of yellow and purple pansies thriving in the sunshine give an otherwise grey façade some vibrant colour. Anna Hopping's home has an indigo-blue door, and matching blue window frames.

'Who the hell is that?' asks Audrey Hubble, gazing at the redheaded woman riding a bicycle like she was born on it.

Anna and her mother are staring at Beth as she enters their front yard, her hat awry. Introducing herself, she dismounts, lays her bicycle on its side and straightens her hat. A fragrant whiff of mint and lavender drifts from the laundry. Sophie, never having seen a bicycle at such close quarters before, goes straight to it with exploring hands. Calmly, Beth points to the spoke telling her it's dangerous for curious little fingertips. Sophie scuttles to nestle into her mother's skirts.

'I'm working for Mrs Lydia Emerson, investigating Mr Eric Emerson's disappearance. We're wondering if you might be able to help us.'

'I'm just one of his clients, what would I know?' Anna asks, wide-eyed.

'I'm interviewing all Mr Emerson's clients,' Beth lies. 'Is it convenient to talk now?'

'Mr Stirling sent me a letter saying he's taking over Mr Emerson's side of the business. That's all I know.'

'I thought you might be able to shed some light on Mr Emerson's frame of mind before he vanished, given you had a special ...'

'We're goin' inside, Ma. Could you keep an eye on Sophie?'

Her mother nods and takes Sophie's hand.

'My nosy neighbours will have plenty to talk about today,' says Anna, gesturing for Beth to enter the tidy cottage.

Beth is seated but Anna remains standing, her hands plonked on her hips. 'Why on earth do you think I could help you?'

'You were very close to Eric Emerson.'

'What's that supposed to mean?'

'I know about the affair, Mrs Hopping.'

'If you're planning to blackmail me you're wasting your time, my husband gives me barely enough for food.' Her big brown eyes mist up as she recalls begging him for a few shillings during his last shore leave.

'I assure you, Mrs Hopping, our conversation goes no further than this house. I'd simply like you to tell me anything you know about Eric Emerson, anything.'

Anna's shoulders slacken, she takes a seat. 'Eric told me I make him happy, he was never down in the dumps with me.'

'What sort of man is he, in your opinion?'

'He's kind and funny, generous too. We went out to fancy places, I enjoyed his company. He's very romantic – he always gave me a rose whenever we met.'

Beth observes Anna, she is young, at least ten years younger than Eric, even in her frayed clothes and stained apron she is beautiful. 'Are you absolutely certain your husband doesn't suspect anything?'

'I wouldn't be here talking to you if Angus knew. Not in one piece anyway. He's a bully and a coward. If he got wind of the affair he'd kill me, not Eric.'

'Does he go away often, Mr Hopping I mean?'

'Not often enough.'

'Is he away now?'

She nods. 'He'll be back in a few days.'

'So you'd meet Eric when your husband was away at sea?'

Anna nods. 'Ma looked after Sophie on the nights I went out. He said he had big investments and when he cashed them in he'd leave his marriage and we'd run away together, Ma and Sophie as well. We planned to go to Melbourne and start again.'

Beth mulls over Anna's comments, Eric must have thought he was due for a windfall, and not simply the sum he'd withdrawn from his bank account. Perhaps it had something to do with O'Halloran's business.

'Eric disappeared on Saturday, the 7th of April. Do you remember if Angus was on leave during that time?'

'Yes, I do. It was Ma's birthday; the four of us were here enjoying a special day together.'

'When was the last time you saw Eric Emerson?'

'He took me out to dinner on Monday 2nd of April.'

'Did he mention he was going away?'

'No, as I said, we were planning to go away together.'

'Where did you first meet?'

'At his office, two years back. Angus inherited his parents' house and needed help with the paperwork. As he's often away he sent me to the solicitor's office. Eric asked me out to dinner and I accepted. Our friendship grew, I wasn't just some slapper on the side – it was more than that.'

Beth nods in agreement. She remembers envying them; their passionate relationship was more than a passing fancy. 'Do you know of anyone who'd want to harm Eric?'

'I can't imagine Eric getting on the wrong side of anyone.'

'Do you know where he is?' Beth fixes her hazel eyes on Anna, hoping to see a tell-tale sign she knows his whereabouts.

Anna shakes her head, rises from her seat, approaches the

window to check on her daughter playing outside, sees all is well and finds her seat again.

'So he hasn't contacted you at all.'

'No, he has not,' Anna answers firmly.

'Have you been to his office since he left?'

'Mr Stirling asked me to come to his office. He told me Eric had left the business and he'd look after my affairs if I was happy to let him do so.'

'Were you?'

'Yes, he said he'd waive the fee for a year. The house deeds are secure in Mr Stirling's safe. Given the chance, Angus would sell the house from under us.'

'I have something to show you, Mrs Hopping.' Beth fishes the button out of her drawstring bag and holds it in the palm of her hand, anchor side up. 'I found it in Mrs Emerson's front garden. Would your husband have gone there?'

'Why would he? Angus doesn't know anything about my relationship with Eric. That button could belong to anyone.'

'The anchor design suggests it could belong to a boatswain.'

Anna sniggers. 'Brass buttons are dear. We don't have money to throw away on fripperies.'

'You've been very helpful Mrs Hopping. I'll give you my card, if you think of anything else please …'

'I don't want your card, don't come back here again. If Angus gets wind of it he'll think I've joined the suffragettes.'

'It's just a matter of time before women are granted the right to vote, perhaps this year, definitely by the time your daughter is an adult.'

'As if that would make any difference to my life, Angus wouldn't let me vote even if I could. Some women got ten, twelve kids. Do you think getting the vote will change their lives? It's easy for ladies who got time on their hands to go out marching in the street, wearing pretty clothes, silk stockings and shiny shoes, but some just don't have the same opportunities. It's a well-to-do ladies club, isn't it? If you don't mind I have a pile of washing to contend with.' Anna rises wearily to her feet.

Anna's views have never entered Beth's mind. There would be many women like Anna, unable to cast a vote because their husbands are bullies or because they don't have the time or the literacy to research the political parties. Beth has one child and lots of help, how do poor women with children cope? After bidding Anna and her family goodbye, and from their point of view – good riddance, Beth moves outside, picks up her bicycle by the handlebars and leaves. Out on the street, before mounting her bicycle, she looks back at the house, and notices the two women and the little girl standing outside near the front door. Beth waves but they don't wave back.

By the time Beth is almost home the sun is high in the trees and streaky red and grey clouds sag across the western sky. She is negotiating a sharp bend in the road when a wagon stops right in front of her. Avoiding a collision, she swerves around it and applies the brakes, just short of storming into Mr Somerville's fruit store. Noticing the wagon has moved off, she dismounts and catches her breath. Now on foot, she guides her bicycle onward. Further along the road, the wagon halts abruptly in front of her again. Anger and shock bolstering her courage, she confronts the driver and immediately recognises him. 'You're blocking the road!' she shouts.

'Bloody thief,' Andrew Hall snarls.

'We both know who the thief is. Leave me alone or I'll report you to the police.'

'I'll crush ya flamin' bike one of these days,' he threatens, through clenched teeth.

Beth remembers the man sitting next to Hall as the one who'd chased her down the road after she'd saved Cupcake. 'Dog snatchers,' she says, already regretting she didn't mount her bicycle and hurry away.

'You're a thief, ya stole my dog!' Hall bellows, he might not get the dog back but she'll pay for it one way or another. That whinging little rat of a dog was just one day away from being sold to a very appreciative buyer. If it weren't for that meddling woman, he'd have filled his pocket with a wad of notes.

'You stole that dog from an old lady, shame on you.'

'Liar!' Hall shouts. His tall friend joins in the insults, standing up now, pointing at her, chanting: SHE'S A THIEF, SHE'S A LIAR!

Within a short time, people are milling around, attracted by the street drama. Pedestrian, horse cart and carriage traffic has built up on both sides of the road. The long traffic lock has infuriated people. A huge man from the crowd bellows, 'She's a suffragette, a trollop!' A missile flies through the air; the rotten egg splatters over her upper arm. Using a handkerchief, she wipes the slimy liquid from her sleeve. Andrew Hall and his friend remain in the wagon, inciting the crowd. A ragged man comes within a yard of her, wagging his finger, telling her to go home where she belongs. An elderly woman raises her walking stick and points it in Beth's direction, 'Shame on you, bicycles are of the devil.' Soon everyone is hurling insults. The mob is inching closer to her and all the while Andrew Hall is spurring them on, telling them she stole his dog, leapt over his fence and off she went, getting away on that blasted contraption. Her hand instinctively clutches her bike; they'll tear it apart if they get their hands on it.

Pointing at Hall, Beth shouts, 'That man, Andrew Hall, is a criminal!' But her voice is lost in the mounting hubbub. Fingers wrapped tightly around the handlebars, she gingerly wheels her bicycle away. Looking over her shoulder, she sees the mob coming for her. Several rotten apples are tossed into the air; one of them strikes her bike, another one slaps her back, followed by a reeking tomato. She imagines her back looks like an artist's palette, colours merging into one murky splodge. Instinct tells her to pick up the rotten food and hurl it back at them, but she keeps moving on. Aware that one should never run when pursued by a dog, she wonders if running from a mob would incite more aggression. A shrieking whistle cuts through the commotion. A policeman arrives on the scene. Young, not more than twenty, he blows his whistle several times. He orders people to clear the street. Sweat dribbles on his forehead and above his upper lip. His blue uniform offers some protection but the frenzied crowd could turn on him as well. Bells are soon heard ringing in the distance; more policemen are on the way. Andrew Hall's wagon pushes through the dispersing crowd. Catching Beth's eye, he draws his index finger across his neck. Her head reeling, she waits with the policeman until the giddiness subsides. To still her shaking hands she clasps the handle bars of her bicycle.

'You'd better go home now, madam,' says the young policeman, in his most authoritative tone. Repulsed by her reeking clothes he steps several feet away from her. 'You've caused enough strife for today.' His shoulders rigid, his head held high, he has dispelled the mob, perhaps saved lives. Poised for take-off, Beth's right foot rests firmly on the right peddle, her left on the ground, she executes a dramatic take-off, within seconds her two feet are pounding the peddles, the screeching bicycle protesting she is pushing it beyond its capacity. Bobbing along the potholed road, she passes a handful of stragglers moving away, they don't even look at her, her twenty minutes of infamy already history. It crosses her mind to stop at the police station and make a formal complaint, but she hastens down the road instead. Twilight is looming and given the stench of her clothing she'd probably be thrown in a cell for offending the nostrils of law-abiding citizens. Besides, Hall would deny his part.

Kensington Road doesn't come soon enough. In the dusky light, home appears in the distance, behind clumps of trees growing along the high-walled barrier that skirts the property. Every so often she turns her head, Hall is not behind her; of course he isn't, too busy celebrating her humiliation by now, perhaps sitting in a warm tavern with a pint of beer before him, surrounded by friends, all joking and laughing at her expense.

She dismounts before turning into the front gate, closes it behind her, wheels her bicycle along the brick path and parks it under the lean-to. The air is scented with eucalypt smoke, Harry has stoked the fire. She enters the house through the laundry door where she removes her soiled boots and jacket.

From the drawing room, Faith hears Beth grumbling to herself and gets to her feet. Moving down the hall, mildly alarmed by the putrid odour, she follows her nose. 'Good Lord, Beth, what is that dreadful …?'

'It's a long story, I'll tell you later.'

'For heaven's sake, Beth, tell me now; you look and smell like you've waded through the sewers.'

'Where's Sam?'

'He's in the kitchen helping Harry with dinner. What's going on?'

Beth launches into an explanation about her confrontation with Hall. 'I expected repercussions from Hall and his mate, but not in a public place. I can't believe how the mob turned against me; even the policeman accused me of causing trouble.'

'Now you're being naïve, Beth. They judged you by your unconventional clothing and a discernible penchant for freedom.'

'What freedom? I can't even ride around town without being judged and bullied.'

'I can't imagine you giving up your beloved mode of transport, and you shouldn't have to either.' Faith smiles. 'Cultural mores are always changing, narrow-minded folks will just have to get used to it.'

'I could have been seriously injured today,' says Beth, now adopting a conciliatory tone. 'Actually, my greatest fear was they'd smash my bicycle to pieces.'

'I'd hug you my dear plucky niece but …' she makes an exaggerated gesture of sniffing the air and holding her nose.

'I'm struggling to find this amusing. My cycling costume will need a good soaking for days. What will I wear?'

'Perhaps Harry will lend you a pair of tweed trousers,' Faith says, throwing her head back with laughter.

'That's so side-splittingly funny, Aunt Faith.' Beth scowls.

'Go and change for dinner, you'll feel better once refreshed. We all will,' says Faith, laughing out loud as she leaves the room to fetch the lavender atomizer. 'And for heaven's sake, stay home tomorrow.'

Beth hurries off, wondering if old age is responsible for making her aunt so fickle of late. Perhaps Harry has influenced her in some way. Nothing seems to faze him either.

Later, cleaned up and relaxed, Beth does her best to forget the unpleasant incident with Andrew Hall and his mate. Singing nursery rhymes with Samuel soon erases the memory of them, at least for the moment.

> 'Pat-a-cake, pat-a-cake,
> Baker's man!
> Make me a cake as fast as you can
> Pat it and prick it and mark it with S
> And put it in the oven for Sammy and me.'

'When I was a little girl Mama would sing that nursery rhyme to me, only the cake was marked with B.'

'Mark it with B for Bethy and me.' Sam grins.

'We'll just have to make two cakes, won't we?'

'One each!'

'But for now it's time to sleep little one,' says Beth, drawing the blanket loosely around his shoulders and kissing him. 'I love you Sam, Sam, make me some jam.'

'Love you, Ma, jam's in a jar.' He chuckles. 'Are we still going on a picnic tomorrow?'

'Yes we are, so you'd better go to sleep now.'

'Will we see ducks?'

'The ducks are invited,' Beth grins.

A wooden train carriage in his hand, Sam falls asleep within minutes. Lying on the edge of his bed, Beth listens to his quick little breaths and kisses his warm face. 'Papa would be so proud of you, little bear.'

Feeling light-headed, she regards the moon shadows falling through the wide gap in the curtains and lets her thoughts wander back to the time she and Arif travelled across the Khyber Pass. The days when life was an adventure and the future was spread out like an immense map of winding roads and endless journeys.

~

The ancient city of Peshawar glimmered in the distance as the train crawled over the hill. Set in a valley framed by mountain ranges, it was a magnificent sight. Beth could already smell the smoke wafting from the fragrant incense sticks. The aroma of spices, masalas, and hot curries in the shops and alleyways made her mouth water. Everyone stood up well before the train came to a standstill. Arif gathered the luggage and told Beth to stay close to him. There were so many people, and she did as he asked, if she lost him she would never find her way back to him. A ten-minute walk took them to a red brick mansion. As if they'd been waiting for them at the front window, an elderly couple emerged from the house, their arms out-stretched. Hugs were exchanged, and Beth liked them immediately. Over a delicious curry lunch, Mr and Mrs Halligan wanted to know everything about life in Australia and how she and Arif had met.

The following day, Beth and Arif strolled in and out of the many bazaars around Peshawar. Everything was new and fascinating: people, scents, sights. Beth was in awe of the ancient Mohabot Khan Mosque with its majestic white marble façade and the Goraknath Hindu temple. For lunch, they ate spicy beef kebabs with yogurt from one of the stalls. During the afternoon, Arif showed her the private English school he'd attended. They rested in the lush park gardens across the road from the school, in the shade of a mango grove. Arif talked about his school experiences, most of them positive. Sadness crossed his face when he spoke of his best friend Paul Halligan. As a child Arif had lived with the Halligan family, he and his friend were often bullied by the senior boys. Too young and too afraid to report the bullies they endured the beatings. They took refuge in creating stories in which the bullies would be harmed in some way. They would fall about laughing following their gruesome scenarios of drownings and tiger attacks. Paul once told a story about the biggest and nastiest bully being bitten by a snake and dying in excruciating pain. A week later, the bully was bitten by a viper. During the funeral ceremony, the dead boy's parents gave a moving speech about their only son, their loss and their suffering. Paul was in tears. He blamed himself; he believed he'd willed the boy's death. Arif and Paul's parents tried to convince him that only God has the power to decide on life and death but Paul would not be consoled.

'What happened to Paul?' Beth asked, dreading the answer.

'He took his own life just days after graduation. He was seventeen, a talented young man with a great future.'

The next day, Beth went shopping with Mrs Halligan who expressed her joy at hosting a female guest as a welcome change from army men and their military conversations. Beth purchased several brightly coloured saris and an embroidered scarf. For three days every moment was filled with shopping and sightseeing. Before their departure, Beth promised she would write to Mrs Halligan. Mr Halligan told them to be vigilant travelling across the Khyber Pass. 'There are many hospitable people on the way, but there are also marauding bandits ready to ambush travellers and steal from them.' Those words produced a mix of excitement and trepidation in Beth's mind, but she felt safe in Arif's company. Besides, she believed that freedom always carried an element of danger and decided it was worth it. She was free. They were free. The alternative was boredom, she would never tolerate that, life needed a certain amount of intensity, an exciting edge. Envisioning several days journey across the Khyber Pass and onward to Jalalabad, they set off with two horses and a packhorse in tow.

They reached camp just as the surrounding ranges were jagged black silhouettes. A popular stopover for travellers, the fireplace was already set with a circle of blackened stones and charred wood. A stone monolith about a yard in breadth and as tall as a grown man stood on the cliff side. Arif called it the 'sentry' due to the two oval eye-socket-like crevices in the stone through which shafts of sunlight and moonlight glow. The sentry marked the beginning of the steep track leading to a ravine where a clear stream flowed along carved caves and furrows beneath the mountains.

The horses tethered, the fire raging, they dined on grapes and bolani stuffed with spicy lentils while the water was heating for tea. They slept under a starry sky. At dawn, Arif woke first and set the fire going. For breakfast, they dunked sweet biscuits in strong tea. With very little water left, Arif asked Beth to wait for him while he climbed down the cliff to refill the goatskin water bag in the stream. She insisted on going with him and he reluctantly agreed. He grabbed the water bag and strung the straps across his shoulders, leaving his hands free for the steep descent. They made their way past the sentry stone, ordering it to guard their possessions and laughed at the absurdity.

Midway, Arif stepped onto a teetering stone and saved himself by leaping onto a wider ledge where he swayed and tipped forward, perilously close to the edge. Rocks plowed into the chasm and exploded on impact. They descended more cautiously from that point on. Cool, moist air washed over them as they stepped into the ravine and strolled along its sandy banks. Arif filled the water bag with at least twenty pints. Parched, they lay on their stomachs and with cupped hands drank the fresh water. Then they rolled over and with hands behind their heads they marvelled at the skating clouds.

Before the ascent, they bathed in the stream, their shrieking voices echoing in the valley as they plunged into the icy cold water. Screaming and laughing, their skin red from cold, they scrambled out of the water and held each other for warmth.

A return to camp saw everything as they'd left it. They hurried to pack up their possessions. Taking hold of the lead ropes, they urged the horses gently along the track. By the early afternoon, a howling wind threatened to sweep them away so they tethered the horses firmly to a tree and set up camp under an overhang, where Arif had camped many times before. They made a fire and sipped sweet tea while Arif told stories about life on his family farm. With conflicting feelings of anticipation and dread Beth listened, she was looking forward to meeting his family, yet she believed the language barriers and culture would be challenging. Their bodies entwined, they slept beneath thick warm blankets. Hours later, the wind fell to a whisper and the resounding howl of wolves owned the night. Arif assured Beth the animals were miles away. Besides, he slept with a dagger by his side.

On the third night, in Jalalabad they were guests of an Englishman, Doctor Michael, a close friend of Arif's. He cooked a delicious meal of roast chicken, basmati rice spiced with turmeric and coriander, yogurt and grapes. Hospitable and interesting, Michael had so many stories to tell, Beth wanted to stay another day or two, but Arif was keen to return home. Michael promised he'd visit them on the farm.

When they arrived at his family's property, the eldest son returned home from abroad, was swamped with attention. Beth basked in Arif's sunny glow but she missed having him all to herself. Days and nights of celebration and fanfare followed. The zerbaghali drum beat and the lute-like rubab instrument that had always taken her to another place strummed, and everyone danced.

Each night she and Arif made love. At first, in the whirlwind of passion she was convinced she'd made the right decision. She was accepted by her extended family, and blessed with fertile land producing fruit, vegetables, milk and honey. Arif's mother,

Nazdana, was affectionate and kind, she smiled easily. Beth was gifted several dresses, multi-coloured and loose-fitting with a pair of baggy tunban pants worn beneath to match each of the costumes. Headscarves were obligatory when outside of the home, but they too were loose-fitting and colourful. Falling into life on the farm, thoughts of leaving faded. Beth was a child in wonderland – everything was new and exotic. In time, they fell into an easy routine. The entire family lived on the farm, working the land, bowing to the changing seasons. Occasionally, a wedding or birth of a child would suspend the routine and celebrations would last for days. At times, Beth missed her homeland, Papa, Tillie and Aunt Faith. There was always the intention of returning to Australia with Arif. He had assured her they would. They still had their dreams of crossing the outback, as far as Stuart, on camels packed with provisions. They would often discuss those plans at night, lying in bed or working in the fields harvesting potatoes. The dream was always there like an extra star in the sky.

SUNDAY, 12TH AUGUST

Beth awakens in her own bed, drowsy and unable to make out where she is for several minutes. Vague recollections of her dreams flicker in her mind, fragmented but comforting just the same. Sitting up against her pillows, her gaze sweeps through the open door and down the hallway, half expecting Arif to enter the room and fall into her arms. But only a current of air wisps down the hall, sending a shiver down her spine. Rubbing her eyes, she sits upright, climbs out of bed, draws the heavy blue curtains aside, opens the window and pokes her head out. Sam is playing in the yard. Nearby, Faith is keeping an eye on him, an expansive newspaper in her hands. Beth regrets sleeping in on this perfect sunny day with the promise of spring in the air. She dresses in a green skirt and white chemise and hurries to the kitchen where she finds a steaming teapot on the hotplate. She fills two cups with tea before joining Faith outside. Sam asks if the picnic is still on, Beth assures him it is, he smiles and returns to his toy soldiers. Beth shares her dream with Faith, asks if it's a good thing, the memories coming back.

'You're coming to terms with the grief,' Faith responds. 'Grief is a tyrant, it won't be snubbed.'

Later, Ayishah, Tillie and her friend Eva arrive. Together with Beth and Sam, they climb into the wagon, their baskets laden with food. Harry drives them to their favourite picnic spot in the Botanical

Gardens near the large pond, home to scores of ducks and croaking frogs. Sam is first to leap from the wagon, he immediately heads for a flock of ducks floating peacefully in the glassy water. His arms waving about, he screams with joy as the startled ducks sweep into the air, their frenzied, squawking, splashing escape producing rippling spirals in the water. Told not to scare the birds Sam bellows 'sorry duckies', his laughter belying true respite. Within seconds, the ducks return to the pond as if accepting Sam's apologies.

Beth spreads a checked picnic blanket across the lawn, she and Tillie set the food in the centre and call the group to settle around it and tuck in. Harry declines an invitation to stay as he has work to do; he wishes them a good day and will collect them later in the afternoon.

'How did you get hold of lettuce and cucumber at this time of the year?' asks Ayishah.

'Harry is growing salad food in the hothouse.'

'And our bees are making honey,' says Sam, dripping the golden liquid onto his slice of bread.

'Perhaps I should ask Harry to grow some spicy herbs for me,' says Ayishah. 'I am sure he would use them as well, he enjoys cooking.'

'Yes, he'd be delighted, he's always on the lookout for tasty herbs,' says Beth, turning her attention to Sam who is throwing chunks of bread to the jostling ducks. 'No Sam, they'll ...'

'Too late,' Eva laughs.

'He'll wonder why he's hungry later,' says Beth, throwing her arms up in the air. 'I hear you've started working at the hospital, that's wonderful news.'

'I stand out like a zebra amongst horses. There's only one other female doctor.'

'Two zebras then,' Beth grins, pouring everyone a cup of fresh orange juice, the oranges plucked from their citrus orchard.

After lunch, Tillie proposes a game of cricket but Sam would rather go on a bush walk first. Tillie and Eva are happy to accompany him along the track that follows the river.

'Are you coming with us, Beth?'

'I'll stay here with Ayishah.'

'We won't be long.' As they move along the track, Tillie and Eva are on either side of Sam, holding his hands, lifting him up and dipping him down in unison each time prompting joyful laughter and Sam's cries for more.

'Are you still travelling to Karachi next month, Ayishah?'

'Yes, I am going to purchase a variety of scented oils for my shop.'

'You must be looking forward to seeing your family again.'

'Very much so. Every so often I need to immerse myself in Indian culture, the food, theatres, emporiums, and most of all, my dear friends and family.'

Beth remembers feeling the same sentiments when she lived in Afghanistan, at times she'd ache to see her homeland and family again.

'I invited Faith to travel with me but she will not leave her darling Samuel. I do not blame her, he is a charming boy.'

'He adores her. He's very fond of Harry too. I don't know what I'd do without them.'

'What about your personal life?'

'I've tried so hard to focus on the present and for the most part I do. But recently the past is coming back to me, especially in my dreams.'

'Arif will always be part of you and part of Sam, but you have to move on, live your life. That is what Arif would want you to do.'

'That's what Aunt Faith keeps telling me,' says Beth, turning her head towards the noisy bushwalkers returning to the fold. Tillie and Eva are imploring Sam to slow down as they cannot keep up with him. Too young to consider the encumbrance of heavy skirts slowing his opponents, Sam's arms are waving about in the manner of a sprint champion.

'They will want us to join the game,' says Ayishah, with a sigh. 'I will volunteer to be a fielder.'

'Me too, we'll carry on our conversation on the field.'

Tillie and Eva set up the wickets. Eva bowls. Tillie hands Sam the cricket bat and instructs him on how to hold it firmly and aim for the ball. He misses several strikes but persists until the fifth attempt when he misses again, and looks on the verge of tears.

'Don't give up,' Tillie presses.

'Go Sam, you can do it!' the group shout, not quite in unison.

Sam grudgingly raises the bat and sets about trying again. His face takes on a tight-lipped determined expression as he holds the bat out, grasping it tightly. With Tillie bowling, he hits the ball into the air and runs as fast as a rabbit, stopping at the wickets just in time before Eva catches the ball. 'I did it!' he shouts, jumping for joy.

Tillie's turn to bat, she slams the ball which veers towards a man sitting on a bench by the duck pond. The man leaps to his feet, catches the ball and throws it back to Eva. She gestures a thumbs-up thank you and carries on bowling. The man sits down again, watching. Beth studies him: tall, wiry, dark hair, well-dressed. Her first thought is to ask Sam if he's the stranger who had gifted him the kite, but Sam is engrossed in his game. As if able to read Beth's musings, Ayishah enquires about the man who has been watching them for some time.

'Since when?'

'I noticed he was there when we were having lunch, I think he arrived about the same time as us.'

'We should be vigilant and keep together just the same,' warns Beth, with no intention of heeding her own advice.

Ayishah casts Beth a quizzical look. 'You are not going to approach him, are you?'

'Wait here, I'm just going to talk to him, no harm in that,' says Beth, before moving away.

When she is within a yard of the man he springs to his feet and hurries off. There's something familiar about his long strides and youthful swagger. She hitches up her skirts and follows him. As he picks up speed so does she. Eventually, they are both sprinting. Some distance away, Ayishah has joined the chase, wondering why Beth is pursuing a complete stranger.

Observing the man from the back, his mane of thick black hair, his wide shoulders, his neat black suit, Beth wonders if he has something to do with Eric's disappearance. Aware of being followed, but not looking around, he melts into a clump of trees. Beth stops in her tracks, looks around and listens, the only sound resonating through the trees is birdsong. If she were clad in her riding costume she'd have a fair chance of keeping up with him. Pity it's soaking in a bucket of lavender soap flakes. The blazing sun in her face, her squinting eyes catch sight of the man several hundred yards ahead, racing across a grassy field. She watches him dash up a steep hill and drop from view. The man is an athlete. Heading back to the picnic area, she finds Ayishah along the way, bending double trying to catch her breath.

'Are you all right, Ayishah?'

'What would …?' she pauses, wheezing. 'What would you do if you caught up to him, Beth?'

'I'd have wrestled him to the ground, and sat on him until help arrived.' Beth laughs.

'That is not the way to find a husband,' quips Ayishah, her lungs now full of air.

'It worked the first time.'

'Brazen hussy!'

The two women break into riotous laughter before trudging back to the picnic area where the others are still playing cricket. Not one of them had noticed Beth's escapade, nor had they noticed Ayishah pursuing her.

MONDAY, 13TH AUGUST

Saturday's calamity with Hall still fresh in her mind, her riding outfit still immersed in soap suds, Beth boards a two-wheeled cab, that looks more like a baker's cart, to travel to O'Halloran's business. Located on the south-west side of Adelaide, on the edge of town, his furniture warehouses take up most of the land running along Mountebank Road. Both sides of the road comprise corrugated iron and timber clad structures except for the two storey office building which is brick. The etched timber sign out front says: *O'Halloran's Quality Furniture*. Squeezing her hands together, stilling her unease, she takes a deep breath and enters. Using her most assertive voice, she introduces herself and informs the clerk she'd like to see Mr O'Halloran regarding Mr Eric Emerson's disappearance. The clerk, a lean young man with a long pointed nose and sleepy eyes, rises from his seat and asks her to wait while he informs his boss. Looking around, Beth observes the walls are adorned with photographs of furniture, employees and smiling customers. By all appearances it's a very successful business. The clerk reappears, escorts her to Mr O'Halloran's office and returns to his front desk.

The man with the handlebar moustache gets to his feet and invites her to take a seat across from him. Two heads taller than Beth, he plonks back into his oversized chair. 'What can I do for you?' Mr O'Halloran asks, his bushy eyebrows drawing together in a scowl, making Beth feel as welcome as a stray cat.

'I'm representing Mrs Lydia Emerson in regards to the disappearance of her husband. I'm making it my business to interview Mr Eric Emerson's clients. I believe he was your solicitor,' she says, sitting up taller, raising her chin and looking him in the eye.

'I've heard about his disappearance, terrible news.' His mouth moves into a side smile. 'Unless he wanted to disappear.'

'Apparently, you gave him a very generous commission when he recommended your business to his wealthy clients.'

'There's nothing illegal about promoting a superior product.'

'Legal, yes, but perhaps unethical given Mr Emerson had a vested interest.'

He glares at Beth, his regard sly and suspicious. 'We're the biggest furniture business in Adelaide. We offer high-quality furniture at a reasonable price. Eric was doing his clients a favour and being rewarded for it. Confident we're the best in Adelaide he even persuaded his business partner to purchase our furniture.'

'Mr Stirling?'

He nods. His countenance is one of a fox that has just gobbled a rabbit. 'Didn't he tell you?'

'Mr Stirling has been most helpful in my investigations,' says Beth, a mix of nausea swirling in her stomach and a strong desire to get up and leave.

'Did Stirling send you here?'

'On the contrary, he advised me not to see you in person.'

'If you know what's good for you, you'll follow his advice.' His eyes are fixed on hers. 'I don't like people snooping around my business, neither does my son.'

Beth doesn't flinch from his glare, she wishes there was a window in his office, sunshine, daylight, birdsong, always calming, but this stuffy room smells of sweat and stale tobacco smoke. 'Just one final question, Mr O'Halloran.' Taking her time, she chooses her words carefully. 'When a customer rents your furniture or opts for hire-purchase, does the price include insurance cover?'

'The insurance premiums are always easy on the pocket and highly reputable. Should a valued customer's furniture be stolen or damaged due to unforeseen circumstances, they're able to recover the lost funds,' he says, the words rolling off his tongue like a child chanting the times tables.

'Does the price of your furniture include insurance cover, and if so, have any of your clients had cause to use their insurance cover?'

'I just answered that question. Will that be all, Mrs Durrani?'

'May I have the name of your recommended insurance company?' Beth presses.

'You've already taken up too much of my time,' he smirks. 'You're not a customer; you're just a meddling nuisance. Now, if you don't mind I'm a busy man.' Getting to his feet too quickly he stumbles and regains his balance by grabbing the back of his chair. He moves to the door, and calls for his son who is working in the office down the hall. Shortly afterwards, a younger version of himself enters the room. About thirty, the man is the same height, with the same thick moustache and eyebrows, and the same bellicose disposition. He is introduced as Raymond O'Halloran, joint owner of the business.

'My son will escort you to the door, Mrs Durrani.'

Raymond ushers Beth out of the building, insisting they have nothing to do with Eric Emerson's disappearance. Why would they? Eric's involvement was good for business. Standing on the threshold, his hands in his pockets, he quietly warns her against coming back. Before re-entering the building, he watches her clamber into the waiting cab. Settling back in her seat, the cart shaking and rattling along the uneven road, she vows to find out the name of their insurance company, if it exists at all.

Beth alights from the cab in King William Street, pays the driver and strolls across the Adelaide City Bridge, stopping in the middle to admire the spectacular Torrens River. The winter sun sparkles on the water, and a flock of ducks floats by, ripples in the shape of fingerprints swirling around them. Beth notices a black mastiff on the sandy bank lapping up water. His thirst quenched he looks about him like a hunted creature. Confident there is no imminent danger, he flops under a red gum, resting his droopy black face on his front paws, dozing yet vigilant. Moving a little closer, Beth recognizes the dog's expensive silver studded collar. Large and intimidating, each of his paws would fill an average man's boots, which is probably why he hasn't been nabbed yet. Beth grasps a lead from her pocket. On her approach, he opens his eyes and his large ears prick up. Recognising her, and despite his bulkiness, he leaps to his feet. Attentive and playful, he looks like a dog waiting for its ball to be thrown. His wagging tail invites Beth to pat his silky short coat. 'Hello Carl, be a good boy now, your Papa is very worried. And so am I, twenty pounds worth of worried to be exact, and I need the money,' says Beth, giving him some biscuits. As his head is downturned devouring his prize, she quickly connects the leash to his collar. His hunger satisfied, his tongue mops up any remaining juice from his jaws. Beth leads him back to the footpath. Buoyed by the promise of more biscuits he obeys.

On the banks of the Torrens River, the teahouse is a red brick building, Victorian in style, with elaborate balustrading enclosing raised timber planter boxes brimming with blooming marigolds and nasturtiums. She loops the end of Carl's lead over a sturdy post, gives him another biscuit and tells him to behave himself while she takes tea inside with her sister. Carl sits as instructed and gives a contented grin, his moist brown eyes wide and angelic. Taken in by his charm, Beth pats him and offers another biscuit before leaving him. 'Growl if anyone tries to steal you.'

Inside a fire is blazing and the air is steamy from hot pastries and teapots. Chinking cutlery and crockery and hearty chatter all around the spacious room complement the warm atmosphere.

'Sorry I'm late, Tillie. I came across Carl just by chance.'

'Carl?'

'The mastiff we've been looking for.'

'Oh, a dog, I thought for a moment ...'

'Mr Burkett will be delighted to get him back, not to mention generous. I've secured him to a post outside, he should be right for a while.' Beth removes her coat and wraps it over her chair, before flopping onto the seat. 'Do you have classes this afternoon?'

'No, just a mountain of marking,' Tillie responds. 'I've already ordered the tea and scones.'

'Thanks. I'm starving.'

'Good gracious, you smell like a wet dog, here use some of this on your hands.' Tillie takes a small tin of lavender balm from her pocket.

'I should get some of that.'

'Have it, a gift from me, you need it more than I do.' Tillie laughs.

'That's very generous of you, thank you. How's school?'

'We have a new mathematics teacher.'

'What's she like?'

'He's male.'

'What's he like?'

'He's young, about my age, good looking in a bookish sort of way, tall, wears spectacles, loves birdwatching and Dickens.'

'You seem to know him well.'

Tillie's blue eyes avoid Beth's gaze. 'We have a lot in common.'

'You should move in with us, it'll save you rent.'

'I like my independence. Besides, my little flat is just a short walk from the school.'

A young waitress with dainty hands sets two porcelain cups, a pot of tea and a plate of scones on the table.

Tillie gobbles up a scone topped with thick cream and strawberry jam. 'Not as good as Papa's but delicious all the same.'

'I miss Papa's scones, I miss him as well.'

'Me too. Aunt Faith hopes he'll join us for Christmas this year.' Tillie pauses to brush crumbs from her lips with a serviette. 'When are you going to tell me the full story about you and Arif? You were overseas for years and you've barely shared any of it, or only the briefest details leaving me to imagine the rest.' Tillie laughs.

'That's a worry,' Beth laughs back. 'Your imagination I mean.'

'I won't hound you. But it's better to talk about it than to mope.'

'For heaven's sake, I'm not moping around. I'm presently working on a missing person's case, possibly my first murder investigation.'

'Sounds like your life is more exciting than mine.'

'It's not always interesting, sometimes it's dangerous. Some people are so aggressive. I visited Mr O'Halloran's furniture business this morning. He's the rudest man you could ever meet. I think if we were alone on a dark street he'd have thumped me.'

'He sounds awful; don't get on his wrong side.'

'Too late. I'll send him a bunch of roses.'

'A bunch of stinging nettle might be more fitting.' Tillie grins.

'Let me know if you hear anything about the company.'

'I'll ask around. I know of one wealthy family using O'Halloran's furniture, I was tutoring their son when it was delivered, it's very luxurious.'

'Ask them if they're happy with the service and anything else you can think of. Aunt Faith is planning a visit in a few days as a potential customer.'

'I think she's enjoying the detective caper. Harry too. What a team of sleuths.' Tillie giggles at the thought of the intrepid trio. 'Are you going to the suffragettes rally next week? We're so close to getting the vote, we have to keep up the pressure.'

'I wouldn't miss it for the world.'

'I hope the anti-suffrage gangs don't turn up.'

'Harry reckons there'll be a lot of policemen on the streets.'

'It's more likely they'd arrest us.' Tillie giggles. 'How's the adorable Sam?'

'He's growing up too quickly; he spends too much time with adults. It'll be good when he goes to school and associates with children his own age.' Beth pauses for a moment. 'A strange man called him to the front gate four days ago. He gave Sam a kite, chatted with him for a while and hurried away when I approached him.'

'Sam's very outgoing; you'll have to teach him to be cautious around strangers.'

'I could be imagining danger where there isn't any.'

'The investigator's curse.'

Outside, an icy wind is blowing as Beth and Tillie leave the teahouse. Tillie asks where the dog is, Beth asks herself the same question as she regards the empty spot where she'd left him. At first, she imagines he used his hefty strength to sever the leash and break away, but the entire leash is gone. Only a human hand could unloop it from the post. Carl would still be wearing his collar with his name tag attached. Strange she didn't hear him barking or snarling. They hurry to the bridge, hoping he is lazing on the grass by the river, but he is nowhere to be seen. Tillie has to hurry off; Beth is left wondering if Andrew Hall had something to do with it. Not about to give up, she spends the afternoon looking for him until the blisters on her feet force her to return home.

Dinner is being served as Beth steps into the house. Harry Fairweather, hobby chef and bee keeper, has prepared baked chicken and vegetables smothered in gravy.

Samuel smiles with delight on seeing his mother, she kisses his forehead before sitting at the table beside him.

'How was your day, Sam?'

'Me and Uncle Harry got some honey from one of the bee hives, we didn't even get stinged.'

'You didn't get stung, that's wonderful.'

'It's so yummy,' he says. 'We put some in the carrots.'

'Thank you for entertaining him, Harry. He's learning so much with you.'

'Clever young chap,' says Harry, tussling Sam's curly hair.

Two years ago, just after the Bank of South Australia crashed and Faith lost most of her savings, Harry was taken in as a boarder. Faith has told him on many occasions that his meaningful contribution to the household has proven exponential and he should not be expected to pay board, but Harry insists on paying his way. Having inherited a comfortable sum from his last surviving relative he retired early from the constabulary to live a peaceful life, or so he thought.

Later, Samuel tucked in bed upstairs, Beth, Faith and Harry meet in the drawing room to chat over a glass of sherry, a roaring fire crackling in the hearth. Beth recounts the story of Carl's getaway and concludes anyone could have done it. 'Perhaps a couple of schoolboys did it as a lark or Hall is involved. I might ride past Mrs Hall's home tomorrow to see if the dog's there,' she says.

'What would you do if you saw him, take him in your arms and heave-ho over the fence? He's as big as a pony and just as heavy.'

'I was going to ask you to do it, Aunt Faith.' Beth chuckles.

Faith flexes her arm muscles in the style of a sideshow performer. 'Thank you for acknowledging my boundless talents.'

'Sounds like a severe case of self-delusion.'

'You're on the money there, Harry,' says Faith, grinning. 'Anyway, how do we get that incorrigible hound back to Mr Burkett?'

'Hall would be holding the dogs somewhere else, less exposed to the public. We're lucky we got Cupcake before he moved her. I'll visit Mrs Hall in a couple of days masquerading as Andrew's mate come to settle an account. His mother might let on where he is.'

'Carry dog biscuits, she owns a very savage looking dog,' Beth warns.

'My formidable dog biscuits would stop a lion in its tracks,' Harry boasts. 'I might give you the secret recipe one of these days Beth; it's been handed down in my family for generations.'

'Why not now, I happen to have a pencil at the ready?'

'Good things come to those who wait.'

Faith claps her hands gently. 'Shall we knuckle down?'

Harry raises his arm like a school boy. 'Eric Emerson has been missing for four months, why has Lydia waited so long to contact us?'

'She recently spotted him entering the Café de Paris in Rundle Street, he saw her and took flight,' Beth responds. 'I think she just wants confirmation he's all right.'

'The fact that he hasn't contacted anyone is concerning,' says Harry.

'The police told Lydia he'd emptied his bank accounts two weeks before he disappeared.'

'Sounds like the bloke was preparing to leave.'

'Anna told me she hasn't seen Eric since early April when they were planning to run away and start a new life in Melbourne, taking Audrey and Sophie with them. Of course, she could be lying.'

'Angus Hopping has a strong motive to harm Eric, maybe he found out about the affair and …'

'According to Anna he was at home celebrating Audrey Hubble's birthday on the day Eric disappeared.'

'It's strange Eric didn't leave a note, making off without a word seems very cruel and out of character given everyone describes him in glowing terms,' says Faith.

'If he intended leaving for good, why did he lock his study door and take the key with him?' Beth asks.

'Maybe he intends returning home and he's just lying low until whatever strife he's in blows over. As for the locked door, he doesn't want Lydia getting her hands on his stash,' Harry speculates.

'Maybe he simply forgot the key was in his pocket,' Faith suggests, throwing her hands in the air. 'Anyway, what do we do if we find him, given he doesn't want to return home?'

'We'll take him back to Lydia in leg irons, his hands manacled behind his back.' Harry bursts out laughing with his entire upper body, his shoulders rising and falling with each burst. His mirth is contagious and soon all three are laughing.

'We return unwilling pets to their owners, why not unwilling husbands to their wives?' Beth chortles, using a handkerchief to dab the tears of laughter from her eyes.

'Come on team, enough shenanigans.'

'You started it, Harry!'

Faith puts on her serious face. 'Why would Lydia engage our services if ...' she pauses, fishing for a suitable expression, 'she'd dispatched him?'

All agree it is unlikely that Lydia has dispatched her husband, but they keep an open mind.

'What about Mr O'Halloran, would he have had something to do with Eric's disappearance?'

'Eric would have enough proof against O'Halloran to land him in the lock-up,' says Harry. 'If Eric threatened to expose him ...'

'O'Halloran wouldn't think twice about murdering anyone who threatens his business,' says Beth. 'He's an infuriating man, when I asked about the compulsory insurance he delivered a tedious sales speech.'

'I'll visit his furniture warehouse in a few days as an interested client. I'll get the address of that so-called insurance company.'

'Are you sure you want to face that boorish brute, Aunt Faith?'

'It'll be fun. The ill-mannered can be very docile and affable when they catch a whiff of money in the air.' Faith laughs so heartily, she spills sherry over her white blouse.

'Don't wear that blouse,' Aunt Faith.

'I intend wearing my best fake jewellery and my most exquisite gown to dupe that awful man. He'll think I'm loaded, believe you me.'

'Another person of interest is Vincent Stirling,' says Beth. 'I can't help thinking he's holding something back. O'Halloran boasted Mr Stirling had purchased his furniture on Eric's recommendation. I'll visit him in a week or so to verify that.'

Using his investigative wisdom gained from thirty-five years in the constabulary, eighteen years in Port Augusta and more recently as a senior detective at the Adelaide constabulary, Harry makes use of a large blackboard and chalk to map out the tenuous evidence and a sprinkling of suspects: Lydia Emerson, Angus Hopping, Stanley O'Halloran and Vincent Stirling.

They declare the meeting closed until further evidence comes to the fore.

'When shall we three meet again, in thunder, lightning, or in rain?' Faith asks, followed by a cackling chuckle.

'When the hurly-burly's done!' Beth joins in.

'When the battle's lost and won.' Harry raises his glass.

TUESDAY, 14TH AUGUST

The railway station in North Terrace is an impressive stone building with red brick dressings and wide verandas. Bidding his several friends farewell, a tall muscular seafarer is making his way through the arched portico, a duffle bag over his shoulder. Looking forward to enjoying two weeks leave, Angus opts to walk home, to get his land legs limbered up. A mile on, he comes to Wilson's Park where the sweet fragrance of blossoming almond trees call to mind the romantic picnics he'd shared with Anna when they were courting. Silky black hair, dark eyes, clear skin, she was young and fresh then, and she doted on him. Now, she's tired all the time. Sometimes, when he has a quid, he treats himself to a night out at Ethel's Dance Hall, he always asks for Ruth, a woman who appreciates his vigour. When he's out at sea, it's the memories of that place that keep him going. He still has nightmares about a particularly horrendous experience. It was during a fierce storm off the coast of Perth, the ship struck a shoal of rock and water began pouring in. The captain ordered his crew to abandon the sinking ship. The officers monopolised the lifeboats and the rest of the men had to leap into the sea and cling to floating wreckage or tread water until a search party arrived. It was the ship's cook who saw Angus floundering about, his head going under. Chef Masterton saved his miserable life by approaching him with a lifebuoy and telling him to calm down and hold on tight. Angus complained of cramps in his legs. For hours, he and the other survivors were at the mercy of the sea, fish nibbling at their skin and numb from cold. Jolted about in the ferocious waves, it was thoughts of Ruth's buxom curves that warmed his body. When help finally arrived, he and the other sailors were pulled from the water, helped into lifeboats and taken to the mother ship anchored some twenty nautical miles away. Thankfully, nobody discovered his inability to swim. He'd never let on he couldn't swim, and if that detail finds its way to his superiors he'd be thrown out by the seat of his pants. It's what he discovered about himself that still haunts him – he hadn't once thought of Anna or Sophie, despite a belief he might not survive. When he returned home, he was wracked with guilt, shedding tears each time he held his little girl in his arms.

A flock of galahs devouring white clover barely flinch as he strolls across the lawn outside his favourite pub. The thought of a refreshing cold beer makes his mouth water. Despite looking forward to seeing his daughter he cannot resist the urge to socialise with the blokes he'd grown up with. A hardworking man deserves some down time. Mixing with a group of old friends, he celebrates being on land again well into the afternoon. By the light of a blood-red sunset, he shuffles out and moves along the road singing a sea ditty, his long legs leading him home as if they've a mind of their own.

Standing at the kitchen window, Anna watches him enter the yard. Wondering if there's any money left for food, she is already dreading his erratic mood swings, especially when he's been boozing it up. Sophie is outside, sitting on a tattered blanket playing with her dolls. He stumbles down beside her, his gangly legs stretched out, his arm wrapped around her, chatting and laughing out loud, until something she says changes his mood. When he hauls himself to his feet, he tells Sophie to wait outside while he goes inside to see Mama. Anna has learned over time that Angus' worst outbursts are demonstrated by slow movement. He stands at the threshold, slips through the door, a predator. Lips shut tightly, eyes narrowed, crimson-faced, he approaches Anna. She knows that look, what it precedes, she fears it, she fears him.

Her pulse racing, she feigns a welcoming smile.

'Our darlin' girl tells me a woman come round here on a bicycle, wearin' blokes' trousers. I hope ya not gettin' involved in them harlot groups. I won't have it, ya understand.'

'I've got no time to join any groups, Angus.'

His hand goes straight to her throat, his large fingers pressing into her skin until she can barely breathe. 'You know what group I mean, them bloody suffragettes who want to run the country like blokes.'

'Let go, Angus, let ...'

When he loosens his grip, the red outline of his hand is imprinted on her neck. Staring at his open hands as if they belong to someone else, he rubs his palms on his shirt, erasing his excesses.

Unable to speak, coughing profusely, Anna stumbles onto a seat. Her fear eased, she swallows a glass of water and speaks. 'The woman came to tell us our lawyer Mr Emerson has left the firm. His partner's takin' over. I've got a letter to prove it if you don't believe me.'

'We don't need 'em no longer, the house is ours now.'

'They keep our legal papers. It doesn't cost much to have 'em locked up safe and sound.'

'Don't let me catch you leavin' the house except for groceries,' Angus warns, pointing his index finger at her face. 'Even when I'm at sea, I'll find out if ya break the rules, I got a lot of friends here about. And no visitors, you got ya ma and Sophie, ya don't need no friends.'

'I live for you, Ma and Sophie. You know that,' says Anna, looking into his bleary eyes and wondering what has sparked his outburst. The thought crosses her mind one of his friends or acquaintances had spotted her out with Eric. But who would recognise her all done up like a princess. Eric had gifted her two beautiful silk gowns and a necklace to match. She'd already sold the necklace but the gowns are still in the house – hidden in the linen cupboard in a purple box beneath the sheets. When Angus is at sea she often wears them, pirouetting across the floor, reviving fond memories. If those possessions were slumber they'd represent a nap of happiness. If Angus found them she'd end up in a box just like the gowns. Short of money, she'll have to sell one of them, maybe both if Angus keeps drinking their paltry savings.

WEDNESDAY, 15TH AUGUST

Harry rises early, dons his best suit and has breakfast with Faith who compliments him on looking dapper and perhaps overdressed for a jaunt in his wagon. 'I have to impress a lady of a certain age today,' he says, combing his hair back with his fingers and smiling mischievously.

'Well, you've impressed this one.'

Harry parks outside of Mrs Hall's home. A tall timber fence frames the entire block. He lifts the latch and opens the gate, the click sets off a dog, a large one by the sounds of the deep and resonating bark tone. Warily, he approaches the front door and knocks, hoping whoever is inside doesn't let the dog out. Beth had warned him to arm himself with magic dog biscuits but he'd forgotten to. A scrawny, balding woman swings the door open and asks what he flaming well wants. A large growling dog is kneeling by her side, she smacks him on the nose and tells him to shut up.

Doffing his hat, Harry introduces himself as Mr Tingcombe, a name he often uses when anonymity is called for.

'Mr what?'

'Tingcombe.'

Mrs Hall moves out of the house, closes the door behind her. The dog is told to sit, he obeys her command. Glaring at Harry with narrowed eyes, she waits for an explanation.

'Would you be Mrs Hall?'

'What's it to you?'

'I've come to settle an invoice, is my good friend Andrew Hall at home?'

The dog starts growling again. 'Shut-up Sweetie or I'll lock ya up!'

Harry makes a point of remembering the dog's name in case Sweetie decides to exercise his authority.

'The old Mr Andy Hall is dead. Young Andy moved out a while back.'

'Did he leave a forwarding address?'

'Which one, old Andy or young Andy?' She grins.

Harry chuckles. 'Most amusing, Mrs Hall.'

'Andy tells me nothin' but he stays over sometimes, comes back like a flamin' boomerang he does. You can give me the money. I'll see he gets it.'

'That's very kind of you, Mrs Hall, but I'd rather pay Andrew in person.' Harry stands there, looking directly at her, urging her to volunteer her son's address. But she clams up, her pale eyes showing neither fear nor friendliness.

'Could he be staying with a relative?'

'Besides Andy, my only surviving relative died a couple of months ago.'

'Sorry for your loss, Mrs Hall.'

'He weren't worth bein' sorry for, the drunken pisspot only ever turned up when he needed a quid.'

'That's most unfortunate,' Harry assumes an empathetic expression. 'Is Andrew still running his dog breeding business?'

'Why?'

'I'm looking to buy a friendly pooch,' he smiles. 'I'm a lonely old man, Mrs Andrews. I'd love a loyal four-legged companion.'

'Mongrel or purebred?'

'I'd prefer a large dog, a purebred.'

'They ain't cheap.'

'What price a good friend?' he chuckles. 'Besides, I'm a man of means.'

'I'll let him know, give me your business card Mr Ting.'

'Tingcombe.'

'Whatever.'

Feigning a search for his cards, Harry fumbles through his coat pockets. 'Oh dear, I seem to be out of cards. I'll pop one under your door during the next few days.'

Without so much as a goodbye, Mrs Hall tells the dog to get inside and slams the door behind her. Disappointed his swish suit and charm had not born results, Harry remains standing on the threshold for several seconds before making for his wagon.

THURSDAY, 16TH AUGUST

Faith asks the hansom cab driver to wait for her. Their expenses are covered and a cab on stand-by is a handy get-a-way vehicle should the necessity arise. Dressed in a fine silk beige dress enhanced by an exquisite ruby necklace with matching earrings, she lifts her fulsome skirts as she negotiates the several steps leading to the office and arrives promptly at the appointed hour. Stanley O'Halloran is yelling at his red-faced clerk when the distinguished lady steps into the room, bidding them good morning. There's an uncomfortable silence while O'Halloran reinstates his decorum and offers his sweaty hand. Faith feels his clammy heat through her lacy glove. He gestures her into his office.

'Please take a seat,' he says, returning to his own seat, more of a throne given its immense size and cushioned comfort. 'What can I do for you, Mrs Ellsworth?' he asks, setting aside some paperwork.

Faith knits an intricate crochet of lies detailing her family's journey to Adelaide from Melbourne. They plan to stay in Adelaide for eighteen months and require quality furnishings in their rented property.

'You've come to the right place, Mrs Ellsworth. I'm sure you'll find exactly what you're looking for here. Our products are of superior quality,' he smiles broadly, his eyes drawn to her ruby necklace and matching earrings. His expression telling, she's a toff with money to burn. Following a discussion of the conditions, prices, and insurance, he calls his son into the office. Raymond O'Halloran of sturdy stature, has a head full of brown frizzy hair, not grey-blue like his father's. Invited to tour the showrooms, Faith follows Raymond as they wander amongst the sturdy furniture. He invites her to run her fingers over the fine timber, she dares not remove her gloves, her recently acquired love of gardening has given her the hands of a potato farmer and dirt in her fingernails would give the game away. When he thinks Faith isn't looking, he regards his reflection in the wardrobe mirrors and preens his hair. The factory is as large as a ballroom, the furniture spread out, well-presented, mostly set up like lounge rooms or theatrical stage settings. Faith is invited to be seated on a sofa, a luxurious chaise longue and dining chairs of various designs and colours. Each time, her guide offers his hand to hoist her up. Following the tour, she is accompanied to the clerk's office where she is urged to sign up immediately and receive the first three month's hire at a reduced rate. Raymond hovers for a long moment, hoping she'd make an impetuous decision as so many do. Faith imagines a few older customers, exhausted after having toured around for an hour, would feel compelled to sign a contract so they could rush home to rest.

'Would you like to complete the paperwork today?' Raymond asks.

'I'm tempted, the furniture is superb and I can't wait to see it sitting in my home. But I must discuss it with my husband first. Could you give me the price details of my chosen pieces? I'll return in a week or so with my husband to finalise the contract.'

'Our very competent clerk can do that for you, Mrs Ellsworth,' says Raymond before leaving the room.

'Did you find what you're looking for, Mrs Ellsworth?' asks the clerk, his pointy nose in the air.

'I did indeed. The quality furniture is most attractive to the eye. Do you have any price lists?'

The clerk hands Faith a list of furnishings, most of which have the prices indicated. All three cost options are listed – purchase, hire purchase and rental. 'There's also an added cost of compulsory insurance should you opt for hire-purchase or rental. Some of our customers have taken out insurance for furniture they've paid outright for. We're very flexible.'

'Would you be so kind as to provide me with the name of the insurance company? My husband's a stickler for details,' she chuckles.

The clerk suggests he can do better than that, he hands Faith a copy of the insurance form, and asks her to complete the document before she returns to the office to consolidate the contract.

'I'm sorry to have entered your office during a heated discussion,' says Faith.

The clerk simply shrugs his shoulders.

'I didn't mean to pry. Mr O'Halloran seems like a very charming gentleman.'

The clerk's eyes move to O'Halloran's closed door before responding. 'He flies off the handle every so often; it keeps me on my toes.'

Faith thanks the clerk and informs him she'll return within the week accompanied by her dearly beloved husband. Looking absurdly uppity, she makes a refined exit from the office.

Sitting in a cab, on her way home, Faith studies the insurance form, the Guaranteed Insurance Company is located in Unley. Her curiosity gets the better of her; she pokes her head through the hatch and instructs the driver to take her to the address indicated on the form. He makes a turn to the right, the cab rumbles along a pot-holed road for a short while, turns left and there she is. In case she has to make a hasty exit, she asks the driver to wait for her. Snooping about has landed her in trouble before. On the street, she studies the house numbers and stops when she sees the number five etched on a brass plaque. Below the number are shiny golden letters: Mr H. O'Halloran. There's no mention of an insurance company.

Before proceeding, she mentally tracks the O'Halloran male lineage, Stanley and Raymond O'Halloran, and the man she is about to meet. She ascends the tiled steps and presses the doorbell. As there is no answer she presses again and waits another five minutes. She is about to leave when a tall man with a long face and a square chin opens the door.

'Can I help you?' he asks, rolling an aniseed lolly round his mouth.

'My name is Mrs Faith Ellsworth, I'm wondering if I could see Mr O'Halloran?'

'Mr O'Halloran is indisposed, good day.' He closes the heavy door. Faith hears the bolt clunking on the other side and waits a few minutes before slapping the doorbell again, this time harder. He answers the door, his steely eyes look directly into hers then move downwards to her ruby necklace. His gaze sits there too long, Faith wonders if he has discerned it's a fake.

'Is this the office for the Guaranteed Insurance Company?' she asks, trying not to look at the depressed scar, a shade lighter than his skin and running from his lips to his left earlobe.

'No, it's the residence of Mr O'Halloran.'

'I'm a customer of Mr Stanley O'Halloran's furniture business. I'd like to discuss the terms of insurance before I sign the contract. I've been led to believe this is the address of the insurance company. If not, would you be so kind as to direct me to the correct address?'

'Please wait there, I'll speak to Mr O'Halloran.' He slams the door and locks it behind him. An audience with Queen Victoria would be easier than securing a chat with the man behind that heavily reinforced door, she tells herself as she ponders whether to leave or not.

Several minutes pass before Faith is invited inside. As she is led into the drawing room she hears the clicking of the lock behind her. The elderly man she sees sitting behind a large desk is an older version of Stanley O'Halloran. But the older face is wan, as if his skin hasn't seen sunlight in years.

'It's all right, William. I'll chat with the interloper,' Mr O'Halloran says, gesturing to him to remain in the room. He looks Faith up and down before asking why she is bothering him with questions that should be directed at his son.

'I was given an impressive guided tour of the warehouse this morning. The furniture is exquisite.'

'Tell me something I don't know.'

'I'm on the verge of signing a rental contract but I thought I'd check on the insurance first. It's expensive and compulsory.'

'I used to run the Guaranteed Insurance Company, but I've since retired. My son uses another company now; you'll have to discuss the new arrangements with him.'

Faith takes the insurance form from her bag and holds it up to the elderly O'Halloran. She asks why the furniture business hasn't changed the address on the form.

'May I see it?'

Faith reluctantly passes it to him. He scans the page, and hands it to his assistant who shreds it into confetti before tossing it into the paper bin.

'You had no right to damage my property,' Faith responds.

Mr O'Halloran turns his attention back to Faith, his stony-faced stare unsettling. 'It's not your property, it belongs to O'Halloran industries,' he snaps. 'That form has expired; the clerk gave you the wrong one. My advice to you is to return to my son's office to request a valid form.'

'Can you tell me the name of the current insurance company?'

'I'm tired of this conversation. William, please show Mrs Ellsworth out.'

'Has anyone else been here to enquire about the insurance?'

'If you want to discuss my son's business activities, see him at his business address.'

Faith gazes at the old man; he must be eighty if he's a day. Turning her attention to his desk, she notices a pistol alongside his writing paraphernalia. She suspects he is cognisant of his son's dubious business dealings, perhaps he's the architect.

'If you know what's good for you and your family you'll leave this house and never come back.' His hand moves to the pistol, his knobby fingers stroking it as one does a precious stone; a subtle beast now replacing a feeble old man.

'I won't take any more of your precious time, Mr O'Halloran. I have a hansom cab waiting outside, the driver must be wondering why I'm taking so long,' says Faith, inching out of the room, feigning a smile, her calm veneer belying a heart palpitating unease.

His hand slides away from the pistol as he bids Faith good day, reminding her that his son will hear about her visit.

'Standing at the front door, she waits for the old man's assistant to unlock it and set her free. His face so close to hers she smells the fruity aniseed lollies on his breath, he tells her to take heed of Mr O'Halloran's warnings as he'd stop at nothing to protect his family.

The door swings open. Faith inhales deeply before hurrying down the steps and onto the street. O'Halloran might reside in a swish residence in a moneyed area but he's a ruthless brigand. She climbs into the cab, thankful she'd asked the driver to wait for her. His insurance company is about as authentic as her fake rubies. She suspects Stanley O'Halloran's clients are paying high premiums for mandatory non-existent insurance; she could kick herself for giving him the form. Customers wishing to claim for loss or theft would find themselves in a blind alley. O'Halloran's no fool; he knows his well-to-do clients would at all costs avoid getting their names in the newspapers, too wealthy and too proud to have their reputation sullied, afraid of being seen as being taken in by a lowly under-handed businessman. And should there be anyone who dares to complain to the constabulary, it wouldn't be above O'Halloran to use the threat of violence to silence them.

Faith directs the driver to the Department of Records where she plans to spend the afternoon making enquiries into O'Halloran's insurance business. With the assistance of a trusted friend who holds a management position in the department, Faith hopes to return home with solid evidence of O'Halloran's criminal conduct.

~

Assembled in the drawing room before a crackling fire, the three members of Bethany's Agency are seated at the round table, a glass of sherry before them. Faith relays the details of her visit to the furniture warehouse and her harrowing experience with the elderly O'Halloran.

'Sounds like the O'Halloran men grow more abhorrent with age,' says Beth.

'His assistant looked like a nasty thug, William I think his name was. He smelled of aniseed lollies. I used to enjoy aniseed drops, not anymore.'

'Did you find out anything at the Department of Records?'

'My friend was unforthcoming about O'Halloran's business dealings, apparently a police detective recently visited to collect all files connected to them.'

Harry confirms Faith's findings; he has heard on the grapevine that the O'Halloran business is being investigated.

'Lydia told me she wasn't aware of Eric's affiliations with the O'Halloran family. We're stumped, aren't we?' says Beth.

'How long did it take you to find Cupcake?' Harry asks.

'About three weeks.'

'We're looking for a human being and you're concerned we haven't found him yet. Something will come up, it always does. What about that dog that got away?'

'I have no idea where he got to. With such a generous reward on offer there'd be others after him. I wouldn't be surprised if Andrew Hall has him.'

'According to Mrs Hall, he moved out a while back and hasn't told her where he lives. She's a cunning vixen, but I think she was telling the truth,' says Harry. 'You're right about that dog of hers; he'd turn a man into mincemeat in seconds. His name's Sweetie.'

'I bet your special biscuits came in handy.'

'I forgot them. Luckily Mrs Hall has total control of Sweetie. To be honest, I'm not sure which of the two is more terrifying.'

'I think Mrs Hall and Sweetie are probably evenly matched,' Faith chuckles. 'Anyway, your covert investigation has confirmed Carl is not at her place.'

'Speaking of which, I'm going to Tillie's school tomorrow to talk to her students about the joys of the investigative profession. Then I'm going to pop in to see Vincent Stirling. I'll probably be late home; can you mind Sam for me, Aunt Faith?'

'Young Sam's company would be a welcome change after today's adventures.'

FRIDAY, 17TH AUGUST

Beth had passed the afternoon at the Advanced School for Girls as a special guest speaker with Tillie's senior students. For the most part, she answered questions and shared her experience as a private investigator. Their questions were absurd and at times amusing: how many murderers had she arrested and how many bank robberies had she averted? She had informed them that a large part of investigating is observation, interviewing people, accumulating evidence and making deductions. People matter the most, she'd explained, you have to dig deep into their past to find out what motivates them. Harry often reminds her that a crime is solved by studying the people involved not the other way around. Surprisingly, the students also enjoyed her stories about reuniting people with their beloved pets. They all wanted to know when women would be accepted into the constabulary, she could only assure them it was inevitable but not for a very long time. She encouraged them to join suffrage groups and to attend organised rallies.

A wintry wind is blowing when she alights from the cab in Pirie Street, the kind of damp chill that bites through clothing. It's only half past five but twilight looms. The street lamps flicker on, their pale light encircled by mist. Beth wraps her scarf around her face and neck and hastens down the street, hoping Vincent Stirling is still in his office. The door leading to the stairs is unlocked; she turns the knob and lets herself in. Noticing a light beaming from his office, she moves along the dimly lit hall and finds him on his feet tidying his desk.

'Mrs Durrani, what brings you here?'

'I've come for a quick chat, Mr Stirling.'

'I'm just about to leave. Would you care to chat over dinner? It's a more congenial place than the office.'

'I'm not really dressed for an evening out.'

'It's a quaint, unfussy little place, no need for elegant attire. I'm not dressed to the nines myself,' he smiles, looking down at his navy blue cardigan over a white shirt. 'Besides, you look ravishing as you are.'

'In that case, I'd love to join you, thank you. I'm not expected home until late, it's been a long day and I am hungry,' says Beth, recalling she hadn't had time for lunch that day.

Vincent dons his coat. They descend the stairs. He locks the solid entrance door and they set off on the short walk to the restaurant. Holding up her skirts as she marches along, Beth does her best to match his stride. The restaurant is warmed by a raging fire. A waiter takes their coats and conducts them to a table near a broad-leafed indoor plant. The menu is handed to Beth, the beverage list to Vincent who orders a bottle of white wine. The waiter arrives soon after and pours a taster for Vincent's appraisal. Vincent clasps his glass, takes a sip, and raises his expressive eye-brows with a nod of approval. Beth wonders what he'd do if the wine wasn't to his liking. The waiter fills their glasses.

'This is hardly an unfussy restaurant, Mr Stirling,' says Beth, pleased she isn't wearing her bloomers.

'I dine here so often it feels like home,' he says, raising his glass.

They clink their glasses and sip the cool wine. Minutes later, another waiter approaches and takes their order. Unaccustomed to the restaurant, Beth simply has what Vincent orders: grilled salmon and baked potatoes.

'So, what is it you have to tell me, Mrs Durrani?'

'I visited Mr O'Halloran's office on Monday. I'm wondering why you didn't mention you'd purchased furniture from him?'

'You didn't ask,' says Vincent, noticing that Beth's hazel eyes become golden when she's touching on a delicate matter.

'I'm asking now.'

'My word, you'd make an excellent lawyer, Mrs Durrani.'

'Mr O'Halloran used your name as a recommendation for his business credentials.'

'I've never given that lying swindler permission to use my name to endorse his dodgy dealings.'

Beth fixes her eyes on his, prompting him to elaborate.

'I took Eric's advice and bought a dining room suite on hire purchase for my seaside residence. During my conversations with Stanley O'Halloran I let slip I reside in Port Adelaide on weekends only. Just weeks after I'd made a final payment the furniture was stolen, and the insurance did not exist.'

'Why hire purchase?'

'It was fifteen percent cheaper than buying outright and included insurance cover.'

'Do you think Mr O'Halloran had anything to do with the theft?'

'He stood to gain from it. Besides, only the O'Halloran furniture was stolen, all the other rooms were untouched.'

'Why?'

'Their own brand of furniture is easily restored and resold.'

'You must have been very angry with Eric for recommending such a disreputable company.'

'I was furious, but not angry enough to harm him, if that's what you're implying. He was just as gullible as I was.'

'Would Mr O'Halloran have harmed Eric?'

'O'Halloran's a thief, but a murderer, that's a stretch.'

'Anyone is capable of murder, given the circumstances.'

'O'Halloran deals in hire purchase and rental furniture with fake insurance. He steals the furniture, restores it and resells it. If I were a murderer I'd have murdered him months ago, and so would any number of his disgruntled customers. But he's still above ground, isn't he?'

'Above ground and above the law,' Beth concedes. 'Aunt Faith visited Mr O'Halloran yesterday as a potential client, and she was handed an insurance form. The address turned out to be his father's home. Following a heated discussion, in a roundabout way, Mr O'Halloran senior threatened my aunt with a pistol. He warned her to stop prying or else. If you'd told me about their spurious insurance schemes she'd have avoided their intimidations.'

'I had no idea the O'Halloran men would stoop so low. I'm sorry your aunt had to endure ...'

'Aunt Faith knows how to look after herself.' Beth gives a half-smile. 'Anyway, she has established the fact that three generations of the O'Halloran family are involved in the fraudulent insurance scheme. But I'm sure you already know that.'

'I'm glad your aunt wasn't hurt and, yes, I've known about it for some time, but I don't have solid evidence that would stand up in court. Here comes our dinner,' he says, noticeably pleased to change the subject of their conversation. The steaming salmon is placed on the table along with crisp bread, butter, potatoes and fresh green vegetables. The waiter refills their glasses with wine before moving to another table.

Vincent takes hold of his cutlery. '*Bon appétit.*'

'It's delicious,' says Beth, her irritation subsiding, the wine soothing.

They eat hungrily, barely saying a word until their hunger is appeased.

'Tell me about Bethany Investigations.'

'I don't run the business alone, Aunt Faith and her boarder Harry Fairweather assist. They also help me look after my four-year-old son Samuel as I'm often out and about.'

'You're fortunate to have a trusted team of sleuths and child-minders. It must be very demanding raising a child whilst running a business.'

'Demanding and wonderful, Sam is the sunshine of my life.'

'Mrs Emerson informs me you've lived in Afghanistan. What an experience that must have been.'

'It's a wonderful place. My late husband, Arif, and his extended family own a large parcel of fertile land, we lived well.'

'Yet you left.'

'I had my reasons.'

Vincent reads her serious countenance as a closed door and is relieved when the waiter hands them the dessert menu. He recommends orange cake served with cream and Cointreau liqueur.

'Sounds delectable, thank you. And please call me Bethany or Beth if you prefer.'

'On condition you call me Vincent.'

'Tell me about yourself, Mr Stirling … Vincent.'

'I enjoy swimming and fishing.'

'A man of the sea.'

'I grew up in Port Adelaide where life revolves around the sea. I still live in my parent's home on days off.' Vincent pauses as the waiter places their dessert before them. 'I'm also an incorrigible sweet tooth,' he smiles.

'Same here,' Beth responds, and adds, almost as an afterthought. 'Were your parents at home when thieves stole your furniture?'

'My parents died five years ago in a boating accident.'

'Sorry to hear that. You must miss them.'

He nods. 'What about your family?'

'My mother died when I was twelve-years-old. Tillie, my younger sister, is a teacher at the Advanced School for Girls. My father owns an outback bakery in Farina.' Beth finds herself wondering why she's divulging personal details to a man who is essentially a stranger and possibly a suspect.

'I know farina means flour but I've never heard of Farina the place, where is it?'

'It's about four hundred miles north of Adelaide. It's a wild and unpredictable place with marvellous tangerine sunsets and star-filled skies.' The luscious dessert and wine has put Beth's wariness on hold, but the thought crosses her mind she should guard against being side-tracked by Vincent's charm and good looks.

'How did your father come to choose such a place?'

'It was inexpensive and he was determined to open his own bakery. At the time, Farina was touted as the 'great granary of the north', Papa expected to find a green oasis. We all did.'

'And did you?'

'Not at first. Farina was in drought and we wanted to return to Adelaide. We soon learned the outback is prone to drought, floods, sandstorms, and of course perfect weather in the cooler seasons. We adapted and grew to love the place.'

'I must be more adventurous and explore the outback one of these days.'

'Arif and I planned to cross the desert as far as Stuart. In the early eighties, hardly anyone white lived there, just a few workers operating the telegraph service. Indigenous people live there, Arif told me they're fascinating people who live off the land.'

'I don't think the rail goes that far yet.'

'We planned to travel by camel train.'

'You know how to ride a camel?'

'They're delightful animals once you get them on side. Perched on a camel, you feel as though you're on top of the world.' Beth doesn't mention the aches and pains experienced after a long ride. 'Anyway, the journey didn't eventuate, Arif's father fell ill and we moved to Afghanistan.'

'You've had some fascinating experiences.'

'Like everyone else, I guess, the full gamut.' Following a pensive silence, Beth asks Vincent if he was in the habit of dining with Eric.

'Yes, we would often meet here to discuss business over dinner. Why?'

'I'm just curious.'

He smiles. 'An essential trait in your business.'

'Does Eric carry any accessories that are of sentimental value to him? Perhaps jewellery, a watch, a pocketknife, a …'

'He wears a wedding ring.' Vincent pauses to reflect and adds, 'When he graduated from university his father gifted him a pocketknife, there's an inscription engraved on it. I can't remember the wording. Why do you ask?'

'I came across it in his home study. It's kept in a drawer all to itself, it must be very special.'

'It's his most prized possession in terms of sentimental value.'

'You'd think he'd have taken it with him, wouldn't you?'

'I guess it depends how hurried he was.'

As they are talking, Vincent's eyes follow a gentleman entering the restaurant. Heads turn as he and his entourage are led to a large table.

'He'd fall over backwards if he held his chin up any higher,' Beth chuckles. 'Do you know him?'

'Mr Ebenezer Ward. He's a former client, an eloquent man yet quite dull, to be honest.'

'He is vehemently opposed to female suffrage.'

'Yes, he's using every trick under the sun to prevent the suffrage bill from passing.'

'I believe it will pass, despite Mr Ward's ruthless opposition.'

'He'll have egg on his face if it does.' Vincent grins.

'That obviously pleases you.'

'He's an arrogant toad.'

'Are you pleased because the arrogant toad could make a fool of himself, or because you believe women should have the right to vote simply because they are human beings?'

'Both those reasons.' He smiles. 'Are you a suffragette, Beth?'

'I can't imagine any woman, or any man for that matter, not wanting the right to vote in elections. I'm sure we'll have universal suffrage before the year is out.'

'You're very optimistic.'

'I'd put money on it,' says Beth, the orange liqueur making her reckless.

'Ten pounds.'

Beth offers her hand and they shake on it.

'There's a street demonstration next Thursday to submit a petition containing more than ten thousand signatures to the minister. That has to count for something.'

'Will you attend?'

'Yes, my sister and her friend are visiting tomorrow to make banners in preparation for the rally.'

'Do you really believe posters and sashes will drive powerful men in parliament to make concessions?'

'We do what we can. It would show them there are many of us who want suffrage and encourage others to join our cause.'

'Will women in parliament make the world a better place?'

'Better maybe, at least for women, but certainly a different place.'

'Well, I hope you win the vote even if it costs me ten quid.' He pats his lips with a serviette and calls for the waiter to bring the bill. Soon after, they fetch their coats and leave.

'I'll walk you down to the tavern on the corner; it's easy to hail a cab there.'

Outside, a thumbnail moon smiles in the sky and the wind has died down. They chat as they stroll down the street until they arrive in a busy part of town. With little time left in the evening and the subdued light making her brave, Beth seizes the moment to discuss a thorny issue. 'As a lawyer you have the means and the expertise to fight Mr O'Halloran in the courts. You know perfectly well he's a ruthless crook.'

'As I already said, accusations need solid evidence. I would not put my reputation in jeopardy without the certainty I'd win.'

'Imagine all the other people he's duped, you could have saved some of them.'

'Most of them can afford it.'

'You don't know that.'

The sound of rowdy chatter takes Vincent's attention. Several young men pass them, their jovial conversations and roaring laughter resounding along the street.

Beth waits for the merry group to vanish before continuing. 'Middle class pride, that's why he gets away with it, the crafty old fox and his equally devious son get away with theft and perhaps murder.'

'It's not that simple. If I went public my clients would consider me a gullible fool and my business would suffer. Who in their right mind would engage a lawyer who can't even manage his own dealings?'

'I would engage a lawyer who stands up for the rights of his clients and his rights as a citizen.' Aware of Vincent's unwavering gaze, Beth feels a pang of guilt. She asks herself if she'd sacrifice her bread and butter, her family, to confront scoundrels like the O'Halloran family in court. 'Sorry, that was out of line.'

'The man's a professional fraudster. Stay clear of him,' says Vincent waving down a cab. 'I'll drop you off home,' he adds, holding out his hand to Beth who accepts his offer and climbs in.

SATURDAY, 18TH AUGUST

Harry and Beth rise early on Saturday morning to set up the work tables. Mid-morning, Tillie and Eva arrive carrying baskets of pastries and fruit, as well as purple fabric for the sashes. Excited greetings and small talk exchanged, they join Beth, Faith and Harry for tea on the front veranda. Alongside them, Sam has a small table set up with pencils and paper for his own artwork which he plans to display on his bedroom walls.

Beth raises her cup. 'Here's to the big day.'

'To the 23rd August, 1894!' they shout in unison.

'With three failed franchise bills under his belt, Robert Caldwell is not about to give up,' says Tillie.

'Mary Lee once praised him as a champion of the Women's League. Let's hope he, George Hawker and their supporters will pass the legislation this year.'

'I'm looking forward to hearing Mary Lee's inspiring speeches,' says Tillie, noticing her sister isn't displaying her usual enthusiasm. 'What's on your mind, Beth?'

'Last week, a young mother told me getting the vote would make no difference whatsoever to her life and in a wider context have no effect on poor illiterate women, especially those with large families and domineering husbands. It occurred to me the Women's League is not only led by well-to-do educated women but ultimately is to their advantage.'

'Women living in poverty are unable to afford a doctor or a basic education, suffrage is on the bottom of their long list of needs,' says Eva.

'Are you still offering medical services to the poor?'

'Yes, Papa usually takes me out in the buggy. I'd ride my bicycle but he worries about me serving women in the slums, especially at night.'

'We need more men like your father. Too many men believe women are incapable of dealing with the strains of medicine and politics,' says Beth.

'Do you think they really believe that or is it just an excuse to exclude women?' Tillie enquires.

Eva suggests it's a little of both. 'Sometimes it's a power thing. Male doctors come up with ridiculous reasons to exclude women from studying medicine: there are no toilet arrangements for ladies, we're too delicate to contend with drunks and prostitutes and the most outrageous reason of all,' Eva assumes a feeble voice, 'we lady doctors are too dainty to manage the sometimes gruesome challenge of childbirth.'

'Dainty! About as dainty as a troop of soldiers on the front lines, you lot!' Faith guffaws.

'It's absurd really, as a female doctor I can patch up broken bodies but I cannot vote unless I own property.'

'The greedy weasels will happily accept your tax payments though,' says Faith, rising from her seat and packing up the tea setting. She asks Sam to help; he nods and follows her into the house, carrying the teapot in two hands like a handful of freshly laid eggs.

'I wouldn't mind joining the constabulary as a fully paid employee earning a secure income,' says Beth.

'You've got the likes of Senator Ebenezer Ward and his fogey friends determined to keep women confined to the kitchen.' Harry shakes his head.

'We have no choice but to assassinate him,' says Beth, her eyes scanning the others who are looking at her in distress.

'Are you serious, Beth?' Tillie asks.

'Of course I am, I'm sick of waiting for men to give me the right to vote. It's time to take it by force. That man must be crushed like a pesky cockroach.'

'There are those in the movement who believe violence is the only way, but murder?'

Beth breaks out in laughter. 'I'm joking for heaven's sake.'

'You had us worried there,' says Eva, joining in the raucous laughter.

'We have to get the vote though. If New Zealand can do it so can we, besides, I've put money on it.'

'That's my sister, not only an assassin but an intemperate gambler as well.'

'I bet ten pounds we'd get the vote by the end of the year so we have to, don't we?' Beth is deadly serious now.

'Does Aunt Faith know?' asks Tillie.

'I won't tell her until I win, so keep it up your sleeve. That goes for you too, Harry.'

'You should tell her, she'd find it amusing.'

'Not if I lose.'

'You won't,' says Harry, looking as though he really means it.

Faith is no longer the staid woman she used to be, Beth muses, partly because of Harry's cheery influence and partly because several journeys to India with Ayishah have broadened her outlook.

Enlivened by tea and good company, the crew begin work. Harry has pre-painted the thin plywood placards white. Using a timber baton, Beth stirs the thick black paint. A first year intern at the Adelaide Hospital, Eva's steady hand pencils the words VOTES FOR WOMEN to be painted in by the others. Soon, a dozen painted banners are drying on the veranda in the gentle breeze and the group moves inside for a late lunch.

Assembled around the large dining table they enjoy sandwiches, cheese, pastries and fruit. Beth pours lemonade into their wine glasses and tells them she's baked a carrot cake for afternoon tea. Harry joins them and Sam insists on sitting next to him, on the men's side of the table. 'The placards look very professional, ladies,' says Harry.

There's a boisterous, collective thank you to Harry for helping.

'My pleasure, it's about time you ladies got a say in parliamentary decisions. Numbat politicians could use some help from the other half.' He raises his glass and sips his lemonade.

'Uncle Harry said I can help nail the handles on,' says Sam, looking to his mother for approval.

Everyone gives a rowdy hurray for Sam. Chuckling, he stands up and bows.

'What's on tomorrow then?' Faith asks.

'We'll finish the sashes.'

'Did everyone leave their brushes soaking in alcohol?'

'I checked, all done,' Harry confirms.

'Just a week to go before women commit to the biggest rally ever conducted,' says Eva. 'Let's raise our glasses to universal suffrage.'

Continuing the festive moment, Faith calls for a second toast to everyone who contributed to the wonderful lunch. Their glasses chink a second time before a brief silence reigns while they devour their lunch.

'Have you discussed O'Halloran's furniture business with any of your student's parents, Tillie?' Beth asks.

'Yes, I have. One of them told me in confidence he'd purchased O'Halloran's furniture. In a matter of months it was stolen and the insurance didn't cover theft despite a firm assurance at the point of purchase that it would.'

'Did he report O'Halloran to the constabulary?'

'I presume he didn't, as he told me not to discuss the theft with anyone.'

'That's why the police can't pin O'Halloran down, his wealthy clients aren't willing to stand up in court and admit to being taken in by a swindler,' Harry says, shaking his head.

'Why would he tell you, Tillie?' Faith asks.

'He's sweet on me.'

'I hope he hasn't made improper ...'

'He's a perfect gentleman, Aunt Faith.'

'A little bird told me there's a new teacher at your school.'

'His name's Edward Fraser,' Tillie pauses, her aunt's astute hazel eyes are asking for more, 'he's covering my classes so I can go to the rally next week.'

'That's very kind of him. Harry and I won't be going, I've always supported the suffrage movement but I really don't like crowded street rallies. Will you invite Mr Stirling, Beth?'

'He's a potential suspect, Aunt Faith.'

'You didn't consider him too dangerous last night when you dined with him in a fancy restaurant.'

'That was business. Anyway, it didn't end well. I implied he was a coward for not reporting Mr O'Halloran to the constabulary. He wasn't impressed.'

'Reporting him for what?' asks Tillie.

'Eric Emerson persuaded him to purchase furniture from Mr O'Halloran. Weeks after he'd paid it off, it was stolen from his seaside home in Port Adelaide, and the so-called insurance cover didn't exist.'

'I like the sound of a seaside residence. Besides being gullible, what's he like?' Faith asks.

'He's ...'

'Say no more, you're as red as a ripe tomato. He's obviously very charming.'

'I'll fetch another bottle of lemonade,' says Beth, marching off to the kitchen.

'What about you, Eva. Do you have any romantic inclinations towards any of the dashing young doctors at the hospital?'

'I'm tempted sometimes but I've struggled too long to get this far in my profession. I'd have to leave it all behind if I married. As for the rally next week, I've been allocated two rosters, so I won't be able to attend, nor will the other female doctor.'

'Others will carry the placards on your behalf. Harry and I will deliver the spares to the Women's Suffrage League on Monday.'

Harry rises to his feet, saying he's going to nail handles to the placards which should be dry by now. Sam, who likes nothing better than woodwork, is right behind him.

Beth returns to the fold and sets the lemonade on the table before going outside to help Harry. With Sam's assistance, the handles take twice as long to complete, but with practice Sam is able to hammer the nails straight in, only once hitting his thumb.

'He's my right-hand man this one,' Harry grins.

'I'm a big boy now,' Sam says, nursing his sore thumb in his mouth.

'I know you are, Sam. Have you finished your drawings?' Beth asks.

'Ages ago,' he responds, mild indignation in his tone. He displays his drawings across the table. There are several pictures of train carriages travelling over vast stretches of countryside, clouds of grey smoke billowing from oversized chimneys. One of the pictures features a man dressed in a black suit standing at the front gate.

Beth's calm tone belying intense unease, she asks if the man in the picture is the one who gave him the kite.

'Yes.'

'Have you seen him again?'

Sam shakes his head. 'He came back.'

'How many times have you seen him since the time he gave you the kite?'

Sam holds up two fingers.

'Never approach him. He might be dangerous.'

'He looks sad and lonely, Mama.'

'Next time you see him tell me, or if I'm not home tell Aunt Faith or Uncle Harry.'

'I will, Mama.'

'Good boy. Let's go inside for tea and cake.'

MONDAY, 20TH AUGUST

The room reeks of rotting food. Dirty dishes are spread across the sink, some of them already coated in a splatter of grey mould. Mrs Bramley clutches her grey woollen scarf, wraps it around her neck and pulls it tight. The thought crosses her mind to yank it so hard she'd choke. There's nothing to live for now her body is all aches and pains. Gone are the days of escaping into the throes of a swashbuckling novel, imagining herself in the arms of the heroic musketeer. Even when her spectacles are sitting on her nose she can barely read the words now. Life isn't the same without her cheerful sister around. At times she sees Irene sitting in her favourite armchair, hears her crackly voice and her silly witchy laugh, only to realize she isn't around anymore. There just isn't anything to look forward to now she's gone. The knocking at the front door draws her away from her anguish. 'Come,' she yells.

Beth pushes the door open, pokes her head in. 'Hello.'

'I'm in the kitchen, Margaret. Don't stand out there in the cold; you'll catch your death.'

Beth finds a woman in her mid to late sixties seated on an armchair, a pale yellow crotchet blanket draped over her legs. The bedraggled woman with the greasy hair has sparkly blue eyes. Beth imagines she'd been pretty before disappointment and age took its toll.

'I'm sorry if I startled you, Mrs ...?'

'Bramley. I thought you was my daughter, she comes every few days to check on me. Who are you?'

'My name is Bethany Durrani. I'm a private investigator.'

Wary, she looks Beth up and down without saying a word. Such a lovely lady and well-dressed too, why on earth would she be an investigator?

'I'm working for Mrs Lydia Emerson, investigating Mr Eric Emerson's disappearance. She's desperate to find out where he is. Your late sister worked for him and I thought you might be able to shed some light on the subject.'

'You think my Irene done it, just 'cause she died on the same day, do ya?'

Beth is taken aback. 'I knew your sister recently passed away but I didn't know it was the same day Mr Emerson disappeared. I'm sorry for your loss, Mrs Bramley.'

'Me too and all, it's bloody lonely in this draughty old place.'

'By all accounts your sister was a respected employee. As for Mr Emerson, we believe he's still alive.'

'He sure as hell don't want to be found though, does he?' Mrs Bramley pulls the blanket up over her chest, and scratches some congealed food from her chin. 'Irene liked Mr Emerson. She said he was a real gentleman, so very kind, funny too, that's all she ever said. She had a nice little job at that house, four hours a day, Monday to Friday. They paid well; it earned her a bit extra for little comforts. We always ate cakes on Friday nights. She'd be here now if she didn't make that terrible mistake.'

'Mistake?'

'Irene thought it were Monday and turned up at work. She suffers … suffered memory lapses. She got muddled up about things, especially the days. I was sick in bed that Saturday, or I would've told her to stay home. She come home so upset that day, went to bed without dinner and never woke up. Two policemen come in the morning, they said she smelled of alcohol, but it's not like my sister to drink. I never seen my sweet sister drink liquor, never.'

'Did you and Irene get a chance to chat that night?'

In deep thought, she purses her lips, looks around the room as if the answer might be written on the walls. 'Irene talked a lot of baloney,' is the best she can do. 'Don't get old luv, if ya know what's good for ya. In a few weeks, I'll probably move in with my daughter Margaret and her noisy tribe of four little rascals. I'm not lookin' forward to it, her husband complains about me all the time as if I'm deaf or invisible.' The thought of moving out of her home triggers a terrible throaty cough.

Beth hurries to the sink and can only find a filthy glass. She fills it with water to the brim and hands it to Mrs Bramley who guzzles every drop.

'Are you all right, Mrs Bramley?'

She nods, clears her throat and tells Beth she used to smoke a pipe and suffers for it now.

'My father has a persistent cough, he's a baker …'

'The flour dust?'

Beth nods. 'Besides that, he's well.' Beth goes quiet for a while, doubts her stoic papa would share his health updates with her. 'Has Mrs Emerson contacted you since you lost your sister?'

'About a week after Irene passed, Mrs Emerson turned up to give her sorrows. She paid me my sister's wages and an extra fiver. The money's handy, but it don't bring Irene back.'

'Mrs Emerson praised your sister as a very kind, trustworthy person, Mrs Bramley.'

'She is … was.'

'Can you think of anything else that might help?'

Mrs Bramley lowers her head, massages her forehead for several minutes, summoning more details. Nothing springs to mind.

'Irene was one of the last people to see Mr Emerson before he left. Did she say anything when she came home that night?'

'Chair', that's what she kept repeatin', chair.'

'Chair?'

'That's what I said.'

'It's an everyday word but it must have been important to her.'

'She was upset about something.'

'Is there anything else, Mrs Bramley?'

Looking into the past, Mrs Bramley is scratching her scalp, her fingernails digging in, perhaps activating her memory. She folds her arms, looks to the ceiling and her clear eyes sparkle with certainty. 'I was lookin' out the window that afternoon thinkin' when's Irene comin' home with some cakes. I seen her gettin' out of a fancy cab. Like lady muck she was, being helped out an' all.'

'Who helped her out?'

'The driver.'

'How did your sister normally travel home?'

'She'd get the bus and walk the last hundred yards or so. She might have been losin' her mind but she had a good pair of pins, walkin' never phased my sister, bless her.'

'Did Irene pay the driver?'

'No, it was paid for an' all.'

On her way home, Beth calls into the police station to make enquiries about Irene Howard's death. A middle-aged, slightly stooped sergeant with luxuriant side whiskers comes to the counter. Beth gives a terse account of her visit to Irene Howard's address and expresses her concerns about her mysterious death.

He casts his mind back to the paperwork he'd filed some months back. 'If I remember correctly, the lady died peacefully in her sleep.'

'Can you provide more details?'

'The medical examiner determined Irene Howard had died of old age and feebleness of mind, her passing hastened by excessive alcohol consumption.'

'She died on the same day as Mr Eric Emerson vanished. Employed as a cleaner at his home, she was one of the last people to see him before he disappeared. Don't you think that's an uncanny coincidence? There could be a connection between her death and Mr Emerson's ...'

'Murder and mayhem might be a financial advantage in your line of business, Mrs Durrani, but the police force is overworked by all manner of petty crime and serious malefactions. In short, we don't look for a crime where it does not exist.'

'Irene Howard's sister told me she was a teetotaller. If she was inebriated as you say, perhaps she'd seen something that made her want to drink or perhaps she'd been forced to drink liquor?'

'By all accounts she was a dotty old lady losing her faculties.'

'May I speak with Inspector Taylor?'

'He's not here today.'

Beth keeps probing until she drains him of patience and is told to leave the office and stay out of trouble. The case is closed, nothing left to say. Not in a month of Sundays would she convince the constabulary to think otherwise. The junior policeman she'd met in the street during her recent confrontation with Andrew Hall is called into the office.

'Accompany Mrs Durrani out the door, Constable Skinner.'

The blushing constable recognises her immediately. He ushers her out of the station without so much as a word until they reach the front door where he asks her to stay away from the constabulary as her presence drives the sergeant into a fury and everyone at the station has to pay, especially the junior officers.

Standing outside on the footpath, with a cold gusty wind blowing, she thinks to hail a cab, but as walking stimulates her mind and soothes her nerves she takes a stroll. Moving along, she tries to piece together the piddling pool of evidence acquired to date. More than a week has passed and there is not one strong lead, Angus Hopping has an alibi and Irene Howard, a teetotaller, was having a bad day and might have been driven to liquor simply from confusion. As for the word 'chair', it's more confusing than helpful, who knows, maybe she was tired and wanted to sit down.

Suddenly aware of a repetitive clacking sound beside her she looks over her shoulder at a young couple ambling along, arm-in-arm yet arguing, the man tapping the pointed end of his umbrella on the cobbled footpath with each step. Mindful he is being stared at, he raises his umbrella and thrusts it open with the subtlety of a pig gobbling apples. The disgruntled couple hurry past, the black umbrella concealing their faces. They disappear into the misty distance. Thick violet-black clouds hover overhead, rumbling thunder is warning anyone still lingering in the elements to take cover. The road has cleared – not a buggy or a soul in sight. Tightening the shawl around her neck, Beth hurries on. The sound of heavy footfalls behind her turns her head. She catches a glimpse of a tall figure wearing a black suit and top hat. At first, she thinks he is the man she'd recently seen talking to Sam, but a second glimpse dispels that idea, the man behind her is heavily built, unlike the wiry man she'd seen outside her home. Uneasy, she hears his boots clomping on the footpath. Suddenly cold, she picks up her pace. Hoping the man will keep going, she turns into a road on the left. The dark figure also turns left. More conspicuous now, he is about fifty yards behind her. Convinced he is pursuing her, she hoists up her skirts and sprints. He lengthens his strides, his long legs easily cutting short the distance between them. Just as she is passing Bottlebrush Park she is grabbed from behind and dragged into the bushes. Muted by a large hand clenched over her mouth she cannot breathe. The hand loosens its grip just in time for her to take a desperate breath. A mix of odours assaults her nostrils: sweat, tobacco and something else – aniseed.

'Scream and you're dead,' warns the deep voice. The pressure of his hand increases then loosens again.

Her pulse pounding, Beth holds her silence.

'I saw you coming out of the police station. My employer wants you to mind your own business. Any more snooping around the

O'Halloran properties and you'll regret it. Do not visit any member of the O'Halloran family, especially the elderly one. Nosy people have disappeared in his house, never to be seen again.'

Beth's quavering voice assures him she was discussing another matter with the police which has nothing to do with his business.

'If we see you anywhere near the O'Halloran businesses again, no matter what the reason, you and your family will come to harm. Don't talk to anyone about it. Understood?'

Bile runs up her throat, stifling her words. She nods.

'Say it, damn it, just say it.'

She swallows, clears her throat and manages a scratchy reply. 'I will not talk to anyone about your business, especially the police.'

'Heed my warnings,' he says, easing his hold on her. 'There won't be a second chance. I'm going to walk away, don't turn around. Wait five minutes before leaving the area.'

All senses heightened, Beth hears his fading footsteps crunching on the gravelly ground and low lying branches snapping as he hastens out of the park. Minutes later, goose bumps prickling her skin, she looks around her, finds herself alone and warily makes for the footpath. The threats on her family have hit a raw nerve. There's no use reporting him to the police, they already think she's a troublemaker or at the very least a nuisance. She hurries off down the street and doesn't stop until she comes to a place where groups of people congregate, a place to feel safe, a place to gather her thoughts. Maggie's Tearooms are open. Pulling her hat over her teary eyes she enters, finds a window-facing seat and orders a strong brew. Despite the raucous thunder, a light shower is falling. Her fingers wrapped around a warm porcelain cup, she sips the calming hot brew thinking she won't leave until she feels safe, even if she has to drink three pots of tea. Leaning on her elbows, staring out the window at the drizzling rain, a memory comes to her.

~

It hadn't rained in months but on Arif's birthday it started as a refreshing shower and gradually swelled to a downpour by late afternoon. Everyone in the household ran outside and rejoiced until they were all drenched to the bone. Rain filled their tanks and promised to plump the fruit in their orchards. Beth and Arif held hands and whirled around and around like children. Later, as they ambled amongst the dripping trees, they shook wet branches over each other and laughed madly. All afternoon everyone celebrated Arif's birthday, singing and dancing to the beating heart of the drums. For dinner there was a feast of shashlik grilled on an open fire, naan, saffron rice, spicy vegetables and baklava slathered in honey. Raindrops intensified the sweet fragrance of the red flowering pomegranates growing close to the house, the scent drifted through the open windows, especially later that night when everything was still.

A week later, strolling around the property, mud up to their ankles, a golden eagle flew through the evening mist. Arif tilted his head to the sky, he didn't comment, nor did he show his usual enthusiasm. That was the first time Beth noticed something was wrong with him, as if the eagle had brought sad news. At first, she assumed it was melancholy, a strong desire for the son she had not borne. He was tired. Once, she caught him crying, it was the rain she told herself, he had always enjoyed the boyish joy of playing in the rain, but his eyes were red. 'Illness,' was his terse reply. He told her to keep her distance from him until he recovered. He was to be isolated in a room of his own until the coughing spells ceased. Beth insisted he remain in their room. In time, her company and nursing revived him, his illness passed.

Gabina's presence always made her life difficult. Once, when dusk was fading into night, Beth had been working in the potato field, directly behind the citrus orchard. Two laden buckets beside her, she rose to her feet and hauled up the buckets one on each shoulder. Approaching the house, she noticed Arif's second wife,

Gabina, relaxing on the porch with Arif's baby daughter in her arms. Gabina nodded a greeting as Beth passed, but she made no secret of her disdain for Beth's strange foreign ways. Despite Beth's attempts to speak Pashtan and foster friendship, Gabina would rather Beth did not exist. It was beyond her why the family hadn't sent the foreign woman back to where she belonged, somewhere south in a British colony. The foreigner was barren and of no use to anyone. Her command of Pashtan was no better than an infant's babble. As far as Gabina was concerned, the only advantage of Bethany's existence was a reduced workload, with Beth doing more than her fair share of chores Gabina was free to entertain her daughter, Roshina. Listening to Beth and Arif nattering in English riled her, their foreign conversations excluded everyone else, except twelve-year-old Ramin who understood more than he let on. Ramin had never been an academic child but the desire to understand their conversations was a strong incentive to step up his efforts. Ramin feared Beth would persuade Arif to leave his country and his family. As far as he was concerned, his older brother was obliged to manage the farm as tradition had always dictated.

Months later, the smell of wood smoke was thick in the air when Beth was summoned to fetch Arif from the fields. She kissed his face thick with dust and sweat. With several more chores at hand, he assured her he would not be long. Beth waited, hoping that Gabina would do some work for a change. A flurry of wind carried a scent of roses in the air; clouds huddled over the distant mountains. Arif finished up; she hugged him and inhaled the smell of him. They returned to the house, talking all the way, hands clasped. That was the day she told him she loved their life on the farm, but without Arif, her soulmate, she would return to Adelaide. He laughed and told her she would always be his first wife and the one he truly loved. Gabina was duty, when her husband died Arif was obliged to marry her. Beth didn't like sharing him. Although not unique to Afghanistan, in her opinion marriage as duty was a strange custom.

That night, time stood still as she swam in Arif's deep affections. Their ardent lovemaking bolstered the belief that all was well in their insulated realm. Afterwards, his breathing shallow, his eyes closed, he told her he loved her. Beth laid her hand on his skin and joked she could bake naan on his brow. Smiling, he said it was his beautiful wife filling him with raging heat. They laughed and it felt like Arif would live forever. He told her not to worry so much, he was just tired, that is all. He asked her not to tell the others as there was too much work to be done to take time off.

'What should we call our son?' he muttered, before nodding off.

Unable to sleep, Beth had long given up on bearing a child. The local midwife had confirmed it, she was barren. That interfering woman was responsible for the family forcing Arif to take a second wife. There simply must be many children, especially sons to work the property. Arif was reduced to a prize bull and Gabina his prize heifer. Gabina had borne his child within eighteen months of their marriage, remarkable, given Arif visited her bed once every other week. In some ways Beth was glad she was childless; her children would never be permitted to leave the homestead and visit their mother's country of birth. Like Adelaide, children belonged to their father and his family. At times she missed her home in Adelaide, missed her family, the smell of eucalypts and the saline sea air. Leaving Afghanistan was out of the question. Arif had a second wife and a daughter he adored. He would never leave them.

The following morning, Beth found herself alone with Ramin in the dining room. She wished him a good day before serving herself a bowl of boiled oats. Ramin mumbled a greeting and ate his food in silence, staring out the window between mouthfuls. Having scraped up the last remnants of cereal, he slid his bowl towards Beth, as if to say clean up after me. He told her in his broken English that she should never think about leaving the farm, not even for a holiday. Ramin had a better command of English than she'd thought.

Using a mix of Pashtan and English she told him to mind his

own business.

'You belong to Arif, you belong to family.'

'People are not possessions. You are a child Ramin, think about what you are saying before you speak.'

He said nothing, simply fixed his dark eyes on hers as Arif entered the room and helped himself to breakfast before sitting beside Beth.

'Why are you upset, Beth?' asked Arif as his brother got to his feet, picked up some naan and ate it on his way out of the room.

'Your brother doesn't like me. Nor does he respect me.'

'I love and respect you enough for everybody,' Arif said, kissing her on the forehead. 'I will speak with him, do not worry.'

'It's not funny, Arif. Please don't make light of it, I am annoyed at that boy.'

'He will grow up.'

'That's what I'm afraid of.'

~

By the time Beth arrives home Sam is sleeping soundly. Chided for her lateness without having told anyone, she is at first belligerent, she is not a child and should not be spoken to like one. Allowing the tears to fall, she apologises, recounts her misadventures and her subsequent entry into a tearoom where she sat drinking tea and feeling sorry for herself.

'Who threatened you, do you know?'

'I think it was the elder O'Halloran's right-hand man, I didn't see his face, but I remember you telling me he smelled of aniseed lollies.'

'We'll keep clear of that family from now on. It's not worth it. Go upstairs, throw your clothes in the wash, don something soft and comfortable, go to Samuel and kiss his lovely little sleeping face, then come down to dinner. You must eat. We'll have a chat directly afterwards with a tipple of sherry and some soothing chocolates.'

Exhausted, Beth allows herself to be made a fuss of. Ascending the stairs she wonders if she should invest in a pistol or take a self-defence course for peace of mind and security. There is another alternative; she has heard numerous stories about women accosted in the streets by unwarranted attention who use a sturdy hatpin to fend off undesirables. More than ten years ago, she'd successfully defended herself using a hairpin. Ultimately, she must exercise vigilance and keep her wits about her at all times.

TUESDAY, 21ST AUGUST

An abandoned homestead on the outskirts of South-East Adelaide surrounded by bushland is an ideal place to set up a dog breeding and holding farm. The entrance track is conveniently covered in thick, patchy yellow grass; most people would not expect to see the ruins of a farmhouse beyond it. Half-eaten by termites and crumbling from dry rot, the house now hosts Andrew Hall, his friend and a handful of recently acquired dogs. They have no idea who owns the farm; they assume it is crown land, an unproductive farm gone to wrack and ruin, bought out by the government. They came across the property by chance while carrying out one of the many sidelines in their business dealings. They'd charged a moneyed client to dispose of his time-worn furniture in the city dump, kept the fees and looked for a suitable spot to dump it free of charge on crown land. By chance, they'd turned down the grassy track and discovered the abandoned farmhouse and tumbledown sheds. They installed the furniture in the derelict cottage and took up residence. After repairing the sheds they considered the place perfect for their dog snatching business. Andrew Hall and his associate expect to make a bundle of money from their holdings, they would not allow anyone to jeopardise their lucrative business concerns. To date nobody has entered the property. The two men enjoy an ongoing joke about feeding intruders to the dogs. Every time either one of them mentions it they end up breathless from uproarious laughter.

Andrew Hall steps outside and stretches in the morning sunshine. The late winter air is refreshingly breezy. He sets the fire going and places the sooty kettle on a thick metal plate. A loaf of bread and a lump of cheese is soon sliced up ready for breakfast. He sets two large tin mugs on a stable log and tips sugar from a jar into each cup before pouring the tea. His friend joins him, a newspaper under his arm and coughing after his morning cigarette. 'Have you read yesterday's paper? There's an article about us,' he says, with a smug grin. 'Page five, no names mentioned of course.'

'Read it to me,' says Andrew. 'My eyesight's no good.' Andrew has never been able to read, as far as he's concerned writing's just a hodgepodge of shapes on a page, and there are never enough pictures. His friend has guessed as much but dares not mention it, the last bloke who made fun of Hall's scholastic shortcomings ended up in hospital. 'Go on, read it then!'

'Keep your hat on mate.' His friend swallows a mouthful of tea and heralds the news:

The hunt is on for a band of dog snatchers following the recent hike in dog thefts in Adelaide, particularly expensive pedigree dogs.

The most recent was a poodle from one of Adelaide's wealthiest suburbs. The dog was snatched from the victim's fenced front yard late yesterday afternoon. The little female dog is described as having bright brown eyes and perfect blue pearl and white markings. Anyone with information about this incident is urged to contact the Adelaide Police Station. Information is treated with the utmost confidence.

Residents are also asked to keep an eye on their dogs, do not let them wander the streets during daylight hours or at night.

'Crikey, we're famous,' Hall cackles. 'Me and you are climbin' up the criminal ladder, eh? Adelaide's gettin' too bloody small for the likes of us, we're runnin' out of places to hide. We have ta leave, if anyone finds that body there'll be coppers crawlin' all over the bloody place. Gotta sell the dogs, horse and wagon then we'll leave for Fremantle. I got good connections there.'

'Ya mean bad connections.'

'Bad and mad.' Hall's grin bares a mouth of sparse teeth.

'What about the mastiff?'

'My contact in Fremantle wants him for thirty quid, that's better than the reward on offer here, not as risky neither.'

'Do you trust him to pay?'

Hall's chafed lips tighten. 'He'll pay or else.'

His mate wants to ask 'or else what?' but he thinks better of it. Looking through the newspaper he finds an advertisement for seats in a steamer sailing to Fremantle in September. He tears it out and hands it to Hall who studies the photograph of the steamer and another picture of the cabins available. 'We'll book a cabin.'

After breakfast, they make plans for their voyage to Fremantle. Already missing his mother, Andrew will leave her some money and a promise to return. Having grown up in an orphanage, his mate has no family to speak of. Later, in the kitchen they carve up kangaroo meat for the dogs, the best cuts set aside for Carl. Whistling as he goes, Andrew approaches the kennels with bucket-loads of meat, his mate still inside cleaning up the mess. There's a deafening hubbub as the hungry dogs set each other off. Hall scoops the food into each bowl and replenishes their water supply. Served last, Carl makes short work of his two pounds of steak. 'That bloody mastiff eats more than a fully grown swine,' Hall grumbles.

WEDNESDAY, 22ND AUGUST

Standing at the bar in a smoke-filled inn that smells of yeast and overcooked meat pies, Angus guzzles his pint and wipes the froth from his lips with his sleeve. Bidding his mates a good day, he snakes around the tightly packed tables and scattered chairs and ambles out the door. Outside, the air is crisp and the winter sun warm. He strolls along the tree lined road, at times stopping to catch his breath and shore up his wavering balance. Moving towards the house he has been living in all his life, he walks between the hanging sheets, one of them flopping over his head. He tugs it hard, brings the line down and curses. The door is locked. Unable to remember where the key is hidden he staggers to the backdoor, usually unlocked. In the kitchen, he expects to find his lunch prepared and set on the dining table. It is not. Displeased everyone is out, he thumps his fist on the kitchen wall. A breadwinner works hard for his family, comes home and they're not even there to greet him. He rummages about the kitchen looking for something sweet, finds a tin of biscuits and scoffs the lot. In the bedroom, he pulls out his working boots, thinking he'd get a patch of ground ready for spring planting. But first, he'd lie on his bed and rest. Dropping off as soon as his head hits the pillow, his nap stretches to a couple of hours. Awakened by cheerful voices, he rises from the bed and ambles to the window; the voices are coming from the neighbour's house, that woman sounds like a bloody fishmonger. Suddenly lonely, the liquor wearing off, he wonders why Anna hadn't left him a note. She should be home to make him a cup of tea. Cursing, he pulls a bottle of rum from the top shelf of the wardrobe and swigs what's left in the bottle. There must be more than that. Anna would have a bottle stashed away in a secret place. He opens her side of the wardrobe, if she's gone out somewhere special she'd have worn her good shoes and blue coat. Not there. Where the bloody hell has she gone? He studies her clothes, a little shabby, he thinks. Better that way, if she looks too pretty she'll attract unwanted attention; especially when he's away at sea. He wonders where she has hidden her grog, surely she'd need a swig or two every so often. A large quilted purple box catches his eye because it's under a pile of sheets and blankets that aren't even folded. Anna is usually neater than that. 'I bet that's where she hides her bloody grog,' he tells himself. The pretty box doesn't fool him. He tosses the pile of linen over the floor and snatches the box, opens it, regards the contents. The fabric is soft, it must be silk. He holds the gown aloft. Mauve or violet he's never been able to tell the difference. Sleeveless. Where the hell did Anna get it? A gift no doubt, she couldn't buy something like that on the paltry sum he gives her. Who'd give her such a gift? A rich man … she's being courted by a rich man. His heart is thumping, sweat rolls down his face and back. His hands are shaking as anger courses through his veins. Voices, the creaking of the front door as it opens and closes again. Laughter, he'll wipe the smile from their faces. He drops the gown and moves to the kitchen. There she is, smiling and pleased to have been on a nice picnic. He could rip her head off. That mother of hers has noticed – she's got the fear of hell in her eyes. He tells Audrey to go outside with Sophie. He has to talk to his wife in private. Audrey hesitates. He moves next to her, his face inches away, speaking through his teeth he tells her to get outside.

'Please, Ma, take Sophie outside, I'll be all right,' Anna says, her lips smiling, her eyes filled with terror.

Angus waits until Audrey and Sophie have left the room.

'Do you want some tea, Angus?'

'Do you want some tea, Angus?' he apes her trembling voice, his eyes narrowed, his lips thin and tight. 'No, I don't want no bloody tea.'

'What's wrong, Angus?'

He drags Anna into the bedroom, throws the gown at her, and orders her to slip it on. She'd sold the red gown and the necklace to buy groceries. Now she wishes she'd sold the violet one as well. Stepping back from him, she tells him she'd stolen the gown with the intention of selling it as he drinks all their grocery money.

'Put it on. Just shut up and get it on.'

He glowers at her, his eyes fierce. She obeys. The gown fits like a glove. The man who gave her the gown knows her dimensions like the back of his hand. Anna's not only a whore; she's a liar. He could never trust her again.

'Who gave it to ya?'

'I already told you, I ...'

His large hand slaps her across the face.

'Who gave it to ya?'

Incensed by her silence, he grabs the bodice, and pulls so hard she pitches forward. Summoning furious strength, he rips it apart at the seams.

'Think ya too good for the likes of me, don't ya.' He keeps shredding the material until the dress resembles a tangle of frayed ribbons.

Anna, in her underwear, leaps to her feet and tries to flee from the room, but he grabs her by the hair and pulls her back to him.

'Angus, please, I'm sorry, it won't happen again.'

'Nobody'll want ya by the time I finish with ya.'

Fearing the worst, Audrey takes Sophie's hand in hers and hurries off to call for an ambulance at the local post office, some several hundred yards down the road.

Struck in the ribs, something snaps. Anna tries to scream but his hand is pressed firmly on her neck, muffling her cries for help. He throws her onto the bed, unbuttons his trousers, drops them to the floor and stands over her, his manhood hanging loosely, too soft to perform the act. It's her fault he's a pitiful wretch. Anna's hands cover her face as the shower of warm yellow liquid spews over her body. The vile smell makes her retch, she tries to get up and run but the final blow to the stomach knocks all the fight out of her. Pain rips through her body as if someone had thrust a knife into her. Angus knows what the clotted blood between her legs means – she is losing the son he has longed for, a brother for Sophie. He raises his bloodied hands as if in prayer and weeps. 'Look what you made me do, Anna, look what you made me bloody well do.' But Anna's eyes are closed, she is not responding. He tugs the remaining remnants of the dress from her limp body, thrusts the soiled fabric back into the purple box, and tosses the box into the wardrobe. After dressing her in a nightgown he removes his bloodied shirt and throws it in the wash basket. He moves to the kitchen, leans over the wash basin and scrubs his face, hands and arms. The soap foaming on his skin, he scrubs until it hurts. Aware of an approaching clip-clop of hooves, he throws on a clean shirt and makes for the pub. He'll shout everyone a drink or two, they'll remember his generosity. If he's going to hang for murder he may as well enjoy his final hours of freedom. On his way, he sees two men in a horse-drawn ambulance, the words *Adelaide Hospital* in large gold lettering on the side panel. A stretcher lying in the back, but it's too late for Anna and worse than that it's too late for the son she might have borne.

THURSDAY, 23RD AUGUST

During the past ten years women's suffrage has been raised in seven separate unsuccessful Bills in the South Australian Parliament. The tide of public and parliamentary opinion is slowly turning due to public meetings, lectures, deputation, petitions and letters to the press. The Women's Suffrage League, formed in 1888, is a driving force behind the struggle for suffrage. Several amendments to the Women's Suffrage Bill have been proposed and defeated, they include: restricting women from voting in the House of Assembly, that franchise only be given to women over twenty-five, and the third proposal allowing women to vote by post if they lived more than three miles from a polling booth or were unable to vote due to illness. Many politicians oppose women's voting rights. Intending to derail the Suffrage Bill, Ebenezer Ward has proposed an amendment to strike out clause four which bars women from becoming members of parliament. An uncompromising opponent of women's suffrage, he believes not one parliamentarian would in their right mind support the Suffrage Bill should there be any possibility of women becoming members of parliament. Supporters of the Women's Suffrage League believe Ward's subterfuge will only serve to strengthen women's suffrage ambitions. Today's rally should get them one step closer to their goal.

By ten in the morning, thousands of demonstrators are marching along the main streets of Adelaide and many spectators are assembled along the roadside watching and rallying behind them. With arms linked women are marching along chanting as they go. Others are carrying large banners or wearing placards hanging from thick straps at their shoulders inscribed with the words: VOTES FOR WOMEN. Large groups of women in wide-brimmed hats and white dresses with purple sashes over their shoulders are flaunting the same message. On every corner, vendors can be seen plying drinks, ice-creams, sandwiches, lollies and fruit. Photographers and reporters are on the lookout for sensational stories. There is also a discernible police presence on the streets as during past demonstrations adamant anti-suffrage gangs had resorted to violence to get their views across.

Amongst the thickening crowd, Beth and Tillie are holding their placards high and chanting. Samuel is between them grasping their skirts. The procession to Parliament House in North Terrace flows like a bubbling brook. At the front of the line is Mary Lee, surrounded by her frontline supporters, two of them in wheelchairs. Women from all walks of life are brought together from all parts of the city and the colony. Women who otherwise might not normally cross paths are calling for the same rights. They may not have the same taste in music, but today they are chanting the same chorus: SUFFRAGE FOR ALL!

Constructed in marble and granite, Parliament House stands tall on the corner of King William Street. Mary Lee steps onto the makeshift stage and addresses the crowd as if she has been a public speaker all her life. Speaking through a brass megaphone, she thanks the men and women who made the effort to join her and her supporters to champion women's suffrage. Her eloquent arguments and her charming Irish accent are mesmerising. The crowd cheers raucously when she asserts that women must have the right to say how and by whom they shall be governed. The qualifications entitling women to vote should be the same as those that apply to men. Unprompted, Mary is speaking naturally and from the heart, amazingly, she has no written speech. Every so often she pauses, letting her words sink in, deciding what to say next, she asks the questions, she answers the questions. What difference would voting women make to society? Women would elect candidates who would legislate to improve society in general and strengthen the position of women and children in particular. Lowering the megaphone for a moment, Mary surveys the gathering. Her fair skin is glistening and red in the warm midday sun. One of her supporters moves to her side and holds a parasol aloft. Mary takes a sip of water and wipes her forehead with a handkerchief before continuing her speech. At times, she steps aside allowing various speakers to take turns in spurring the crowd on, driving the belief that suffrage is a human right and ultimately inevitable. Mary gives thanks to the Women's Suffrage League, the Working Women's Trade Union, and the Women's Christian Temperance Union for their assistance in preparing the petition: 400 feet in length with its pages glued end to end and signed by more than 11,000 South Australians. The mention of the petition being presented to the South Australian Parliament, in a matter of hours, provokes a roaring applause.

Finally, Mary Lee declares the petition and today's rally will go down in history as the momentum that turned the tables on women's struggles for the right to vote in elections. Beth wonders how a person could develop that kind of charisma and power to move thousands, and for the good of humanity. Universal suffrage, education and health services are good for women, good for families and ultimately good for the colony.

Later in the day, inside parliament, the Honourable George Hawker, member for North Adelaide, presents the petition and Mr John Cockburn introduces the Adult Suffrage Bill to the South Australian House of Assembly. The Bill is read and debated in parliament, and some men in the room are laughing out loud at the prospect of women voting. All sorts of outlandish arguments are put forward to vote against the Bill, yet supporters effectively put

Colleen Dumaine

forward their case, citing amongst other things the fact that female ratepayers have had the vote in South Australia since 1861 with no adverse consequences.

Hoarse from chanting slogans, thirsty, and pink-skinned from the glimmering sunshine, Beth, Tillie and Sam make for a popular teahouse. With excited voices, patrons are all talking over one another and laughing out loud. Enjoying his chocolate cake, Sam is not really following the conversations, but he is amused by the adults around him who are sparkling with optimism and the satisfaction of having participated in a defining moment in Australian history.

By the time they leave the teahouse, the sun is resting on the treetops. They set off for home, carrying placards ready for the next rally. Sam isn't holding Beth's hand as he is licking the last of the chocolate icing from his fingers. A well-dressed man approaches them. At first he seems polite and introduces himself as a member of an anti-suffrage group. The smiling fox advises them to return to their kitchen as the street is no place for ladies. Tillie will have none of that – she suggests he go back to his cage as the street is no place for a narrow-minded ape. Furious, he lashes out with a swift shove in the shoulder. Tillie almost tumbles just catching herself in the nick of time. Beth intervenes by striking him with her placard. In response, the man raises his fists ready to strike but Tillie, now recovered, upthrusts her placard and together she and Beth pummel him until he flees, calling them enemies of the state and other more unflattering names.

'Samuel!'

Sam is nowhere to be seen. He must have run off during the scuffle. They plough through the crowd, shouting his name over and over again. But their calls are muted in the hubbub of a noisy, dispersing crowd. They find a policeman who assures them he'd keep a lookout for Samuel. He suggests they report him missing at the nearest police station. They bin their broken placards and hurry off.

At the station, the sergeant on duty tells them it's not the first time a child has gone missing, especially amongst an excitable mob.

'The suffragette groups were orderly.'

'I would have thought a private investigator of your calibre would keep track of her own son, Mrs Durrani,' the sergeant snipes.

'We were otherwise occupied, busy defending ourselves against a violent, anti-suffrage thug. There weren't enough policemen at the rally today.'

'We're doing our best.'

Observing Beth's face is beetroot-red, Tillie grabs her hand in an effort to silence her. 'Someone will bring him here, Beth,' she whispers.

'While I'm here, there's something else I have to report. On Thursday, 9th of August, a young man lured Samuel to our front gate for a chat. When he saw me approaching he hurried off. I fear he might have something to do with Sam's disappearance.'

'Did he tell your son his name?'

'No.'

'Why didn't you report it then?'

'I wish I had.'

'What did he look like, this stranger?'

'Tall, dark, a tidy beard, wearing a dark suit.'

'A tall, dark stranger. Sounds like a character in a detective novel, Mrs Durrani. There's no law against talking to children but I have noted your misgivings. Anything else?'

'A few days later, the same man was sitting on a bench watching me and my family enjoying a picnic in the Botanical Gardens. After lunch, he was still there observing our cricket game. When I approached him for a chat he fled. I followed him for a short while but he was too fast for me.'

'It's not a crime to watch a cricket match.' The sergeant raises his chin and assumes an officious stare. 'However, stalking is a crime.'

Beth glares at the sergeant, her son is missing and he is treating her like a criminal.

'You were involved in a skirmish several days ago.'

'I was verbally attacked by a man called Andrew Hall, otherwise known as a callous dog snatcher and fraudster. He stopped his buggy right in front of me, I was almost run off the road. When I confronted him, he and his friend stirred up the crowd. I was attacked and humiliated.'

'I've read Constable Skinner's report. He noted you were dressed in riding apparel.'

'That's probably because I was riding a bicycle,' says Beth, clenching her fists and pressing her nails into her skin.

'You're asking for trouble getting around in men's garb,' he rumbles, gathering his notes into a neat pile. 'Wait in the hallway. We'll do our best to find your son.' Perhaps conceding he has gone too far, the sergeant lightens up and assures Beth that all parents think the worst when their children go missing but most of the time they've just wandered off. He assures her when the first few constables return from their rosters he'll send them out again to scour the streets for her son.

'When do you expect them back?'

'In about twenty minutes.'

'I think I'll get some fresh air.'

'Don't wander off too far. Someone will probably bring him in.'

Outside, Tillie and Beth sit on a public bench beneath a lofty eucalypt, home to shrieking cockatoos, normally a welcome sound touting all is well, but now it pierces Beth's heart. She aches for her darling son, wants to hold his small hand in hers, needs to hear his spontaneous laughter. Weaving her arm into Beth's arm, Tillie does all she can to hold back the tears. There is nothing she can say to reduce the tension. They remain sitting there in silence until they notice several police officers returning from duty, followed by an overweight Inspector Taylor straggling behind, dabbing his forehead with a white handkerchief. Beth and Tillie follow them inside. The desk sergeant shakes his head before Beth has a chance to ask after Sam.

'I'll send a couple of constables out in a few minutes. In the meantime, you're welcome to sit in the waiting room. We'll let you know if someone brings him in.'

An hour later, a young family is approaching the police station. Their little girl is carrying a puppy and chatting animatedly with a boy about her age. When they enter, the parents inform the sergeant on duty they have a little boy lost. Captivated by their friendly daughter and her puppy, he followed them down the street and was separated from his mother and auntie. His name is Samuel Durrani.

On hearing her son's name, Beth leaps to her feet and moves to the reception area. 'Samuel! Where've you been?' she says, before planting kisses all over his face. Wondering what all the fuss is about, he hugs her back.

'I was playing with Pearl and Frankie,' he says, pointing to a little girl wearing a blue dress overlain by a white pinafore. Beside her is a little puppy on a leash.

'Are you Sam's mama?' asks Pearl, letting the puppy go free.

'Yes, I am. Thank you for bringing him back to me.'

The puppy, now let loose, runs around the room before lifting a leg and urinating on the bare timber floor.

'Look Mama, Frankie did a whizzy,' says Sam, still in Beth's arms.

The children giggle with glee and are told to keep it down.

'Having heard the hullabaloo, Inspector Taylor emerges from his office, almost treads in the yellow pool and barks at the constable to clean it up, pronto. Then, turning his attention to Beth he comments it is good news her son is unharmed. Surprisingly, he smiles and pats Sam on the back, before returning to his office and closing the door behind him.

Satisfied Sam had wandered off, the sergeant thanks Pearl and her parents for returning Samuel safely to the station. Beth thanks them for their troubles, in return they give a polite good day, but their disapproving countenance tugs at her conscience. Pearl takes her mother's hand, smiling and bellowing a joyous farewell to Sam.

Oblivious of all the trouble he has caused, Sam assures his new friend he'll see her at the next rally.

Outside, soothed by a late afternoon breeze infused with a scent of jasmin, Beth, Tillie and Sam stroll away, Sam declaring it was the best day he has ever had.

FRIDAY, 24TH AUGUST

The Adelaide Public Hospital in Hindley Street is a grand building with two tenements appropriated to the males and the one adjacent to the females. Beth goes directly to the admissions office and asks if she could visit Mr Nolan Lloyd. Advised of the visiting hours, only twenty minutes left, she hurries along. He is in room number sixteen on the second floor. She climbs the stairs two at a time and strides down the stark white hall, the strong smell of disinfectant making her eyes water.

A patient with sunken eyes catches sight of Beth as she wanders into the shared room. The other two male patients are fast asleep, one of them on his back, his mouth agape, the other one propped up on pillows, his chin resting on his chest. She asks the only one awake if he is Mr Lloyd. 'Last time I looked in the mirror I was he. Nice to see a pretty smiling face,' he says, sitting up. 'I've had some surly nurses lookin' after me. One of them hasn't cracked her face with a smile in years.'

'They're probably overworked, Mr Lloyd.' Handing him a box of chocolates she introduces herself. All skin and bones, his thin fingers are slow to open the box. He chooses a strawberry flavoured chocolate. With eyes closed, he savours the sweet bite as if it were a slice of heaven. 'Would you like one?' he asks, offering the box. Thanking him, she declines.

'More for me.' He winks.

'I'm sorry about your illness, Mr Lloyd.'

'Not as sorry as me.'

Several chocolates later, he gazes at Beth. 'No such thing as free sweets from a lovely lady. I'm not the marrying kind if it's a husband you're after.' His roguish grin bares a mouth of brown teeth.

Beth laughs, amazed one so ill could have such a jolly sense of humour. 'I'm working for Mrs Lydia Emerson, investigating the disappearance of Mr Eric Emerson. I'm advised you worked for him as an odd-job man. I'd like to ask you a few questions, if you don't mind.'

'Not at all, I read about it in the papers a while back, terrible thing but it weren't me who done him in, I couldn't crush a raw egg.'

'We believe he's still alive, Mr Lloyd.' Beth sits on the chair beside his bed, notepad and pencil in hand. 'I'm wondering if you could tell me anything about Mr Emerson.'

'He gave me instructions, I done what he said.' Aware of Beth's pressing gaze he adds, 'Mr Emerson's a cordial, cheery type.'

'Can you think of any reasons why he would leave home without telling anyone?'

'Nothin' comes to mind.'

'Do you know of anyone who might want to harm Mr Emerson?'

He shakes his head, his mouth full of chocolates. 'Oh, there was a sour-tempered bloke come once to the door, blimey he was angry.'

'When was that?'

'A long while back, months.'

'Did you catch his name?'

Nolan rubs his chin, has a pained look on his face as if thinking hurts. He pops another chocolate in his mouth, chews it up and speaks, 'John? No, it was Jack, that's it, Jack, but I didn't hear his other name or nothin'.'

'What did he look like?'

'About the same age as Mr Emerson, looked a bit like him, light brown hair, medium height, well dressed. I didn't take much notice, too busy in the garden.'

'Do you know what they were arguing about?'

'I didn't catch every word, but they was arguin' about furniture.'

'Did you hear any other details?'

'Na, but the police was mentioned.'

'You say the man, maybe Jack, had light brown hair, wasn't he wearing a hat?'

'When they got into a scuffle, he lost it.'

'Scuffle?'

'It started at the front door and ended up out front in the garden, then the man picked up his hat and left.'

Beth wonders who the other man was, perhaps it was Vincent Stirling. But the description doesn't fit, Vincent has black hair.

'How did you get on with Mrs Emerson?'

A blush crosses his face or perhaps his blood pressure is acting up. 'Three years I worked for them, and she sacked me for no reason at all.'

'What did Mr Emerson have to say about that?'

'He said he was sorry to see me go, gave me a reference and ten quid.'

'You've been very helpful, Mr Lloyd. Thank you for your time, I hope you feel better soon.'

He says his goodbyes, telling her he'd welcome another visit.

She assures him she'll return with more chocolates and bids him farewell, thinking he is incapable of getting out of bed, let alone kidnapping or harming anyone.

Making her way out through the maze of halls and staircases Beth bumps into Audrey Hubble.

'Hello, Mrs Durrani, what are you doing here?'

'I'm visiting an old friend. And please call me Beth.'

'My name's Audrey.'

'Are you visiting a friend as well, Audrey?'

She takes a moment to answer. 'Yes.'

Responding to Audrey's apparent distress, Beth offers her morning tea. Audrey wipes her teary eyes and accepts. Familiar with the place, she leads Beth out of the building. They make their way to the teahouse across the road from the hospital. Within minutes a tray of tea and four patty cakes are placed on the table. Beth pours the steamy tea into porcelain cups and hands one to Audrey. Looking into Audrey's red eyes, Beth guesses who she'd been visiting.

'How is Anna?'

'How did …?'

'Just guessing.'

'Angus went berserk. One of these days he'll go too far and kill her. Thank heavens she's recovering, but she might lose her baby.'

'Oh, I didn't know she was with child.'

'He makes her life hell.' Suddenly thirsty, she pauses to drain her cup. 'I know about her affair with Mr Emerson, can't say I blame her, Angus is a mongrel of a man.'

'Why doesn't she leave him?' Beth asks, refilling Audrey's cup.

'Where would she go? The house is in his name. Anna has two choices: suffer regular beatings or sleep on the street and worse than that, lose her daughter.'

'How terrifying.'

'She's not looking forward to going home.'

'Should I visit her?'

'God no, if Angus finds out it'll be the end of her.'

'Do you think Angus had something to do with Mr Emerson's disappearance?'

'I wouldn't put it past him.'

'By coincidence, Mr Emerson disappeared on your birthday, I understand you were enjoying a family lunch that day. Was Angus home for the entire day?'

'He had lunch with us but he went to the pub during the afternoon.'

'Has Angus always been violent?'

'When they first got hitched he was kind enough, but then he changed, started acting like he owned her.'

'Does he hit Sophie?'

Audrey shakes her head. 'She's scared stiff of him though.'

'It must be comforting to have you living in the house.'

'At first it was, he dared not attack her when I was home, but now it's different. When he's in one of his wild moods he sends me and Sophie outside. This time Anna was screaming so loud I rushed off to call an ambulance. She might have …'

'You did the right thing, Audrey, you saved her life.'

'Angus has no shame, he refuses to pay the ambulance fee and doctor's bills, he reckons it was her fault he beat her. Anna has money hidden under the floorboards, but it won't last forever. I left Sophie with a neighbour today, I'd better go. Thanks for the tea.'

'We haven't touched the cakes, take them home to Sophie.' Beth wraps the cakes in serviettes.

'That will bring a smile to her pretty little face,' says Audrey, placing the treats in her basket. 'I'll tell her they're from her mama if you don't mind.'

'Not at all.' Beth gives Audrey her card and invites her to write or call in anytime. Feeling angry at Angus, a man she has never seen or met, she leaves the tearoom and decides to walk home, the promenade certain to settle her nerves. On the way, she stops in a leafy park and finds a timber bench. Seated, she observes a group of mothers and their young children chatting and laughing as if they have all the time in the world. She'd like Sam to be there with her, he'd approach those children and make the most of those playful moments in the sun. She remembers making every moment count during Arif's final weeks. All the years they'd planned to spend together condensed into weeks. Every minute, every second, savoured. Staring ahead without really looking, her mind wanders back in time.

~

Arif awoke in the middle of the night and squeezed her hand with such strength she was sure he'd recovered from his illness. She lit a candle. Unaided, he sat up smiling, his green eyes bright and cheery. Her fingers trailed the outline of his pale face and neck, his skin warm but not feverish. Those brief moments of wellness were blissful. A truce in a fierce battle of survival, they held each other tight, afraid to let go. In the morning when they awoke, Arif tried to climb out of bed and almost fell. Too soon he complained; if he had one wish he'd be the robust man he once was. He wanted to live long enough to meet his son, the heir to the farm. His son would become a champion polo player like his father and grandfather before him. Arif would encourage him to become a scholar; he'd master three or four languages. The thought crossed Beth's mind their child might be a scholarly female but she kept her peace, the anticipation of a son uplifted his spirits.

Within days Arif was able to walk unassisted. He wanted to work but his father would not allow it, not yet. Feeling optimistic, he and Beth announced their good news before the entire family. Everyone cheered. Beth was praised, she had nursed her husband to health and God had rewarded her with a son. It was as though the rope that was tied around her chest had slackened and was thrown to the wind. When the fourth month of her pregnancy passed Beth asked Arif if he would agree to name their son Samuel after her father, with Arif as his middle name. He assented. Beth's father was a good man, his son would be a good man.

One blustery morning, awakened by the bedroom door slamming shut, she turned to Arif and noticed his eyes wide open. A frisson of alarm coursed through her body. Her hand moved to his brow, he was warm and clammy, breathing, alive, a sigh escaped her lips. 'What are you doing staring at the ceiling?' she asked, pulling the blanket from him. 'You're too warm. I'll get you a glass of water.'

Arif smiled and told her not to fuss.

'It's Roshina's birthday tomorrow. Your beautiful, clever little girl is turning one.'

'I will spend time with her.'

'You must stay healthy, Arif. Your sister is getting married soon. You couldn't miss her wedding.'

'I dare not miss her special day; she would strike me with a saucepan if I did not attend.' He laughs. 'You bring so much happiness into my life. God willing I will live long enough to hold our son in my arms.'

'Don't sound so mournful, my love.' She kissed him, over and over again, her tears falling on his face and down his neck, until his skin was glistening with love.

'Soon I will be in God's hands. You must think of all the joys of life, our child, the sun setting over flowering orchards, an ocean-blue sky before a storm, fields of red tulips in spring, there is so much to live for.' Smiling, he asked Beth to leave him to his prayers.

~

In preparation for their meeting in the drawing room, Harry had laid a fire in the grate earlier that day and as the room is damp and cold he puts a match to it. He and Beth move the occasional table up close to the fire and Faith pours three glasses of sherry and sets a silver salver of shortbread biscuits in the centre. Beth gets the ball rolling by expressing her frustration at the constabulary, for their mocking behaviour and dismissive attitude regarding her harassment complaints against Andrew Hall, her enquiries about Irene Howard's sudden death, and more recently Sam's disappear-ance. Harry advises her not to take it personally, the policemen are simply protecting their livelihoods, the last thing they want is women entering the constabulary and taking over their jobs. Her confidence crumbling, Beth laments the fact that it's already been more than two weeks and although there are a few suspects, very little has been established. Again, Harry tells her not to lose heart;

even the most intelligent criminal eventually makes a mistake. To prove his point, he recounts a case he was investigating involving a serial killer who didn't leave one clue for the first few murders but on his fourth homicide he left two vital clues. Enjoying his captive audience, Harry tells the entire story of a man who had killed a woman and two men in Adelaide's west side. The killer believed he'd murdered his fourth victim, but the male victim was actually unconscious. A week later he woke up in hospital and was able to speak. When asked to describe the killer, he said his face was concealed by a mask, but as he'd been kicked relentlessly, he'd noticed two important details. The killer was kicking with his left foot and something even more important – his shoe had a three-inch heel. Just before the victim blacked out, he'd noticed the killer's right shoe had a half-inch heel. In sum, the killer had one leg shorter than the other and was left handed. Those details led to the killer's arrest. The detectives interviewed every cobbler in Adelaide and got the names and addresses of men who'd ordered bespoke shoes to address leg length discrepancies. A few customers were deceased which left five possible suspects. Out of the five men they discounted three for one reason or another, which left two potential killers. Each of their homes was ransacked for evidence. One of the suspects had mementoes from the murders hidden in his garden shed. He was subsequently arrested. That was after six months of plodding.

'Why did he kill them?' Beth asks.

'Good question. The three male victims had made fun of his handicap, mimicking his gait at work. The female victim had refused to dance with him, teasing his dance steps were lopsided. He didn't appreciate the joke, strangled her.'

'I suppose we do have a few clues,' says Beth, smiling.

'Exactly, and we'll find out more,' says Harry, studying the diagram on the blackboard, an intricate web of names, places and motives, all leading to Eric Emerson. Lydia was at her mother's home in Port Adelaide. He reminds the team that people have been known to hire a second party to commit murder. With unemployment and poverty rife in Adelaide, there'd be plenty of men willing to murder a stranger just to put food on the table. Lydia certainly has the means to hire a killer. Of course, Eric could still be alive, in which case he'd probably have contacted his lover Anna Hopping or his good friend Vincent Stirling.

'I really don't think Lydia would have engaged our services if she'd had anything to do with his disappearance,' says Beth.

'Life Insurance,' Faith offers.

'Insurance isn't a strong motive, she's very wealthy.' Harry taps the side of his nose. 'Keep it under your hats, her bank accounts have been scrutinised, her fortune's in her name and so is the house she'd inherited from her father. If she wanted to get rid of Eric she'd have simply told him to pack his bags and go.'

'Talk about a wild goose chase. At least we're being paid for it.' Faith grins.

'An old mate with good connections in the constabulary called in this morning. The O'Halloran family are still being watched. The police don't want us getting in their way.' Harry raises his thumb and index finger to show an inch, 'They're this close to nabbing them for insurance fraud and theft.'

'I visited Nolan Lloyd today, the Emerson's former odd-job man; he's in hospital and looks very ill. He mentioned a male visitor who'd argued with Eric outside his front door around the time Eric disappeared. Here's the interesting bit, the visitor looked like Eric: early thirties, medium height, light brown hair, and well-dressed. Furniture and police were mentioned in their heated conversation. I think Nolan knows more than he's letting on. On my way out I bumped into Audrey Hubble. Angus Hopping assaulted Anna, she's in a bad way – she's pregnant and might lose her baby.'

'That mongrel should be thrown in the clink,' Harry says, shaking his head.

'For heaven's sake, why isn't he?' Faith asks.

'The constabulary don't get involved in domestic matters until it's too late. All too often, battered and bruised women suffer in silence. If a woman's breadwinner is locked up, she and her children go hungry.' Harry carries a defeated expression as he remembers the domestic felonies he'd witnessed over the years and the orphaned children left to carry the burden. He'd sought comfort in gardening but the images often kept him up at night.

Faith places her hand on Harry's forearm and asks the team if there's anything else to report.

'A couple of weeks ago, Anna told me Angus was home the day Eric disappeared as they were celebrating Audrey's birthday,' Beth says. 'This morning Audrey let slip he'd gone out to the pub that afternoon.'

'Angus has motive and opportunity,' says Harry.

'Eric could be hiding from him, if he's still alive that is.' Beth pauses to recollect her recent findings. 'Another thing, as we know, Irene Howard turned up for work on the day Eric disappeared and she died in her sleep that night. I can't help wondering why an elderly teetotaller would drink liquor at work. Apparently she returned home inebriated and talking gibberish. Her sister told me the only word that made any sense at all was *chair*.'

'I'd be calling for a chair if I were sozzled.'

'I've never seen you sozzled, Aunt Faith.'

'I could count on one hand the times I succumbed.'

'As usual, we have more questions than answers,' says Harry, adding Irene Howard and Nolan Lloyd to the list of persons of interest and writing the word *chair* next to Irene's name.

'I have some fascinating news to share.' Faith rubs her hands together as if about to enjoy a delicious meal. 'I had a coffee with my friend from the State Records Office today. She told me, in private of course, that Charlotte Bechard is Anna's birth mother. Audrey Hubble adopted her soon after her birth. I wonder if the two women have kept in contact over the years.'

'That's extraordinary, Aunt Faith,' says Beth. 'Now that I think of it, Anna looks a lot like Charlotte, same big brown eyes and stature. I'll visit Charlotte in a few days.'

'We look forward to hearing what she has to say. What's next?'

'We enjoy another drop of sherry,' says Beth. 'I'm taking Sam to the Botanical Gardens tomorrow. I won't think about this baffling case at all, nor will I allow myself to think of the O'Halloran clan.'

'Cheers,' says Faith, raising her glass.

A sudden thud and crash at the window startles the group.

'What on earth was that?' asks Faith, moving to the window. 'Can't see a thing out there, it's such a dark night.'

'Could be possums, I'll take a look outside,' says Harry, already moving to the front door.

Beth hurries upstairs to Sam's room where she finds him sound asleep. She locks his door and moves back downstairs and locks all the windows.

Faith lights two candles and hands one to Harry. Together they make their way to the window in question. The garden is trampled. An intruder had taken the bricks from the garden edge, stacked them one atop the other to make a platform on which to stand so he could see and hear the goings on inside the house. Whoever was at the window had lost his balance on the unstable platform and grabbed onto the window sill to break the fall. The alarming crash resulted from a ceramic pot plant toppling from the window sill.

'He's run off,' says Faith. 'I wonder how long he's been looking through the window; it mightn't be the first time.'

'We'll have a good look around in the morning,' says Harry

SATURDAY, 25TH AUGUST

At first light, Harry inspects the area all around the window. There are too many crushed plants and pottery shards to find any foot-prints and the intruder left no evidence behind. He spends the morning cleaning up the mess and aligning the bricks along the garden edge near the window. Harry and Faith had planned to enjoy an afternoon out with Beth and Sam, but they decide to stay home and keep an eye on the property, although Harry doubts the intruder would return to the house.

After lunch, Beth and Sam climb into Harry's wagon and set off for the Botanical gardens, singing as they go. He drops them off at the entrance gate and leaves soon after with Sam bellowing farewell as if he'd never see Harry again.

A tall cast-iron palisade fence runs all along the boundary of the Botanical Gardens, the gates are wide open inviting guests to spend time in the lush surroundings. The warm weather during the past few days has persuaded spring flowers to bloom early in the raised garden beds on either side of the entrance, their spectacular palette of warm colours glowing in the sun. Inside the park, wallabies and kangaroos are grazing on close-cropped grass and flocks of ducks and swans are floating along the sparkling Torrens River.

Keen to explore the many streams that meander throughout the park, they set off. Hemmed in by she-oaks, tall red gums and stocky banksias, they inhale the sweet-scented brush flowers. A sudden flapping of bird wings turns Beth's head towards a thicket of yellow flowering wattles. Realising they'd roamed away from the main track they turn back and retrace their steps. Bark, twigs and brittle leaves snap underfoot. Above them, spider webs, home to black spiders with squiggly orange markings, some plump, others like stick-drawings, stretch as wide as hammocks. Beth stoops to avoid damaging their ornate webs, Sam moves easily below them.

A startled rabbit scampers out of the scrub and disappears just as quickly. Beth flinches and grabs Sam's hand. Sam laughs and declares a little rabbit wouldn't harm anyone. Beth immediately chides herself for over-reacting. It's their day out, she doesn't want to be so edgy, but recent confrontations leave her perpetually wary.

Following the signage now, the view of a glistening pool sends Sam running ahead with Beth calling after him to watch out for snakes. He removes his shoes and paddles in the water while Beth sits on a tree stump watching him, in awe of his fearless sense of belonging in a natural idyllic setting. Two girls arrive with their father in tow. Competing for Sam's attention, the two girls are talking over one another, and Sam can barely get a word in edgewise. When their papa says it's time to move on, Sam hurriedly dons his shoes in a bid to follow them. But the peppy girls, several years older than Sam, are so far ahead he gives up trying to catch up with them.

Alone now, they stroll along on the shady side of the leafy trail. Every so often they pause to listen intently to the twangy call of banjo frogs or to observe the myriad of birds or reptiles basking in the sun. Yet, Beth cannot dispel a creeping feeling they are being watched. All around them are lofty trees, scrub and amorphous shadows. Looking askance, she thinks she sees a tall figure in the brush, its shadow elongated by sunrays and obscured by thick foliage, it looks like a man.

'Stay put, Sam. I think I heard a kangaroo, listen.'

They hear the snapping of twigs, and the thud of kangaroo paws.

'Can you see him, Mama?'

'No, he's gone.'

Beth takes hold of Samuel's hand. He pulls away, wanting to move freely, she lets him dash ahead, while she, with her skirt hiked up, follows him. Moving along the track, she senses someone is observing their every move. She wishes she'd already armed herself with a pistol. Harry would know where to get one. He might even teach her how to use it, although he's not in favour of carrying weapons, he'd warned if an assailant managed to get hold of her pistol he could just as easily use it against her.

Delighted to have caught up with the two girls, Sam tells them he'd seen a giant kangaroo in the bushes. Cupping a hand over an ear in the style of a pantomime, they listen attentively. 'No there isn't!' one of them insists. They giggle and move on, skipping along after their father, their ponytails swinging from side to side. The bush track leads to a wide open area of endless lawn, the busiest section of the park. Sam spots the girls and their father standing on an arched footbridge enclosed by a squat balustrade of rough-hewn branches. He joins them while Beth looks on. Soon after, they all set off on the final lap of their adventure, the three children chatting boisterously, until they find themselves back where they'd started – at the park entrance. With a hearty farewell, the father and his daughters go their separate ways. Beth looks for a place to rest by the river.

It takes a minute or so to recognise the man sitting cross-legged on the grass eating a sandwich, his bicycle beside him. Vincent Stirling looks younger dressed casually in knee length cycling breeches and long socks. Noticing Beth, he calls out a greeting; she approaches him and introduces Sam. Vincent shakes his hand telling him he is glad to make his acquaintance.

'We've been for a bushwalk.'

'Good on you, Sam.'

Vincent offers them ginger beer and Sam looks to his mother for guidance. Beth nods, smiling. When Vincent returns from the kiosk he hands out the bottles. They sit on the manicured lawn watching two competing boat racing crews stroking along the river, their swiftly moving oars in perfect harmony.

'So you're not going to Port Adelaide this weekend?' Beth asks.

'No, I have a lot of work to catch up on tomorrow.'

'Where've you been riding?'

'Along the river's edge.'

'Not on the bush track?'

He shakes his head. 'Too rough on tyres.'

Vincent notices Sam has finished his drink and offers him a ride on his bicycle.

'My legs are too short.'

'I'll help you along.'

Vincent lifts Sam onto the seat, and supports his back while his free hand steers the bicycle along. Beth follows close behind. Now convinced there wasn't anyone following them in the bushes, she resolves there's no reason why anyone would be following her, she's not even getting close to finding out what happened to Eric Emerson.

Later, Vincent gifts Sam a ball he'd purchased from the kiosk. They play games until the sun melts over the treetops and the breeze turns chilly. Vincent, wheeling his bicycle, accompanies Sam and Beth home. Standing at the gate, he asks Beth to join him the following evening for a concert. As Beth takes a while to answer Sam gets in first and offers to accompany him.

'Maybe another time, Sam. The performance is too late in the evening for you.'

'Can I keep the ball, Mr Stirling?'

'It's yours, I bought it for you.'

'Thank you,' says Sam, throwing the ball into the air and catching it.

Beth accepts his invitation and is told he'd collect her around five the following afternoon if that suits her. It does. Bidding them farewell, he mounts and rides down the road, his bicycle wobbling as he waves a little too vehemently.

SUNDAY, 26TH AUGUST

Having previously arranged a visit, Beth and Sam are tapping on the solid timber door of Tillie's small flat. There's no answer, nor is there any sign that she's home. They wait several minutes before moving to the backyard where they hammer on the back door. Beth is about to let herself in when she hears murmuring voices inside. Moments later, Tillie appears, still in her nightgown, her wavy blond hair falling over her shoulders. The two visitors are asked to wait outside while Tillie's friend Edward Fraser slips on his suit and hat. With a swift peck on her forehead he bids Tillie goodbye and wishes Beth and Sam a good day as he scuttles away, still buttoning up his coat.

'It's ten o'clock in the morning, Tillie.'

'Come in. Sorry, I didn't realise it was so late.' Tillie draws open the curtains and sunshine pours into her room furnished with: a bed, a single lounge chair, a desk, a bookshelf, a table, chairs and a washstand. Located next door is the communal kitchen and bathroom which she shares with three other residents.

'I've brought you a butter cake and some ginger beer.'

'Mm. Thank you, big sister. I'm starving.'

Piles of paper, crayons and pencils at his disposal, Sam sits at the table drawing while Tillie pours the ginger beer into glasses and Beth slices the cake.

'Is what I saw before what I think it was, Tillie?'

'I'm an adult, not a little girl, and you're not my mother.'

'If you're found out you'd lose your teaching position and you could say goodbye to your independence.'

'My fellow teachers would never snitch on me and should the headmistress pass and catch a glimpse of Edward leaving we'd tell her he'd come over to borrow a book, or to help me with my plumbing or some other such fabrication.' She giggles.

'Plumbing sounds about right.' Beth joins in the laughter.

'She's unbelievably gullible.'

'You're making light of it, Tillie, but I worry about you.'

'We're being careful in every way. Eva has shown me how to prevent the thing you're alluding to, douching, rubbers and the like.' Tillie is careful not to spell it out given Sam's proximity and Beth has to concede her sister is an adult and deserves a private life. She wonders if Eva would help Tillie should the contraceptives fail.

'Is it serious, the relationship I mean?'

Tillie's hands spring to her hips in the fashion of a recalcitrant school girl. 'I'm very fond of him, but I'm not after a husband if that's what you mean. I love my position in the school and I'm keen to keep it. But I'm not a nun either.'

'Good for you,' Beth smiles. 'I don't mean to pry.'

'What about you and Vincent Stirling and I do mean to pry?'

'He's invited me out to dinner and a concert this evening.'

'At least you won't lose your job over it.'

'We're just friends.'

'I hope I get to meet him soon.'

'Can I go with you and Mr Stirling, Mama?'

'Not this time, Sam. I'll be home way past your bedtime. Auntie Faith will look after you tonight.'

'We'll read a book after morning tea, Sam. What would you like to read?' Tillie asks, her blue eyes smiling.

'Something scary!'

'Jack and the Beanstalk?'

'Fee-fi-fo-fum …'

'That would be a yes.' Tillie laughs.

At dusk, the sun is high in the jacaranda tree painting its barren branches golden. Seated on the front veranda beside Faith, Beth is dressed in her most elegant gown, blue silk with embroidered lace trimmings, she wonders what she would wear if he invites her out again. Tillie would lend her a gown, but she's a size smaller than Beth and her aunt is a size larger. A widow for almost five years now, she feels enlivened in Vincent's company, desirous, awkward; romancing is an unexpected new experience, at once frightening and exhilarating.

'I'm looking forward to meeting your mystery man. Sam likes him. Children know instinctively who is genuine.'

'That sounds like wishful thinking, Aunt Faith. Besides, my relationship with Mr Stirling is platonic.'

'You've been a grieving widow for long enough, it's time to start enjoying life's many pleasures while you're still young and attractive.'

'I'm out of practice.'

'I'd been a widow for about six years when I fell head over heels for a handsome young man.' Remembering he was ten years her junior she smiles and adds, 'We were inseparable, at least during the first few months. You'd have been a young girl then, you probably don't remember him.'

'I do. He was very debonair, dark, a manicured beard, witty and charming. Mama told me you were smitten.'

'I confided in your mother, she was very understanding. I knew he was after my fortune but I strung him along because I loved him. He was passionate, fun loving, gentle and generous with his affections.' Faith pauses as a fleeting youthful glow crosses her face. 'A year into our relationship he gave me an ultimatum, marry him or he'd leave me. As you know, before the women's property act was introduced ten years ago, a married woman had to sign over everything she owned to her husband, including her home. I wasn't going to sacrifice my wealth and independence for him.'

'You must have been heartbroken when he left.'

'I was devastated for months, but I've never regretted the fling.' Faith goes silent for a short while. 'What I'm trying to say in my unseemly fashion is enjoy a full life. Permit yourself some time to be lively and frivolous, because the years go by too quickly. I've been around long enough to know that.'

Beth can barely speak, she remembers as a child listening to her parents discussing Aunt Faith's lover, the fortune hunter they'd called him. Beth had never imagined her aunt had entered the relationship fully cognisant of the man's intentions. She opens her arms and hugs her aunt who seems to have opened Beth's mind and looked inside, as one does a jar. 'It's better to have loved and lost than never to have loved, as the saying goes.'

'I agree wholeheartedly, Beth. Thanks to the Bank of South Australia collapse a couple of years back, I've lost my fortune anyway. Needless to say, I'd have lost it years earlier if I'd married him.'

'At least you have a beautiful home.'

'I'd probably have lost that as well.'

'I think we can say with certainty, Mr Stirling is not after my fortune.'

'He's after something.' Faith grins. 'Speaking of which, looks like your fortune hunter is out front. My word, he's a looker, isn't he?'

'Behave yourself, Aunt Faith. I'll introduce you to him.'

They descend from the cab in Kent Town, a short distance from the concert hall. Vincent guides Beth to a small restaurant where they dine before strolling down the street arm in arm and entering the Norwood Town Hall. Beth remembers going to the hall every two weeks for music lessons when she was a girl. Faith was wealthy then and determined to provide her nieces with as many opportunities as possible. Beth had enjoyed the lessons, but she soon gave up as her hands refused to work in harmony. Content to listen to others play, she has heard that the Quintrell family of musicians, vocalists and bellringers are considered exceptional performers. Mr Quintrell, his two daughters and three sons enter the hall amid wild applause and the first part of the concert is performed without a hitch.

During a fifteen minute intermission, Beth notices three women wearing exquisite gowns more suited to a grand opera performance. As they wave and walk towards her, she recognizes Lydia and Charlotte. The older woman in their company approaches Vincent first; he introduces her to Beth as Mrs Mooney, Lydia's mother who resides not far from his Port Adelaide home.

'I adore living by the sea, but theatre and entertainment are sadly lacking in Port Adelaide,' Mrs Mooney responds. 'Except for the Italian restaurant that offers piano performances and mouth-watering food,' she adds.

'Mama often stays over when there's a concert or an opera performance.'

'I love an opportunity to dress up and wear my sparkling jewels,' Mrs Mooney chuckles.

Beth praises Charlotte for her beautiful gown. Charlotte's usual attire is drab and overlaid by aprons, but tonight wearing a black, sequined, short-sleeved gown she looks stunning. The skirts seem a little short and Beth wonders if Lydia gave her the gown.

'Charlotte joined us this evening to help Mama manage the interminable stairs one comes across in central Adelaide,' says Lydia.

'That's very kind of you, Charlotte,' says Beth.

'It is all my pleasure. Madame Mooney is a charming lady and I adore music.'

They discuss the performance until the call comes for the audience to return to their seats.

~

Thrust out of Ethel's Dance Hall, the inebriated man stops on the terrace to grab the hitching rail and holds onto it for a long moment to regain his balance. Feeling nauseous, Angus thinks if he brings up the two beef pies he'd gobbled earlier he'd feel better for it. He thrusts two fingers down his throat in an attempt to vomit, but all he can muster is a loud belch. His body aches, his nose is probably broken. He's supposed to report back to work tomorrow, what will he tell his superiors? He regrets having lost his temper. He'd always taken pride in his swift right hook, but the bloke he picked on was built like a gorilla. The thought of his favourite whore dallying with another man drives him to distraction. Ruth is the most beautiful woman he has ever met, or seen for that matter, obliging too, although she would never let him kiss her on the lips. He remembers one time he tried to force her to kiss him, for his efforts he'd received a deep fingernail gash down his cheek. Blood is streaming down his face and neck. Bowing his head, he pinches his nose, waits. It's almost closing time, his last chance to re-enter the place; Ruth might be available now, but she'd probably look down her nose at him. He hammers the front door, curses and bellows he's never coming back. A loyal patron, he deserves special privileges. In the past, they always made him feel special, like a king in his castle. He always sat on the same sofa, drank the same drinks, requested the same whore. And now, thrust out like a flea-ridden cur, he wishes he'd never set foot in that place. He feels like smashing all the windows but he can barely stand up. If it weren't for his drunken antics he'd stand out as an elegant man about town, not a gentleman by any means, but a man who owns his own home and pays his rates.

Angus again holds onto the rail and straightens his shoulders in an effort to reinstate his dignity. Staggering off, his head heavy, he passes another drunk who bids him goodnight and continues on, singing as he goes. Angus grunts and shuffles on. Traditionally, his legs take on a life of their own and walk him home along the well-trodden path, but tonight he is disorientated. Perhaps it's the thick mist that hampers his sense of direction. The dark streets are empty.

Coming to a clump of trees, he loses his balance and tumbles. Moving on his hands and knees, he sits up against the smooth trunk of a ghost gum, his long legs straight out in front of him. He looks up at the starless sky, the moon sifting between branches and casting splinters of light. Drifting clouds make him feel giddy. Tears are dribbling down his face; only the chirping crickets hear his wheezy moans. His painful wrist, cracked knuckles and broken nose are already throbbing. It'll be worse when the liquor wears off. He has to stop drinking before he loses his job. He's already had a final warning due mostly to the booze. What was that fancy word they used? Addiction. Bloody alcohol addiction, my arse, I'm a man who likes a bit of fun. Put a fancy word on it and suddenly it's a serious offence. There won't be any more warnings. Anna would ask for money he hasn't got. He works hard for that money, why should he share it. He'll beat her again if she keeps on about it. Without so much as a second thought he'd put that whore back in hospital. As the master of the house he might end up throwing her out onto the street. There are plenty of women out there who'd idolise a man who owns his own home. He'd find someone more obedient, more willing to accept his fancies. Her mother can stay and mind Sophie. His little girl is the only ray of light in his life. She might have had a brother or sister if Anna hadn't been a cheating whore. It's getting bloody cold. He should get up and walk home. Home sweet home, he sniggers at the thought, there's no heart in his home. He lights another cigarette, draws it deep into his lungs. He chuckles thinking about his nose, probably triple the size by now. There'll be an onslaught of Pinocchio jokes at the pub next visit. Should see the other bloke he'd tell them. In sympathy, they'll shout him a pint or two. Distracted by smoke streaking through the misty air, he doesn't notice the figure in the dark watching him, wondering how much he has in his purse, eyeing his fine suit and leather boots. Confident the drunk is incapable of defending himself, the watcher rushes at him wielding a knife. Angus doesn't feel the blade pierce his neck, doesn't feel the gush of warm blood streaming down his torso. He doesn't notice the hand going through his pockets, nor his expensive boots being yanked off. Angus lies under the tree, blood running into soil, there are no cries, no moans, just a peaceful sleep.

~

Beth is escorted home in a cab. Vincent walks her to the door, thanks her for her charming company and hopes she'll join him again sometime soon, his tone more like a business transaction than a romantic dalliance. He bids her good night, without so much as an embrace. Beth responds in much the same manner before moving inside. Faith and Harry are before the fire enjoying a glass of sherry. Beth is persuaded to join them and share the night's events. Later, she checks on Sam before going to bed. Nodding off, she dreams of being in Vincent's arms.

MONDAY, 27TH AUGUST

The fluffy Pekingese dog snuggled on her mistress' lap looks more like a brown feather duster than an animal. Mrs Mooney breaks up a generous slice of cake onto a saucer before giving it to her little pooch.

'Cake isn't good for dogs, Mama.'

'Nonsense, Polly is thriving.' Polly displays her vitality by breaking wind. When the air has cleared Mrs Mooney tells Lydia to purchase a little Pekingese as they're all the rage.

'I'd rather have Eric back. I really don't think a dog would replace the love of my life.'

'I'd die of loneliness without my little Polly pooch. Unlike husbands, a dog is a loyal friend.'

'Perhaps I should have married a dog.' Lydia sniggers.

'Vincent Stirling tells me you've engaged a detective to find your wayward husband.'

'I don't have any choice, the police have given up. It was audacious of Vincent telling you my business.'

'He assumed I knew about it and I didn't tell him otherwise. He often calls in for a chat. The poor man misses his parents. Anyway, I enjoy his company; he keeps me informed about the goings on in Adelaide.'

'He misses Eric; they've been friends for years.'

'If they're such good friends he should know where Eric is.'

Lydia shrugs. 'If he does he's not telling anyone.'

'He seems keen on Mrs Durrani, doesn't he?'

'They make a splendid couple.'

'Anyway, Charlotte is a marvellous cook; I must say I've been looking forward to every meal. I'm sure my gowns are getting tighter by the minute.' She chuckles. 'I think I'll stay another day or two, but no longer, I already miss my afternoon stroll along the seaside. You should come back to Port Adelaide with me, and stay for a few days.'

'I'd rather stay here, Mama. In case ...'

'My poor darling girl, he's not coming back.'

'If he does, I'd rather be here.'

'You should employ live-in staff, at the very least a cleaner and a gardener.'

'I've asked Mr Stirling to look into hiring a company to do the cleaning and gardening on a casual basis. I don't want to employ permanent staff.'

'Why on earth not?'

'I can manage the day to day maintenance and Charlotte looks after the food and the kitchen. Besides, I'd like to travel overseas, perhaps England or France, it's about time I started seeing the world.'

'Will that be before or after you entice Eric back home?'

'After, I won't feel at ease until I know Eric is safe. He might be tempted to travel overseas with me.'

'I used to think Eric was bland and homely like your father, but after his fling with that young woman, I don't think I knew him at all.'

TUESDAY, 28TH AUGUST

After a busy morning in the vegetable patch, Sam has fallen asleep on the lounge beside Beth, his stockinged feet on her lap. Faith is comfortably seated in an armchair reading *Wuthering Heights* when Harry enters the room carrying the *Adelaide Herald*. 'Angus Hopping has been murdered,' he announces, handing the newspaper to Faith. 'Page two,' he adds.

Faith places her book on the side table and reads the report aloud:

DEFENCELESS MAN STABBED AND ROBBED

The body of Angus Hopping was discovered near Summerset Park yesterday by a retired sea captain walking his dog. Mr Hopping was last seen in Ethel's Dance Hall on Sunday night around ten before being attacked and robbed on his way home. He had been asked to leave the premises due to violent, offensive behaviour.

The police are asking anyone with information to contact the constabulary.

'There goes our prime suspect,' says Faith. 'If he's the culprit he won't be able to tell us where Eric is, will he?'

'Eric might have killed Angus so he could reunite with Anna,' Beth suggests.

'Could be a random killing,' Harry says. 'There are plenty of desperate men roaming the streets at night on the lookout for easy pickings.'

'What was Angus Hopping doing at Ethel's Dance Hall by himself?'

'He wasn't dancing, Faith. It's a notorious bawdy house.'

'Charming.'

Harry offers to make some clandestine enquiries as the constabulary never divulge all the details to the newspapers.

~

That afternoon, Beth rides to Lydia's home to discuss the case. As she pedals along, she finds herself sifting through the meagre evidence. There's no reason why Charlotte would want to cause Eric harm, besides being her employer he was a perfect gentleman to her daughter. As for Anna, he was the love of her life. There's another possibility, Eric is still alive. Perhaps life had become too chaotic for him, his personal and professional life in disarray he left town to start anew. But now, with Angus out of the way Eric may approach Anna.

Beth leans her bicycle against the handrail edging the front porch. Invited in and seated in the parlour, a jittery Lydia asks Beth if she has heard about Angus Hopping's death.

'Yes, I read about it this morning.'

'Do you think Eric killed him?'

'It might have been a random attack. What do you think, Lydia?'

'Eric isn't prone to aggression. He's witty and eloquent; he'd use words to defend himself.'

Beth recalls Nolan Lloyd's account of Eric's scuffle with a man in his front yard, perhaps Eric is not as placid as Lydia thinks he is. 'Have you seen him again?'

'I've been to the Café de Paris at least twice a week since I last spotted him there, but I haven't seen him since. I gave the staff photographs of Eric, they told me they'd look out for him. To be honest, I'm starting to wonder if I'd seen his ghost.'

'Seeing the person we miss is a common symptom of grief.'

Lydia nods in agreement. 'When he was home we'd go about our respective habits and occupations and join for conversation over dinner or in the garden for tea. Now he's gone, I wish to see him all the time. It's very foolish of me.'

'You miss him. It's completely understandable, Lydia.'

'It's surprising how many men resemble him, especially from a distance. Then I walk up close to them and look into their eyes to discover they're nothing like him at all. It's extremely humiliating, especially when they misconstrue my honourable intentions and invite me to join them for a drink.'

'Do you want me to continue with the investigation?'

She sits up straighter in her seat. 'Yes, of course I do. No matter how long it takes, I need to know he's all right and, if not, what happened to him. It's the not knowing why he left and where he is that haunts me.'

WEDNESDAY, 29TH AUGUST

Several doors from Lydia's home, the once grand mansion now operates as a boarding house divided up into small flats. Standing out front, it occurs to Beth that should Aunt Faith fall into harder times she could join the boarding house community. Though, it'd be a last resort as Faith cherishes her independence. Her bicycle left in the front garden, Beth approaches the door and raises the tapper. A squat woman with a huge, shiny forehead and deep-set eyes answers the door. After an introduction, Mrs Zambetti, the landlady, accompanies Beth to Charlotte's room, located on the ground floor.

'*Vous avez une visitor, Mademoiselle Bechard!*' she bellows, then having displayed her impressive command of the French language, she gives a haughty nod and moves slowly down the hall, turning to ensure her boarder has answered the door.

Beth asks Charlotte if it's convenient to chat. Charlotte nods and ushers her into the room, patches of sunlight illuminating the space. A bed, cupboards, sofa and a thick rug on the floor make up the simple yet comfortable abode.

Beth notices Charlotte's black sequined gown arranged on a coat hanger fixed to a hook on the wall, exhibited like a prized sculpture. 'That's a beautiful gown and you looked ravishing at the concert the other night.'

'*Merci*, Mrs Emerson gifted it to me.'

'That was very kind of her.'

With a graceful sweep of the hand Charlotte invites Beth to sit. 'I must go to work soon,' she says, sitting beside Beth on the sofa.

Promising not to take too long, Beth grasps a notebook and pencil from her vest pocket and goes straight to the point of her visit. 'I've recently learned that you are Anna Hopping's birth mother. I'm wondering why you didn't mention that before.'

'My business, n'est-ce pas?'

There's a brief uncomfortable silence between them.

Charlotte gives a reproving look. 'Did Anna tell you?'

'No, we found out by other means.'

Charlotte slips her stockinged feet into her boots.

'How is Anna?'

Leaning over and lifting her legs, one at a time, Charlotte ties her laces into triple bows. Her boot laces secured she sits up and fixes her eyes on Beth. 'Anna is free.'

'Does Mrs Emerson know your daughter was having an affair with her husband?'

'Please do not tell her. I will tell her, maybe today, maybe tomorrow.'

'It would be better coming from you. Does Anna ever visit you here?'

'Sometimes Anna and Sophie come 'ere.' Charlotte gets up, moves to the cupboard and grasps a recent photograph of her daughter and hands it to Beth. 'Elle est belle, n'est-ce pas?'

'She is, and so is little Sophie,' says Beth, gazing at Charlotte, hoping for an explanation.

Charlotte opens up and tells her story, at times during emotional moments slipping into French. A newly arrived migrant, at fifteen, unmarried and alone she gave birth to Anna. She knew she wouldn't be able to keep her child so she cherished the hours she cradled her daughter in her arms. She and Audrey were in hospital beds, side by side. Audrey's stillborn daughter was taken away from her, whereas Charlotte's child was alive and healthy. Charlotte knew she was unable to support her child given she was unemployed and didn't have any family or close friends to assist her. Charlotte allowed Audrey to adopt her child with conditions: Charlotte would have the right to visit her daughter and see her growing up. Anna would be told about her birth mother and her reasons for giving her up. Audrey and her husband kept their word. Charlotte knew Anna would be well cared for. When Audrey's husband died four years ago she moved in with Anna and gave Angus all her savings, to be used for Sophie's education. Over the years, he squandered it all on himself. Charlotte's dark eyes tear up when she explains how peaceful life was when Anna first married. Angus allowed Charlotte to be part of their lives, but when Sophie was born he became surly and possessive, as if someone would take those he loved away from him. He forbade Charlotte from visiting her granddaughter. Over time, alcohol became his first love and violence became routine.

Beth lets the words sink in.

'When Angus beat my daughter I told her to come live with me, but Madame Zambetti has rules: no children, no animals.'

'Evidently, Madame Zambetti considers children and animals as one and the same,' Beth scoffs.

'She only loves money.'

'Do you think Eric Emerson had anything to do with Angus' death?'

'Maybe.'

'With Angus out of the way, Eric can reunite with Anna, the woman he loves. Do you know if he has contacted her at all?'

Charlotte shrugs her shoulders dismissively. 'I 'ave to go to work now.'

'I'll accompany you, if you don't mind.'

Charlotte's gives a half-hearted nod.

Along the way, Beth learns that Anna had been discharged from hospital early that morning. Standing at the gate of Lydia's home, Beth watches Charlotte stroll down the footpath and let herself into the house, the security of employment no doubt giving her the means to help Anna until she is on her feet again.

Wheeling her bicycle a little further down the road towards the bush track, Beth's attention is caught by a pair of multi-coloured rosellas flying low. She observes them landing together in a bushy young eucalypt crowned with clumps of vivid red flowers. No wonder Eric enjoyed tramping along the bush trails, the natural world is at once sublime and daunting. Wheel imprints are cut into the road and Beth wonders who would be using the track. She remembers Lydia telling her about an abandoned farm down the road, perhaps occupied by squatters now. Considering Eric's proclivity for bushwalking she feels compelled to explore the area, but for now a chat with Anna Hopping is more pressing.

Beth turns into Anna's Road, happy she'd purchased a cake from her favourite café in Rundle Street – tasty offerings do wonders for extracting information from ill-disposed sweet tooths. Entering the yard, she inhales the fresh minty scent of laundry pegged on the line, mostly men's clothing. She props her bicycle against the side wall and takes hold of the cake box before approaching the front door. She taps lightly. Despite her grandmother telling her to wait, Sophie appears at the door.

'Hello, Sophie, may I come in?'

'It's the bicycle lady, Grandma!' Stepping aside, Sophie's pretty plump face bursts into a broad smile as she invites Beth to enter.

The room smells of toast and brewed tea. The stove is hot, the teapot steaming. Audrey tells Beth she is just in time for morning tea. Beth offers the cake. Ushered to take a seat she chats with Sophie while Audrey pours the tea and slices the cake.

'Papa isn't coming home no more, he's in the sky,' says Sophie.

'Yes, he's in peace now,' Beth responds. 'How is your mama?'

'Mama is sleeping,' says Sophie, helping herself to a slice of cake. 'Mmm, chocolate icing is my favourite.' Sophie wolfs down her cake, licks her fingers clean, and takes her rag doll and several other toys to play on a threadbare rug nearby.

'Anna's been sleeping on and off since she got home this morning. I don't think she got much shut-eye in hospital,' says Audrey. 'She's getting stronger, though.'

'Does she know?'

'Of course she does. I can't believe she wept for that man.'

'She might be focussing on the good times.'

'Three months of joy followed by years of hell,' Audrey laughs, more an expression of distain than merriment. 'She'll have to find work now he's gone; at least we got a roof over our heads.'

They hear a thud coming from one of the bedrooms. Audrey asks Beth to prepare a tray of tea and cake for Anna while she hurries to her daughter to find the distressing sound was a book tumbling to the floor. Sophie follows them in and leaps onto the bed and hugs her mother who hugs her back. Soon after, Beth slides the tea tray along the bedside table while Audrey props Anna up against two pillows.

'We'll leave you two to chat, come on Sophie,' says Audrey. 'It's time to go next door to play with your friend.'

Beth sits on the chair facing Anna's bed. 'Would you like your tea, Anna?'

'Thank you.' Anna quickly drains her cup.

'How are you faring?'

'I almost lost my baby.'

'I'm glad you didn't lose your child. I wish you well.'

'I'm not showing much yet, but I already love him. I'm going to call him Eric, if he's a boy or Erica if she's a girl.'

Beth offers her some cake, a poor consolation for her troubles. Surprisingly, she accepts a large slice and eats ravenously. Beth looks about the small room. Several photographs adorn the walls. There's a framed one of the family, professionally taken in a studio, Angus, Anna, Sophie, Audrey and an elderly woman, the only one seated, perhaps Angus' mother, snapped during happy times, probably before Angus hit the bottle. There's a picture of Sophie, nursing her rag doll. There's another photograph of a young woman, broad-shouldered, black hair, intense looking and beautiful in her own way. Her dark eyes and eye-brows call to mind a gypsy. Then it dawns on her, the woman in the picture is Charlotte, Anna's birth mother.

'Who is that pretty woman in the photograph?' asks Beth, her head turning from the photograph to Anna and back again, the resemblance between the two women is striking.

'My mother's friend,' she turns away from Beth, grabs her cup, remembers it's empty and decides there's no use lying. 'As you no doubt know, I have two mothers and I love them both. But two mothers didn't protect me and my unborn child from that cad I married.'

Beth nods. Tells Anna she's going to the kitchen to refill their cups and returns five minutes later.

Anna brushes the crumbs from her nightgown and sits back sipping her tea. They chat for a while until Anna's eyes are heavy. Beth gathers the tea things and leaves her in peace. 'Thank you,' Anna murmurs, nodding off.

Audrey is removing Angus' clothes from the line when Beth moves out into the sunshine and tells her Anna has fallen asleep.

'That's good, she needs plenty of rest.'

'His clothes are in good condition.'

Audrey nods. 'We'll sell his clothes and shoes. We'll need the money until Anna is well enough to find employment.'

Beth follows Audrey into the house and helps her fold the clean washing.

'What did the police tell you about Angus' death?'

'They turned up here the day after he was killed, said he was stabbed with a steak knife. Whoever did it, took his clothes, shoes and wallet.'

'If his possessions were stolen, how did the police identify him?'

'The man who found him recognised him. Strangely enough, he was once Angus' captain before he retired some months ago. He ended up identifying the body. Anna was in hospital and couldn't do it.'

'Do you think the killer was someone Angus knew?'

'Are you investigating Angus' murder now?'

'His death could be linked to Eric's disappearance.'

Audrey wrings her hands together. 'I have no idea about all this. If you don't mind I have work to do. The funeral's this afternoon, his elderly uncle organised it. Anna's not well enough to attend but me and Sophie are going.'

'I'll be on my way then. You have my card if you need to contact me in person or by mail.' Beth fixes her eyes on Audrey and asks if she has seen Eric recently.

'Do you think Eric killed Angus?' Audrey smiles, but there's tension in her manner.

'I don't know what to think.'

Audrey's thin fingers cover her eyes for several seconds, as if she needs darkness in order to think clearly. The dark circles below her eyes evidence of a lack of sleep. 'Eric is dead.'

'How do you know that, Audrey?'

'If he was alive he'd come to Anna, but we haven't seen hide nor hair of him in months.'

THURSDAY, 30TH AUGUST

Cycling home from the corner shop, a wicker basket strapped to the handlebars and laden with groceries, Beth enters Sunny Corner Park to rest and reflect on her recent visit to Anna's home. Wheeling her bicycle, she strolls beneath the giant oak trees now in bud, a few branches already spurting leaves. Carefully, she leans her bicycle against the shoulder of a bench and is seated. Overhead, a mature wisteria vine is entwined in a wire trellis and bunches of fragrant purple flowers dangle between the gaps, some clusters still in bud. She removes her hat and tilts her head towards the sun, the wispy breeze and the warmth on her skin as soothing as fingertips. Her heartbeat slows. Gathering her thoughts, she turns her conversations with Audrey over in her mind, visualises Audrey's countenance as she spoke, and wonders why she was so nervous, perhaps out of concern for Anna. Her relief that Angus is out of their lives is normal, given the circumstances. Though, with another child on the way, the breadwinner deceased and Anna still convalescing, Beth wonders how they'll get by.

She smells him before she sees him. The familiar scent of sandalwood oil engulfs her senses, Arif's preferred scent. She glances at the man sitting beside her. Although dressed in a neat black suit, he smells like a labourer, or someone who has indulged in vigorous exercise. The mix of sandalwood and sweat reminds her of Arif's skin when he returned from working in the fields or the orchards.

An earthy manly smell she had always liked.

Beth looks askance at the man sitting a few feet away from her, a string of beads in his hands, his fingers moving the beads up and down the thread as if he is rehearsing the words he is about to voice. With a scornful countenance, he turns to her and their eyes meet. The man beside her is not Arif. She studies Ramin's young face: intense brown eyes, a prominent nose and wide lips. He is handsome in a hard way, not the gentle face of Arif. She looks about her, others are strolling around the popular park.

Ramin holds her gaze, his glare burning her eyes. He studies her face as if it pains him to be in her presence. No longer a gangly boy, he is strong, bearded, a head taller than the last time she'd seen him. He must be nineteen now, no wonder it took her a while to recognise him.

'Do you still speak English, Ramin?'

'A little.'

'How long have you been in Adelaide?'

'Two month.'

'I sensed I was being followed, so many times. Perhaps I knew it was you all along but I didn't want to believe it.'

'I am not dead like you think.' He sneers.

'I received word from Michael that you were alive and well.'

Casting his mind back, Ramin goes quiet as he reflects on the day Beth absconded from the family home. Mina's wedding of all days. He'd noticed Beth leave the party, followed her and watched her disappear into her room. It was obvious she was intending to leave. Alarmed, he'd looked for his father, to tell him, to warn him, but his father was presenting a speech. Ramin had to deal with the situation himself.

'Arif told me to leave weeks before he died, but I wanted to be by his side when he passed.'

'You lie.'

'No, he knew I was missing my homeland, he knew I wouldn't

stay in Afghanistan without him. He advised me to leave before he died. He said you and your family would not let me out of your sight after his death. Arif was right, wasn't he?'

Ramin looks ahead, taking in Beth's words. He had never imagined she had left with Arif's blessing.

'Was it you who gave Sam the kite?'

He nods.

'Instead of sneaking around our home and stalking me, you should have come in to visit us. That's what family members do, they arrange visits.'

'I do not come to visit. I come to take the son of Arif home to Afghanistan.'

'I can't believe what I'm hearing.' She pauses to make sense of what he is telling her. 'Did your father send you?'

'Baba is old man. I make decisions now. Mother cry every day for Arif, she not stop until grandson is in her arms. She lose Arif and you take his son away.' He pauses to allay his emotions at the thought of his mother who stayed in bed for days following Arif's death. 'Samuel look like Arif,' he adds, his tone softening a little.

'Yes, he looks like Arif, same green eyes. I'm sorry for your mother. I'm sorry for your loss, but I cannot let my son leave with you, he would be unhappy away from everyone and everything he knows and loves.'

He looks directly at her, a look of indignation on his face. 'I not ask permission, I telling you, he come with me.' His fingers are again weaving the worry beads up and down the string.

'He's my son. I have borne him, fed him, loved him, he is mine.'

'You are bad mother, you go all over town, see men.'

'I'm a private investigator; it's my job to interview people, women and men. I have to make a living.'

'You are dog catcher. You shame Arif, dishonour family.'

'I enjoy what I do. Arif would want me to be happy.' Beth pauses for a time and considers Ramin's world view, he would never understand the love she and Arif shared. 'Go home, Ramin, go home to your mother, she needs you.'

'Give me the son of Arif and I go home.'

Beth regards his young face. He really believes she'd hand over her son to him. Words, explanations are useless; nothing will alter that man's determination to have his brother back in the person of Samuel.

'The boy come with me, I leave soon on ship, he is safe with me.'

'I would never give up my son, he is my world, he is a part of Arif, the man I loved and still love. But Arif is gone from me, I have a life to live, my son has a life to live, Arif would want us to be together. Samuel may choose to travel to his father's home when he is an adult but until then he will stay with me.'

'He come with me,' Ramin says, getting to his feet. He hasn't travelled across the world to be harangued by this woman who doesn't deserve Arif's beautiful boy. Without a goodbye, he scampers off into the trees, a man with a mission, a man still grieving the loss of his brother, a man wanting his nephew beside him, a part of Arif to take home to his mother.

Watching Ramin disappear into the afternoon arouses memories of her final heartbreaking days with Arif. She'd have gone anywhere in the world with Arif, but when he died there was no reason to remain in Afghanistan. And now, it is time to move on, time to live in the moment and accept Arif's passing, and in so doing free Arif and Sam as well. The intensity of her love for Samuel is over-whelming at times, but he is not Arif reborn, he is Samuel Durrani, an individual who has his own identity and his own life to live. If Ramin takes her darling boy abroad it would be almost impossible to get him back again. Beth pulls her hat back onto her head, adjusts the pins and grasps her bicycle. Holding the handlebars, she walks along for several minutes before mounting and hurrying home to share her distressing news with Faith and Harry. From now on they must not let Sam out of their sight.

~

Beth is working in the office when Faith enters accompanied by Vincent Stirling. He confesses he was in the area and could not forego the opportunity of visiting the Bethany Investigation Agency.

'You're welcome any time, Mr Stirling,' says Faith.

'What an interesting office,' he says, casting an eye all around the room. 'Who painted the seascape?'

'My late husband dabbled in art.' Faith answers.

'It reminds me of the amazing view from my home in Port Adelaide.'

Noticing his eyes moving to the self-portrait Beth is quick to point out her uncle painted it when he was terminally ill.

'Very moving,' he says.

'Very something.' Beth shakes her head.

'How's business?'

Faith responds before Beth can get a word in, 'A handsome male with big brown eyes, large ears, an imbecilic grin and wearing a sleek black coat has disappeared and we're on the case. His name is Carl Burkett, and a hefty reward is being offered for his capture.'

'Capture?'

'We'll find him, we usually do. You'd be surprised what wealthy people pay to get their beloved pooches back.'

Vincent breaks into laughter. 'I thought you were referring to a missing person.'

'We'd rather not shackle our missing persons, but sometimes it is necessary,' Faith grins.

'Mr Stirling doesn't want to know the ins and outs of our business, Aunt Faith,' Beth says, her lips pouted in a silent shush when she sees Vincent isn't looking.

'Please join us for a cool glass of ginger beer, Mr Stirling?'

'Thank you, Mrs Ellsworth, I'd be delighted.'

Faith leaves the room, the glass door almost shattering as she slams it behind her.

'I thought it would fall off its hinges,' says Vincent taking a seat. 'I'd better be virtuous at all times to avoid being assaulted like that wretched door.' He laughs and his dark eyes find hers and she would like nothing better than to throw her arms around him for bringing merriment to the office.

'Aunt Faith may have damaged a few doors about the place, but rest assured she is very kind to humans.'

'That's a relief,' he smiles briefly, but his expression becomes more thoughtful. 'You've no doubt read about Angus Hopping's death?'

Beth nods. 'We've also learned that Charlotte Bechard is Anna Hopping's birth mother. Unmarried and poor, she had to give Anna up so she could make a living. There was an agreement with Audrey that her daughter would ...' Beth stops talking to study Vincent's stony face. 'You don't look surprised, Vincent.'

'It's Vincent again, is it?'

'Stop trying to change the subject.'

'No, I'm not surprised. Eric told me in confidence.'

'You'd have saved us a lot of time if you'd shared that information.'

'I abide by the words: *in confidence*.'

Beth considers herself to be a trusted friend with whom confidential information could be shared, but she holds her tongue. 'So if Eric had told you *in confidence* to keep his whereabouts secret you'd keep it to yourself.'

'Of course I would. But I assure you he has not contacted me.'

'The two mysteries could be linked. If Eric's alive he could have killed Angus, it would leave the way clear for him to reunite with Anna.'

'Good Lord, Eric's not a violent man.'

'He was certainly well liked by everyone who knew him. Amiable, generous, cheerful, but nobody's perfect, are they?'

'I consider myself to be perfect,' says Vincent, straight-faced. 'I cannot for the life of me think of any flaws in my character.'

Beth is speechless for a long moment until Vincent cannot hold his deadpan expression any longer and bursts out laughing.

'You had me worried there, Mr Perfect.' Beth grins.

'I like to think I don't take myself too seriously, Beth. So where do you go from here?'

'Eric enjoyed long treks in the bushland across from his home. It'd be worth exploring some of those tracks.'

'You think Eric is living in the bush like a caveman?' he asks, an amusing glint in his eyes. 'Eric loves his creature comforts.'

'I'm open to any ideas, any direction other than going around in circles chasing my own tail.'

'Bushwalking often leads inexperienced hikers around in circles,' he smiles.

'It's just a question of staying on track.'

'Let me know when you're planning to go.'

'You'd accompany me?'

'I really don't think you should go bushwalking by yourself.'

'I'm going tomorrow morning. Are you able to take the day off?'

'I'm confident Verity will hold the fort in my absence.'

'I've already arranged to meet Lydia for tea before the bushwalk. Shall we meet there, around nine-thirty in the morning?'

'Certainly.'

Faith enters the office to announce afternoon refreshments are served. They are soon seated on the veranda sipping ginger beer, laughing, chatting and generally enthralled listening to Vincent's more controversial courtroom dramas performed in the legal halls of Adelaide. Soon after, Harry and Sam emerge from the garden to join them. Later, they erect a series of square-topped hoops on the lawn and invite Vincent to participate in a game of croquet. Each player is given a mallet and several wooden balls. Harry reminds Sam that the goal is to hit a ball through the course of six hoops.

They play several games until the sun is high in the trees. As sunset casts her mellow glow, Vincent takes his leave, thanking everyone for a delightful afternoon.

'Those eyes, like shiny black pearls,' says Faith, watching him walk briskly down the footpath to the front gate.

'He is rather dashing, isn't he?'

'Is he wealthy?'

Beth shrugs her shoulders. 'Comfortable.'

FRIDAY, 31ST AUGUST

Despite the misty air and scudding clouds, Lydia and Vincent take tea on the front porch. A mischief of magpies are carolling their melodious songs from the tree peaks across the road, perhaps announcing imminent rain.

'How's the tea?'

Vincent takes a moment to come up with a tactful reply for the over-brewed, murky liquid. 'Rejuvenating, I won't sleep for a week. And the cake is delicious.'

'I prepared the tea but I can't take credit for the cake; we can thank Charlotte for that. I've never had to cook in my life, spoiled really. I've been doing a bit of tidying up around the house as well. I'll keep it up until I engage a cleaner. The exercise is most beneficial, I haven't felt so fit in years.'

'Perhaps you should join us for the walk.'

'The bush is too full of insects, arachnids and reptiles for my liking. I don't know what you and Mrs Durrani think you'll find in there. Eric loves nature but not enough to take up residence in a humpy.'

'Beth seems to think we should traipse around and see. We'll put it down to an investigator's intuition.'

'On first name basis, are we? She's a handsome woman; she could simply want to spend time with you.' Lydia grins.

'I took the liberty of inviting myself. It's too dangerous for a woman, or a man for that matter, to go bushwalking alone. Besides that, she's still mourning her late husband.'

'Some people never recover from their first love.'

A whirring sound of spinning wheels turns their attention to the road out front, in the near distance a woman is speeding along on her bicycle, her hat released, her red hair trailing behind her like a runaway cape.

'Good Lord, swift as a galloping horse,' says Vincent, standing up for a better view.

Looking very sporty in her cycling suit and hiking boots, Beth dismounts at the gate. Her wide-brimmed straw hat is attached to her neck by a loosened chin strap, she pops it back on her head and tucks her hair in before wheeling her bicycle along the footpath. Still panting, she greets Lydia and Vincent, props her bicycle against the handrail, and flops onto a seat. Lydia pours her a cup of tea and hands it to her. Beth takes a large gulp and does all she can to stifle a groan as the tea tastes like raw spinach. To get it over and done with she quickly drains her cup.

'Goodness, riding certainly produces an ardent thirst,' observes Lydia, her thin white hands covering her mouth as she chuckles.

Beth nods, sloshing a piece of sweet coconut cake around in her mouth to neutralise the lingering bitter taste of tea. Vincent has noticed and is smiling wickedly, his cup still three-quarters full, his cake devoured.

'May I leave my bicycle here while we're gone, Lydia?'

'Of course you may. Let me know how you go and please don't leave the main track, it's easy to lose your way in the bush. Eric told me the tracks are ill-defined and sometimes non-existent.'

'If we're not back by dusk please alert the constabulary,' Vincent grins.

'I suspect you're jesting, but I will expect to see you well before dusk.'

The two bushwalkers set off on the wide track that cuts through the forest and seems to go on forever. 'Does anyone live at the end of the road?' Beth asks.

'Not sure, Eric told me there used to be a thriving farm down there, apparently the old farmer died of snake bite and his grief-stricken wife died soon after. I think it's crown land now. Eric used to harp on about how the land should be preserved for human recreation. He was always fearful it'd be developed for housing.'

'It'd be a pity to destroy virgin forest.'

'There's always a need for more housing though, only last week almost two hundred migrants arrived on a steamer from Great Britain.'

Beth pushes images of the pristine bushland being felled from her mind. 'Did Eric ever invite you on a bushwalk?' she asks.

'A few times, but I never got around to it. Pity, I'd know his favourite haunts.' Vincent stops to examine the deep furrows in the track. 'Looks like wagon marks in the sand, bogged by the looks of it. Possibly one of those pesky people dumping rubbish; Eric used to complain about them littering the bush to avoid paying waste disposal fees.'

They stroll along talking continuously for a good mile until the track tapers to a width just wide enough for a wagon, as if nature has mapped out a plan to close in and block access. When they come to a sheltered clearing they stop for a break. A flat sandstone boulder serves as a seat. Beth grasps two mandarins from her bag and offers one to Vincent.

'Mmm, thank you. Where did you come by such fresh fruit?' Vincent asks, inhaling the tangy zest.

'Aunt Faith's garden. Harry Fairweather, her boarder, has turned a large section of her grounds into a cottage garden; we hardly ever go shopping for fruit and vegetables.'

'Sounds like an ideal boarder.'

'He's like part of the family,' she says, still unsure exactly how close her aunt is to the ever cheerful Harry.

A large kangaroo leaps across the clearing and stops amongst the trees, glaring at them, asserting his territory. His ears pricked, he is at home and they are intruders. They dare not approach him. Seemingly cuddly creatures, Beth knows never to pat them as they consider that an invitation to a boxing match. Their claws are as sharp as knives. Satisfied the human intruders are no threat, the kangaroo hops away down the track.

'Amazing how strong their hind legs are, looks like they've carved a path through the scrub,' says Vincent.

'It's a well-trodden trail. Shall we see where it goes?'

Leaving a scattering of mandarin peels behind them, they move off, Vincent in front. The only sounds are their boots trampling sticks and brittle leaves and the occasional flutter of startled birds. Looking down, Beth observes a faint impression of zigzagging wheel tracks imprinted in the sandy trail, superimposed by footprints, as if someone had wheeled a bicycle through the bush. Or more than one person, perhaps the cyclists were expecting a more amenable track and turned back disappointed. Vincent suggests they could be snake tracks. That comment urges them to move through the bush more cautiously. As the trail gets steeper they find themselves walking on a smooth stony track. On either side, there are vast stretches of solid sandstone with a few hardy shrubs pushing through rock crevices here and there. The two trekkers cheer when they reach the crest of the hill and find themselves standing on a rocky plateau near a steep escarpment.

'Forest as far as the eye can see, it's so wild and beautiful. I'd love to fly like a bird over the valley,' says Beth, her raised arms held to the side as if she's about to take flight.

'It is spectacular,' says Vincent, tilting his head towards the blue-grey clouds gathering across a bleak sky and wondering if they should turn back. 'Engineers like Lawrence Hargraves reckon it's just a matter of years before people take to the skies in flying machines.'

'A bird's eye view of the world would be stunning.'

Beth moves closer to the edge of the escarpment and looks down into the gully below. 'There's another track down there.'

'I'd like to climb down to see where it goes. Do you mind waiting here, Beth, I won't be long?'

'Yes, I do mind, I'm coming too. The cliff's not as sheer as I first thought.'

'It's a challenging descent. I'll go first so I can catch you if you fall.' He grins.

'I'll hold you to that, Mr Stirling.'

Gripping protruding rocks and deeply rooted shrubs and using deep indents in the stone to lodge their feet, they descend slowly and without incident. Stepping into the gully, the air is damp and the landscape is marked by thick scrub, lofty trees and green tree ferns that stand tall like sweeping parasols. Using their strong hind legs, mobs of kangaroos have hewed a myriad of vein-like narrow trails through the virgin bushland, but the wide track heading north is the most used.

Somewhere in the distance, thunder rumbles and the wind picks up. 'We'll end up in Port Augusta if we keep going.'

'I can't imagine anyone else I'd rather be lost with.' Vincent gives a playful smile. 'I suppose we should turn back, I wonder if there's a way of returning without having to climb back up the cliff.'

'There's that kangaroo again.'

'How on earth do you know it's the same one?'

'He has the same big brown, upturned nostrils and large pointy ears.'

'Very observant, Detective Durrani.'

'A knack for remembering faces is vital in my vocation.'

'Indeed, especially when tracking down missing kangaroos.'

They laugh together.

'We might be headed for that farmhouse you were talking about, Vincent.'

'Do you think we should turn back?'

'No.'

Half an hour later they come to a wide grassy clearing just as a light shower sets in. A fallen giant lays nestled at the foot of a lofty red gum, hollowed out by time and climate, its jagged mouth wide gaping. Daubed in emerald-green moss and jade-blue algae, ferns flourish all around its rotund girth. Posies of white orchids huddle along the northern side of the fallen eucalypt.

'I've never seen a dead tree hollow this thick before.'

'It must have been a majestic giant before succumbing to a storm or old age,' says Vincent, dropping to his knees and craning his neck to see inside. Pale light falling through the large gaps in the roof of the hollow illuminate the bones, tattered clothing, and boots. 'Good God!' He bolts out backwards as if he'd seen a snake. 'A body, bones, human I think,' he says, moving away from the hollow before standing upright. 'Eric loves ...' says Vincent, struggling to keep his emotions in check, 'loved this place.'

Beth takes his hands in hers and suggests the body might not be Eric's.

Besides a few wispy ferns, the hollowed entrance has been kept clear, perhaps by animals in search of shelter. Beth kneels at the opening and peers inside. She inhales the mouldy smell of rotting wood and something else, death. The shrunken clothing flecked with white spores has peeled from its host. In that splintery cist where time trails the four seasons, a pocket watch lies idle on the mulchy floor. The skull is pointing towards the back of the hollow, suggesting the victim had crawled in. The question is why? Normally bones would not provoke intense emotions, but imagining those bones are Eric Emerson's has a strong effect on her. She recalls her last memory of him cavorting arm in arm with Anna Hopping, laughing, joyous, in love. And now, bones.

Entirely consumed by their macabre discovery, they don't notice the distant roll of thunder and the sky turning black. Within minutes, the mizzling shower becomes galloping rain.

'We'll have to inform the constabulary,' says Beth, dreading another visit to that place almost as much as traipsing back in the rain and the mud.

'The quickest, safest route back to the main road is probably the way we came. We'll have to be careful, everything'd be slippery now.'

They walk back to the escarpment in silence, their thoughts taken up with the body in the hollow. Thankfully, the cliff face is gently sloping and reasonably accessible to novice climbers. Beth ascends first, digging her boots into the stone crevices between the layered sandstone and gripping the jutting rocks and scrappy plants to hoist herself up, careful not to slip. Vincent is behind her. A lightning flash beaming across the sky makes her jump, she waits, stunned. Vincent urges her to keep going; they're almost to the top. She clutches a shrub, pulls at it to ensure its roots are fixed deep within the earth, and lifts her body a yard higher. Rain is streaming down her neck and back, icy cold on her skin. When her hands grip the ridge, she hauls herself up onto the ledge and crawls away from the edge before getting to her feet. Vincent arrives soon after. The surrounding bushland is now blanketed in thick clouds. Emotions running high, they hug each other for a long moment before moving on. Traipsing along the narrow track through the drooping, slapping, wet foliage, they continue until they come to the clearing where they'd left the citrus peels, now a vivid orange on the grey, sloshy earth. Mist swelling through the trees, they continue up the main track to Lydia's home, the rain easing, a bitter wind biting through their clothes, a layer of mud caked thick and heavy beneath their boots.

They enter Lydia's property and stand on the threshold, dreading the news they must impart. When the door swings open, Lydia reads their drenched faces before they utter a word. Despite their assertions, the body could be anyone, Lydia almost collapses and Charlotte appears from nowhere to console her and help her move to the parlour, while Vincent hurries off to alert the constabulary of their gruesome discovery. Beth is invited in, but given her clothes are soaked through, she remains on the sheltered porch. Charlotte provides a warm blanket and a cup of hot chocolate.

By the time two police wagons arrive, the rain has ceased and pale sunlight is struggling to shed light on a sodden landscape. Four police officers wait in the wagons while the sergeant follows Vincent onto Lydia's property. Charlotte emerges from the house to announce that Mrs Emerson has taken a sedative and is fast asleep. Before Charlotte goes back inside, the sergeant informs everyone they must not make assumptions about the victim's identity at this early stage, at least not until the medical examiner has submitted his report. He whips out a notebook and pencil from his coat pocket and asks Beth and Vincent to briefly relay the events of the day while he jots down the main points. He tells them to report to the constabulary on Monday to provide a detailed statement. Vincent is called upon to direct the policemen to the hollow. Already exhausted, he is not looking forward to another bushwalk. Beth bids Vincent farewell and sets off for home where she hopes a warm fire is blazing.

The policemen pull up near the clearing; the mandarin peels now floating in puddles. A constable stays behind with the wagons whilst four policemen climb out. With rucksacks strung over their shoulders, they set off carrying a light stretcher, ropes and an axe. Vincent leads the way. When they come to the escarpment the policemen observe the drop into the gully with some consternation, but they have been instructed to return to the station with the body before nightfall and will comply with orders. The sergeant asks Vincent for detailed directions to the hollow and sketches a map in his notebook. Vincent is thanked for his assistance and told he should return home as the way to the hollow seems straightforward from that point.

'I'd like to keep going if you don't mind, Eric was a close friend.'

'It's police business, Mr Stirling. Besides, the body hasn't been officially identified yet.'

'When will …?'

'Hours, days, weeks, who knows? Don't discuss this case with anyone, especially newspaper reporters.'

SATURDAY, 1ST SEPTEMBER

Inspector Taylor calls in the medical examiner who is not at all happy to be dragged out on his day off, but an augmented hourly rate boosts his willingness. By early afternoon, he concludes the cadaver had been in the hollow for almost five months. The victim had fallen from a substantial height and on impact with the ground his pocket-watch ceased working on Saturday, 7th April, 1894. This date corresponds to the skeletonised condition of the cadaver. Given the size of the bones and the skull having pronounced orbital ridges, the bones are those of a young male of average height and average boot size. His hair colour is light brown. There is no evidence of dental work having been carried out.

Decomposition has occurred at an accelerated rate due to the humid conditions in the hollow and organisms such as insects and carnivores having attacked the body. The cadaver has lost most of its mass. Hair, bones, cartilage, and other by-products of decay remain. There is evidence the neck and face had been interfered with post-mortem, probably feral cats.

The victim had sustained three fractured lumbar vertebrae and severe spinal cord injury. There is evidence of a mild skull fracture. His olecranon bones are mildly damaged on both arms suggesting the victim used his upper body, especially his elbows, to propel himself along a bush track as he was unable to stand up and walk due to paralysis. Similarly, the victim would have utilised his upper body to crawl into the tree hollow as a refuge for the night and subsequently died there from his injuries.

Items found near the cadaver include: a wedding ring, pocket watch and a pocketknife. The pocketknife is engraved with an inscription dedicated to Eric Emerson.

Following the post-mortem examination, the medical examiner is satisfied Mr Eric Emerson's injuries were accidental.

SUNDAY, 2ND SEPTEMBER

On Sunday afternoon, Inspector Taylor studies the medical examiner's report before sending one of his officers to fetch Mrs Lydia Emerson. He'd known Eric well, had on many occasions socialised with him. He finds it baffling that an experienced bush walker could fall from a precipice. Perhaps he'd been drinking.

Within the hour Lydia is escorted into his office. The inspector asks her to take a seat before imparting the sad news.

'Mrs Durrani said it could have been anyone, but I knew it was Eric. He'd often spoken of the tree hollow, it intrigued him.' Lydia sobs quietly. 'How did he …?'

'He fell from an escarpment, Mrs Emerson. Despite his injuries, he summoned the strength to crawl along the track and enter the hollow for the night.'

'My darling Eric was close by all along, if only I'd known.'

'Are you able to identify his possessions?'

Lydia nods, rises from her chair and moves to the table. Inspector Taylor removes the sheet covering an array of items: tattered clothing, leather shoes and various personal possessions.

'Do you recognise any of them? Take your time, Mrs Emerson.'

Lydia grasps the solid gold wedding ring, remembers it had cost her a fortune. She reads the inscription: IN LOVE FOREVER engraved within the band. While toying with the pocketknife she affirms all the items on the table belonged to Eric.

'I'm sorry for your loss, Mrs Emerson. Eric was a good man, I always enjoyed his company.'

'Thank you, Inspector.' Feeling light-headed, she returns to her seat.

'Could you read and sign the paperwork, Mrs Emerson. It's an administrative requirement. If you're presently unable, I understand. You may return tomorrow.'

'Tomorrow would suit me better, thank you.' Lydia tries to get to her feet and falters. 'If you could allow me to rest a while, I feel unsteady on my feet.'

'Constable Skinner will bring you a cup of tea in a jiffy.'

'Following the church service this morning, I sought counsel with Vicar Appleby. I told him in confidence about Friday's ordeal and my now verified fears it was Eric. He advised Eric be laid to rest without further delay. I booked a funeral service for Tuesday. Will Eric's body be released by then?'

'Most certainly.'

MONDAY, 3RD SEPTEMBER

Beth and Vincent meet outside the constabulary before entering the building. Instructed to sit in the waiting room they discuss Friday's events until Inspector Taylor emerges from his office. A teary Lydia is by his side; he bids her farewell and disappears down the hall. Judging by Lydia's swollen red eyes the news isn't good. Holding a handkerchief beneath her nose she sniffles into it before placing it in her reticule.

'Thank you for finding Eric, at least he can be laid to rest now.'

'Do you mind if I ask what happened to him?' Beth asks.

'An accidental death, he'd fallen from the escarpment and ...' she briefly drifts into her own thoughts then continues, 'I didn't sleep a wink last night.'

Beth and Vincent express their condolences. Beth wants to ask if the evidence is irrefutable, but she holds her silence.

As if she has read Beth's mind, Lydia asserts the medical examiner's report has dispelled any doubts she may have had.

'Will you be all right getting home, Lydia?' Vincent asks.

'Charlotte should be outside waiting for me.'

Before leaving, Lydia invites Beth and Vincent to the funeral and the wake arranged for the following day. They accept the invitation.

Ten minutes later, Inspector Taylor leads them to the interview room. He seats himself behind the wide oak desk, a notebook and an array of writing material neatly assembled before him. He invites them to take a seat. Constable Skinner stands at the door.

'So we meet again, Mrs Durrani. You seem to be a regular visitor to the station.' He smiles smugly.

'Not by choice, Inspector Taylor.'

'You and Mr Stirling provided a brief account of your bushwalk on Friday, today we require a detailed statement of events.' He informs them he'd like to interview them individually, starting with Mrs Durrani. Constable Skinner accompanies Vincent to the waiting room.

Beth remains seated while the inspector dons his spectacles and riffles through his papers. When the underling returns and is seated, fountain pen in hand, he writes the date and Beth's full name on the form before him, ready to transcribe the interview.

'Mrs Emerson has informed us she engaged your services to find her husband, Mr Eric Emerson. Is that correct?'

'Yes, she feared Mr Emerson was in danger, she just wanted to put her mind at rest.'

'Did Mrs Emerson ask you to search the bushland across from her home?'

'No, it was my idea. I'd been advised by those who knew him well that he enjoyed bushwalking. It occurred to me he could have been injured or attacked whilst out walking. Turns out I was right.'

The inspector pauses to study the notes before him.

'Was Mr Emerson's death accidental?'

'I'll ask the questions if you don't mind, Mrs Durrani.' He fixes his baggy eyes on hers. 'You're on record as being a public nuisance. What's your connection to Andrew Hall?'

'Among other things, Mr Hall is a dog snatcher. I've come into contact with him on several occasions as I'm often employed by dog owners to find their missing pets. I was recently harassed and bullied in public for saving a client's dog from his clutches. Thanks to Constable Skinner I was relatively unharmed.'

The constable stifles a smile as he recalls the day Beth was splattered with rotten tomatoes.

Half an hour later, Beth's version of Friday's events transcribed, she is asked to sign her statement before being dismissed. Mr Stirling is called upon to give his version of events.

Inspector Taylor greets Vincent and thanks him for helping the police recover the body of Mr Eric Emerson. Smiling inwardly, Vincent informs the inspector that it was Mrs Durrani's sense of intuition, extraordinary deductive ability and unerring persistence that produced the outcome.

'Mrs Durrani is an amateur detective and on this particular occasion she was lucky,' the inspector asserts, his eyes narrowed, his opinion delivered like a challenge.

'We'll just have to agree to disagree, Inspector Taylor.'

The inspector pauses to smooth his moustache, then he asks Vincent to describe his relationship with Mr Eric Emerson, Mrs Lydia Emerson and Mrs Bethany Durrani.

Vincent explains that Eric had been a close friend and colleague for many years. He was concerned his friend had not contacted him in months and felt obliged to offer his assistance to Mrs Emerson and Mrs Durrani during the investigation.

'With no further ado, we'd like you to give an account of events that took place on Friday 31st August – starting with your departure from Mrs Emerson's residence and ending when you returned. Constable Skinner will transcribe your statement.'

Satisfied Vincent's story correlates with Beth's account, the inspector asks him to sign his statement before being dismissed.

'Was Mr Emerson's death accidental?' Vincent asks before leaving the room.

'It would appear so.'

Outside, on the street, Vincent congratulates Beth and her agency for having given Lydia some peace of mind.'

'Mixed blessings though, isn't it?'

'Not the one we were hoping for. He'd fallen from the escarpment, it was a terrible accident.'

'Did Inspector Taylor confirm that?'

'Yes.'

'He virtually told me to mind my own business.'

'Lydia told you.'

'Yes, but I wanted to hear it from Inspector Taylor, my investigations led to Eric's body for heaven's sake.'

'That's just it though, isn't it?'

'It's such a lot of nonsense.'

'Will you join me for lunch?'

Beth declines. Her stomach nauseous, her head reeling, she needs to cuddle her child. Furthermore, she must return home so she and her sleuthing partners can finish up writing a final report for Lydia while the information is fresh in their heads.

TUESDAY, 4TH SEPTEMBER

A small group of mourners are assembled in the courtyard when Lydia arrives, accompanied by her mother and Charlotte, their faces obscured by fine silk veils. Beth and Vincent arrive soon after. Inspector Taylor turns up just before they file into the imposing sandstone church. As a child, Beth considered the church an intimidating space. Her mother insisted she and Tillie attend each Sunday. They resented losing their precious free time and having to spend an hour dressing up to the standard expected on Sundays. When their mother fell ill, they passed weekends at Aunt Faith's home where they would play hide-and-seek in the spacious garden or run wild around the house with its long halls and over-furnished rooms. Tillie, an accomplished pianist, would play their favourite songs and they would sing as loud as they wished. Aunt Faith had little time for religion, although, over the years she has donated many hours working tirelessly alongside religious institutions to raise funds for orphans and poor families.

The vicar scans the room and gives a dimpled smile before welcoming the congregation. Following his uninspiring sermon and accompaniment by the organ player, Lydia's mother performs Eric's favourite opera, *The Merry Wives of Windsor*. Her high notes resonate with a twangy vibrato, a detail that does nothing to curb the resonance of soft sobbing. After the vicar's final blessings, mourners move outside into the stark morning sun. The vicar intones the prayers then the coffin is lowered into the grave, Lydia lifts her veil and leans over to cast the first handful of soil onto the coffin. The gravediggers begin their work. Soon the ornate box is covered in stiff, clayish soil. Wreaths are laid and the mourners gather around a weeping Lydia. Inspector Taylor hurries off to the station where a stack of paperwork awaits him.

Beth wanders off on a solitary tour of the gardens. Looking all around, she wonders if Anna is watching from afar hidden behind a hedge, or perhaps she is too ill to pay her respects. In the rose garden, the subtle sweet scent in the air stirs up memories of Arif's final days. His room was a floristry of roses, as if their beauty and fragrance would dispel the grief of his passing. Seated on the sturdy stone wall that borders the gardens and staring into space, Beth remembers.

~

Arif hadn't left his bed in days, how strange it was to see her friend, lover and protector so frail. Falling in and out of consciousness, his skin burned with fever. Beth never left his side. His mother assured her it would pass, her son had always recovered quickly from illness, and he'd always been strong. Arif's friend from Jalalabad thought otherwise. Michael, an expatriate Englishman working as a doctor for local people and English soldiers, believed Arif was seriously ill with consumption. He advised plenty of bed rest and a well-ventilated room, but he feared Arif had little chance of survival considering he was so thin and coughing up blood.

Gabina rarely came to Arif's bedside, but at times Nazdana brought Roshina to visit. Arif loved holding his daughter in his arms and planting kisses on her little face and Roshina giggled, blissfully unaware of her father's illness.

A regular visitor, Michael always wore a mask and advised all Arif's carers to do so. Once, out of the blue, he asked Beth what she'd do if she lost Arif. Unwilling to grapple with reality, she convinced herself that Arif would recover. His mother had said as much and mothers are always right about their children. Michael maintained he had previously recovered but now there was a dangerous complication. Arif's brother had asked his father to stop Michael from coming to their home as he was upsetting Arif and speaking too often alone with Beth. He argued Beth was shameful the way she conversed with the Englishman away from her ailing husband and in a language no one could understand. Arif's father reminded Ramin that Beth rarely left Arif's bedside, she was devoted to him. Michael was permitted to visit as he was Arif's closest friend. Besides, he delivered the family's mail and saved them a tiresome trip to town.

Once, in Beth's presence, Arif told Michael that he would soon be in God's hands. 'I am wasting away, my dear friend,' he smiled, his voice weak and raspy. 'Beth would like to return to her homeland. Please protect her; she will need your assistance.'

'I am here you know,' Beth said in a strident tone. 'Don't talk about me as though I'm not here.'

Arif took Beth's hand in his. 'Go with Michael today, please Beth. He will help you. As you are carrying my child, the family will never let you go.'

'I won't leave you alone, Arif.'

'I will be with Allah. But you have a long life ahead of you. Please go with Michael today.'

Again, Michael pressed her to leave, he would get her safely across the Khyber Pass with army officers and she could stay with Mrs Halligan in Peshawar before travelling home to Australia. He warned her not to wait too long as a stormy voyage on a steamer would be dangerous for her and her unborn child. Holding onto the fading hope that Arif would rebound, Beth insisted on staying by his side.

Beth hadn't received mail from Tillie and Faith in months, which only intensified her yearning for home. She wondered if Ramin had been withholding her mail from her, he'd told her on many occasions to forget her Australian family. Her suspicions were proven correct when she discussed her missing correspondence with Michael. Fearing reprisals against Michael, she did not confront Ramin, rather, she asked Michael to deliver her personal mail directly to her. Each time he visited, she gave him a letter to post home.

Weeks later, Beth lay in bed beside Arif, her arm over his torso, aware of his heart beating, normally at first, rhythmically like her own heart. But in the early morning hours he awoke gasping for breath. She knew she was losing him. They held hands, tightly at first, as if he was suspended over a bridge and she was pulling him back. Then his hand fell away from hers. There was no heartbeat. Stunned, she lay close to him until the morning sun bowed through the window. She kissed his cold face, rose from bed, dressed and made for the kitchen. Nazdana read Beth's teary face and rushed to her son's bedside. Beth waited outside, heard the gut-wrenching drawn-out scream coming from her throat, her mouth, the core of her body, her soul. When Beth entered the room Nazdana was holding her son in her arms as one does a child, tears streaming down her face. Then his father, Karlan, appeared, a man of few words, even in his grief quietly broken-hearted, all hopes of a miracle recovery were gone, his beloved son gone from him. Later in the morning, all the family members huddled around the bed praying.

Following Arif's funeral, melancholy gripped the homestead. It was as though life had begun working in slow motion, although everyone kept busy, the days and nights seemed endless. Crowing roosters always marked the arrival of mornings in the Durrani household. The quiet chatter, clattering of crockery and steamy hot food had always been so welcoming in the dining room, but the absence of a loved one from the table was palpable and grief floated in the room like words unsaid. Arif's mother and Beth helped each other through the saddest times. Still, Beth wanted to return home. She was fond of Nazdana, it pained her to think of the unhappiness her departure would cause, Nazdana was looking forward to holding Arif's son. Despite being kept under watch all the time, she would find a way to leave. She had entrusted Arif's good friend Michael to dispatch her letters to Aunt Faith, but mail often goes astray. She'd send telegrams from Jalalabad, Peshawar and every other city she passed through on her way home. Aunt Faith would be expecting her. In time, just as Arif had foreseen, she was forbidden to travel to Jalalabad alone, and told she was never to visit Michael, even if she needed a doctor she was advised to use the local midwife. Everywhere she went there was another shadow besides her own.

~

Vincent moves closer to the woman sitting alone and seemingly lost in thought. He considers tapping her on the shoulder but thinks better of it.

'Beth?'

Awoken from her reverie, she turns swiftly, her eyes wide and damp.

'Are you unwell?'

'You startled me. I was miles away in another world.' Smiling wistfully, she takes a handkerchief from her sleeve and dries her tears. 'The scent of roses made me a bit sentimental, it happens sometimes.'

'Solemn occasions invite nostalgic thoughts. They call to mind the people we miss.'

Beth nods, thinking so many sights and sounds produce the same effect on her: a warm breeze on her skin, the soughing of pine needles, palm fronds flapping. At times, she busies herself, pushes the memories aside, but recently she has fallen into the habit of surrendering to them.

'Should I leave you alone?'

'No, please stay.'

He offers his arm, inviting her to walk with him in the sunshine. 'It's surprising how happy memories can make us feel miserable, and regretful ones can make us laugh out loud at our own folly.' He grins.

Beth laughs. 'You have the knack of cheering me up, Vincent.'

'Rather that than make you cry.'

'Perhaps we should join the others.'

'Most of them have gone.'

'It's strange Eric died in a place where he'd often sought solitude and calm, isn't it?'

'He often boasted he knew the bushland like the back of his hand.'

'If he knew the bush so well why did he fall from the escarpment?'

Vincent shrugs, admits he has no idea. 'You still have doubts, don't you?'

'I wouldn't say doubts, just a niggling feeling that something's not quite right.'

'You need a break by the sea. Would you and Samuel like to join me this coming weekend at my beach house in Port Adelaide?'

'Samuel would love that, but the time isn't right at present. I'd like to know you better before ...'

'Wouldn't spending the weekend together do exactly that?'

'Yes, but not yet.'

'It's an open invitation,' he smiles. 'Let me know when you and your young chaperon are ready.'

'I'm a grown woman, Vincent. I don't need a chaperon.'

'You'll join me?'

'Yes, if Aunt Faith is able to mind Samuel.'

'I have a cab waiting, would you like a lift to the wake?'

'Thank you.'

WEDNESDAY, 5TH SEPTEMBER

The hansom cab pulls up outside of Vincent Stirling's office. Lydia steps out and asks the driver to wait for her. Entering the building and ascending the stairs she breathes in the familiar aroma of coffee, beeswax furniture polish and the vanilla scent of old paper. She remembers the times she'd meet Eric for lunch and how they'd stroll, hands joined, to their favourite restaurant. Even today, she doesn't know why they'd drifted apart, why their thriving romance ended. She'd thought their relationship was simply in drought, perhaps linked to the parched economy. Even when she discovered he was having an affair with Anna Hopping she believed he loved her, favoured her. Anna was simply a fleeting distraction. Wishing Verity a good morning, she takes herself directly to Vincent's office. Gestured to a seat, Lydia notices that Eric's will lies before him. Vincent is one of those people who smiles readily, but today he is wearing a serious expression, one that concerns Lydia.

'As you know, Eric appointed me executor of his will. I don't know whether Eric informed you of the changes he'd made to his will.'

'I wasn't aware of any changes.'

'I'm sorry, Lydia. Mrs Anna Hopping is the only beneficiary of his will. No doubt he bequeathed his inheritance to Mrs Hopping because of her dire circumstances. He had told me many a time that his affections were always stronger for you.'

'Thank you, Vincent. What about his life insurance?' Lydia

believed she would receive the large insurance payout, after all, it was she who had initiated his life insurance policy and it was she who had been paying the monthly premiums.

'He has bequeathed his life insurance policy of five thousand, six hundred pounds to Mrs Hopping. She is named as the sole beneficiary on his insurance policy. Given the current findings, his insurance payout should be released once the insurance company receives the medical examiner's advice on Eric's accidental death.'

Lydia is speechless, she wants to scream, to weep, but she sits in silent shock. A wealthy woman, she can live comfortably without Eric's inheritance, she simply wants confirmation he'd always loved her more than his lover.

'The insurance payout is the bulk of the inheritance; he'd recently withdrawn his deposits from the bank.'

'Yes, the police have informed me of that detail. Is Mrs Hopping aware of her windfall?'

'As far as I know, she is not cognisant, I wanted to inform you first. Eric told me he would leave his inheritance to Mrs Hopping because she is a poor woman who would escape her brutal husband should she have the means. He was aware of your comfortable situation and knew you would not suffer from this. He pitied Mrs Hopping but he loved you, Lydia.

'But not as much as Anna Hopping, it would seem.'

THURSDAY, 6TH SEPTEMBER

With a feeling of mild trepidation, Beth steps into Mr O'Halloran's business premises. Disappointed he is out of his office; she asks if she could wait for his return as she has a pressing matter to discuss with him. The clerk reluctantly accedes. Moving around the room, she studies the photographs pinned to the walls and notices the business awards. She wonders if they're genuine. There must be a few satisfied customers, family members perhaps. There's a large photograph of Jack Spencer, a handsome, well-dressed salesman – he bears an astounding resemblance to Eric Emerson, in another context they would pass as brothers.

'He's a handsome man.'

The clerk looks up from his work and sniggers. 'He certainly thinks so.'

'He's very fashionable. Look at those lovely anchor buttons.'

'Mr Spencer believes anchors bring good luck. He sold a lot of furniture, that's for sure.'

'Is he still working here?'

'No, he left months ago.'

'Does he live in Adelaide?'

'He lives in a house a couple of doors down from the public baths.'

'If he was doing so well here, why did he leave?'

'Some people are never happy.'

A guttural cough coming from the front steps brings their conversation to an abrupt end. The clerk's head drops back to his work. Stanley O'Halloran enters the room, removes his coat, hangs it on the coat rack stand, glances at his clerk who wishes him a good morning and looks Beth up and down as if she were a farm animal at an auction. 'What are you doing here, Mrs Durrani?'

'May I speak with you?'

'Five minutes,' he says, checking his fob watch and determined to order her out of the building after that precise time allotment. She follows him into his office, leaving the door open. As Beth is not offered a seat she remains standing while he is comfortably seated on his oversized throne-like chair, its ludicrous height almost placing them face to face.

'I've just come to tell you I'm no longer investigating the disappearance of Mr Eric Emerson.'

He gives her a mocking, lopsided smile. 'Back to dog catching then, is it?'

'As my investigation into the disappearance of Mr Emerson is concluded I won't expect any more intimidations from your family.'

'Leave us be and we'll leave you be, that's the recipe for peace, isn't it?'

'I'll have nothing more to do with you, Mr O'Halloran, please be assured of that. I won't think about you and your business dealings ever again.'

'You say that like I care. Listen lady, you're no threat to me or my business.' He gives a disingenuous smile before tugging at his fob watch and informing her she has used up her five minutes. Without getting up he bellows for his clerk to escort the busybody out of his office and out of the building.

Keen to explore the notion that Jack Spencer was the victim in the hollow, Beth hurries to the hansom cab. Nolan Lloyd had said as much, a young man arguing with Eric about furniture and insurance. If the button she'd found in Lydia's front yard is from

Jack's shirt there may be a connection.

Dropped off near the public baths, Beth pays the cab driver and makes her way to Jack Spencer's cottage. Standing out front, she observes the knee-high weeds in the front garden. The gate is wide open and hanging off its hinges and the letterbox plinth is crumbling with wood rot. She pounds on the front door but there is no response from within. The door is locked, as are the windows. Moving down the side of the house, she looks over the neighbour's fence, they appear to be out. The back door is locked. Harry once showed her how to pick a lock with a hat pin. She tries it. The lock gives way and clicks open. She turns the doorknob and pushes the door open. A cricket bat leans against the wall. A musty smell hits her nostrils. Sparsely furnished, there's a shabby single couch, a table covered in food scraps and one chair. More worrying, drug paraphernalia is spread across the surface. The white walls are unadorned by family photographs. The resident of this home is a loner. She moves to the bedroom and finds a suitcase full of clothes; it seems the owner doesn't intend staying long. She rummages through his expensive clothing, some with the labels still attached. Who can afford to spend nine pounds on a silk shirt? Not a salesman. Hoarse guttural sounds send her to the front window. A scrawny young man is moving into the property. He stops to lean over a shrub and clears his throat. Beth makes for the back door and scuttles to the garden shed. The dusty window gives her a hazy image of the figure moving slowly down the side path and approaching the back door, a bag of food in his hand. Noticing the door wide open he looks all around him, sets down his shopping. He goes to the window on the side of the house and looks in. Whoever was there has gone. But just in case, he enters the house, grabs a cricket bat and surveys each room. Still carrying the bat, he moves outside and notices the door to the shed is wide open. Beth has no choice but to run for it, but the man puts himself in the way, holding the bat aloft like a cricketer about to slam a ball, he asks her what she's doing in his shed, on his property.

Taking a deep breath, she assumes a melancholic expression. 'I'm looking for a dear friend of mine, Jack Spencer, he used to reside here.'

He steps a bit closer. 'It's my place. I live here now.'

The man hardly looks like a property owner. Not much older than twenty, scraggy, and judging by his sour smell he hasn't washed in weeks. The elegant clothes on his unwashed body are incongruous. Beth suspects he is helping himself to Jack Spencer's wardrobe, which is way too large for him and in another context would be comical, especially the clownish shoes, too broad and a good inch too long. 'I'm leaving now, if my friend doesn't live here anymore, I'll look elsewhere.'

'What ya want with 'im?'

'I'm a very good friend of his, I just want to know where he is, that's all.'

He considers her request, scratches his head, and lowers the bat. 'He disappeared 'bout ... I dunno,' he scratches his head again and Beth suspects he has head lice. 'Some time back, he didn't say nothin'.'

'About five months ago?'

'Somethink like that.'

'Have you seen him since then?'

'What's it to ya?'

The black rings around his eyes call to mind a pug dog Beth once reunited with his family, only the pug was friendly. 'I'm worried about him. If you see him, please tell him to go and see Victoria, that's my name, he knows where I live.'

'Victoria what?'

Harry's alias comes to mind. 'Victoria Tingcombe.' There's no way that man would remember such a name, Beth speculates.

'What?'

'Tingcombe. Didn't he tell you we're engaged to be married?'

Jiggling the bat, he looks at her suspiciously, 'Ya bloody full of it, lady.'

She thinks about the times she'd felt intimidated by aggressive dogs and how she could simply toss them a few biscuits and run – no such luck with an angry man. 'I just want to know where he is, that's all,' she answers, inching away. 'I'm sorry I entered your home without asking, I'm desperate to find Jack.'

Overcome by an urgent desire for cocaine, he waves his arm in the air directing her to go away before turning on his heels and making for the house.

Beth lifts her skirts and walks swiftly down the side of the property and onto the street where she fills her lungs with fresh air. It crosses her mind she could have been smashed over the head with a cricket bat. Vincent's invitation to stay by the sea in Port Adelaide is looking more and more appealing. It is time to live a little.

FRIDAY, 7TH SEPTEMBER

Beth has never passed a night away from Sam, let alone two nights. The anticipation of romance and excitement is tinged with guilt. Seated on the front veranda, a carpet bag brimming with clothes at her feet, Beth is waiting for Vincent to arrive when she hears Faith's shoes clacking on the floor boards. Faith sits heavily beside her and hooks her arm in Beth's.

'I've already said goodbye to Sam,' Beth declares, wondering if a reproach is brewing.

'I know you did. Don't worry about Sam, we won't let him out of our sight. He's very excited about tomorrow's outing to the clay pigeon target practice.'

'He's just as excited about going for a ride in Harry's buggy.'

'Young children marvel at the world, everything is new, everything exciting. Harry promised he'd teach him how to use a shotgun.'

'I wish he'd teach me,' Beth chuckles.

'I'm glad you're finally enjoying the marvellous experiences life has to offer. I want you to be happy.'

'You really don't mind me going away?'

'Not in the least. Mr Stirling is very affable and handsome. Speak of the devil, there he is, off you go, enjoy your weekend.'

Bumping along in the carriage, Beth regards the rows and rows of citrus trees, now dotted with fragrant white flowers. Further on, there are vast fields of newly ploughed land, interspersed with thick bushland. Conscious Vincent's leg is resting against her skirts, she wonders if the heat between them is emanating from his body or from hers. Turned away from him, she maintains her silence; a breathless voice would give her away. Swamped by intense emotions, she has to admit she is drawn to the attractive man beside her, has been since they first met. During the past few days she has given far too much time to thinking about his sparkling dark eyes and the way his black eyebrows arch when he is animated about a topic of conversation, which is most of the time.

Rolling fields soon give way to light bushland which in turn thins out to houses as they travel through the town of Port Adelaide. The carriage jolts along wide streets bordered by solid buildings, some several storeys high. A calm shimmering sea comes into view. Ships, sailing boats and a clear blue sky fill the horizon. When the cab turns into a wide coastal road, Beth regards several mothers wearing wide-brimmed hats watching their children cavorting in the shallows, the gentle white-tipped waves slithering to the shore.

Vincent inhales the saline air. 'We're almost there,' he says, briefly squeezing her hand and letting go.

The carriage stops outside a single storey home constructed in solid sandstone blocks and set on an acre of land. The driver climbs down and collects their bags. Vincent pays the agreed fare, adds a generous tip and bids him farewell. He carries the ports to the front door where fragrant freesias bloom in wine barrel planter pots on either side of the entrance. The key is hidden beneath the doormat. The door swings open, a well-lit entry greets them. Beth's eyes move all around the room with its large windows and double doors that lead out to the veranda and beyond that a sparkling sea. Sparse furnishings give the house a neat, uncluttered feel. The austere décor calls to mind her aunt's home, although Faith has sold all unessential furnishings out of necessity, not style.

'The best part is the view,' says Vincent, setting the bags down.

'It's like standing on the ship's deck. Land ahoy, me hearties!'

'Shivers me timbers,' Vincent says, using a gruff voice and grinning. 'How about I prepare some orange juice for the parched pirates? The cleaner usually leaves a bowl of oranges in the kitchen. She comes every Friday, cleans and airs the house ready for the weekend.'

'What's her name?'

'Mrs Wellington. She and her family of eight manage a farm not far from here. They grow all manner of fruit.'

Beth follows him into his immaculate kitchen; either he never cooks or Mrs Wellington is a magician. One after another he presses the fruit over a glass juicer until two glasses are filled to the brim.

'Mm, the zesty aroma of orange is making my mouth water.'

'Sadly, it's the last batch of the season.'

'And you're sharing it with me, I am honoured.' Beth grins.

He looks at Beth in such a way she feels her pulse leaping to a scale that must be obvious, perhaps dangerous. Biting her lip, she turns her head away from his gaze, when all she wants to do is to look at him and feel the joy that impulse brings.

'Sorry, I didn't mean to stare at you.'

'Thank you for taking it slowly, Vincent. I've been a widow for so long it's …'

'I'm not used to courting either. Over the past so many years my life has been filled with work and more work.'

Beth wants to ask him if they are courting but she leaves it hanging in the air and decides that certain feelings don't need words or explanations, they simply exist.

They move to the front veranda where they finish their drinks and chat.

'Would you like to see your room?'

'I wouldn't mind unpacking my things and freshening up.'

He takes hold of her carpet bag and leads her down the hall. The room is large with a double bed in the middle, a towel and a cake of lavender soap on the embroidered quilt. Double doors open out to an east facing veranda; the morning sun would greet her when she wakes. Vincent boasts there's an indoor bathroom with a view to the sea. 'It's very private, only the gulls can see into the room,' he says, smiling. 'I'll leave you to unpack, come to the front room when you're ready.'

'I shouldn't be too long,' says Beth, wondering if Vincent feels as awkward as she does.

'Take your time; try the bed if you like.'

Alone, she removes her boots and lies on the bed, just to see if the mattress is comfortable. The pillow is imbued with the scent of lavender oil. It is perfect. Perhaps everything is too perfect, Vincent, the house. Recently, she has not slept well, her mind consumed by Eric's puzzling disappearance and Ramin's determination to abduct Sam has often kept her awake at night. Wondering where Vincent's room is, she tries to stay awake but fatigue closes her eyes and she nods off.

Awakened by the shrill cry of gulls, she sits up and glares at the wall clock, ten past four; she'd been asleep for almost an hour. She pours herself a glass of water from the jug on her side table before getting to her feet. Standing before the wall mirror, she brushes her hair and straightens the creases in her skirts before leaving the room. Vincent is still seated on the veranda facing the ocean. Beth sits beside him.

'I can't believe I fell asleep in such a well-lit room. It's far too relaxing here.'

'I'm glad you think so. I must confess I did creep down the hall to check on you. You looked like sleeping beauty.'

'I probably sleep like most people, mouth agape and eyes barely closed.'

'Not at all, but you do snore like a grizzly bear.'

'Papa snores as well. I fear it may be hereditary.'

'To be honest, all I heard was a soothing swish resembling a breeze sighing through rustling pines.'

'Delightful, you express snoring as a thing of beauty. Please take a bow, Vincent.'

'Thank you, but I am too comfortably ensconced in my armchair.'

They laugh together.

Beth helps herself to the newspaper from the side table.

'Old news, I'm afraid.'

'My aunt thinks I should keep abreast of the news,' she says, reading a short article about Eric Emerson on the front page. Thankfully, very few details are given, except that his body was found in bushland, a victim of a terrible accident. 'I'm glad our names are not mentioned in the text.'

'It'd be free publicity for your business, Beth.'

'A woman bushwalking unchaperoned with a man would not do my business any good at all. An unchaperoned widow is only marginally more acceptable than an unchaperoned spinster.'

'That's the unjust world we live in.'

'We shouldn't just accept it,' Beth insists.

'Isn't not wanting your name in the paper accepting it?'

Beth ponders Vincent's question and wonders if a suffragette who never takes risks is a fraudster. After all, equality and justice requires those able to take risks to take them. She resolves it was a lost opportunity.

'I'm glad you're here, Beth.'

'Thank you for inviting me.'

'You and your family are always welcome. I'm not here during the week, but you've seen where I hide the key.'

'Yes, you make it very easy for burglars to let themselves in.'

'O'Halloran's henchmen broke in through a window. I should have left the key in the door.'

'You'd think they'd be familiar with the usual hiding places.'

'O'Halloran's days in business are numbered.'

'I hope so,' says Beth, wondering if Vincent is aware of the ongoing police investigations into O'Halloran's dodgy business ventures.

They sit in silence, gazing at the gulls wheeling over the glimmering sea, a vivid red and orange sunset sprawled across the horizon.

'If I had a creative bone in my body I'd paint that amazing vista,' says Vincent.

'Why would you bother? You have the full gallery before you.'

'Unlike a painting, it changes colour and visual texture hundreds of times a day and night.'

'I'm sure I could never tire of that view. Where's Mrs Mooney's home from here?'

'Several doors down. She's probably seated on her front patio now, she'd be enjoying a cigar and a large cognac, her Pekingese perched on her lap. She never misses her afternoon ritual.'

'She's a character. Can we visit her?'

'Work or play?'

'A bit of each.'

'She's already informed me Lydia was with her the entire week of Eric's disappearance. The police also interviewed her. I really don't think we should bother her with any more questions.'

Beth accedes, studying Vincent's face which is now looking away from her. She hadn't noticed his dashing profile before, his Roman nose with a long, well-defined nasal bridge, and a slight down-pointing curve. Conscious he is being stared at he turns to Beth. 'To be honest, I don't want to share you with Mrs Mooney.'

Beth smiles, tells him the feeling is mutual.

'Would you like to see the rest of the house?'

'I'd love to.'

'Follow me.'

From the hall they enter Vincent's spacious, well-organised study, photographs displayed on each of the four walls.

'Is that you with your parents?'

'Yes, taken about twenty years ago.'

Beth points to the two children standing next to Vincent. 'Are they members of your family?'

'No, that's Martina Manassero and her older brother Joseph. Their parents were close friends of my parents. We spent a lot of time together as children. Mr Manassero owns a restaurant, not far from here.'

'What did your father do?'

'He worked locally as an engineer for more than thirty years. He'd only been retired for a few years when a fishing trip came to a disastrous end. He and Mama sailed out on a perfect morning, but a storm reared up when they were too far out at sea to return.'

'How frightening. I'm sorry.'

'Their bodies were washed up on the beach.' He pauses to brush his fingers across their photograph. 'At least I could bury them.'

Beth nods.

'They'd weathered so many storms they probably thought they were invulnerable.'

'Judging by the photographs they were very adventurous.'

'I always admired them for that.'

'What about you?'

'I don't seek danger.'

'Do you want to travel?'

'When I was young my parents took me on some of their trips, I loved Italy. But I'm not really interested in crossing the Sahara or gallivanting around the world as they'd done. It's paradise here, why look any further?' Vincent's mind turns to Beth's travel experiences in Afghanistan but he chooses not to mention it, he suspects she has not let go of the memory of her husband. He asks her to follow him to the kitchen and dining room on the eastern side of the house. From there, double doors lead onto the veranda where several steps descend into a wild rockery of ferns, tall feathery grass and a myriad of palms. Clumps of red and yellow flowering grevilleas soak up the sunshine in the background. In the dabbled foreground, a shallow pond sits in the centre – home to small golden fish. Cool air emanates from the lime green algae carpeting the rocks.

'It's like being in a rainforest.'

'I like a garden that looks after itself,' he smiles, fixing his gaze on Beth. 'Will you join me for dinner at my favourite restaurant this evening?'

'I'd be delighted.'

'I dine there most Saturday nights. Chef Manassero's food tastes more like home cooking than the usual restaurant fare. He'll be surprised to see me; I usually stay in Adelaide Friday nights. I'm allowing myself an extra night to spend more time with you.' Vincent looks away from her, perhaps thinking he'd said too much. 'Shall we leave in an hour or so?'

'That suits me, I'm famished.'

Vincent collects several gardenia flowers and presents them to Beth. Closing her eyes, she bows her face over the flowers and inhales deeply. 'I'll wear one in my hair this evening.'

Her honey-red hair brushed and swept into a chignon at the nape of her neck, Beth appears in the parlour wearing a pink satin gown she had borrowed from Eva who prefers study over socialising with men. Beth asks Vincent to pin the gardenia to her hair. He tells her she looks beautiful. Accustomed to hearing those kinds of compliments from Aunt Faith or young Sam, she finds it strange coming from a man.

'It's a pleasant walk from here,' says Vincent, dressed casually in light trousers, a black waistcoat over a white shirt, and a black bowtie and cape.

'I love walking along the seashore,' she says, draping a woollen shawl around her shoulders.

The last vestige of a streaky pink and violet sunset meets the sea in the west as they stroll along the coastal path towards the restaurant quarter. Beth weaves her arm in Vincent's. A noisy family of six is scampering along the beach, their bellowing children playing tag and tumbling onto the sand, their mother cheering them on. Several yards behind the family, a tall man is strolling along on the firm wet sand. Beth slows down, watches him askance, some fifty yards away now.

'Do you know that man?' Vincent asks.

'He's been following us since we left the house,' says Beth, now halted and openly staring at the man who responds by slowing down and looking out to sea. In the fading light she cannot make out his features, but she is certain the man is Ramin. Aware of being looked at, he marches off in the opposite direction, his swinging arms powering his body forward. Beth takes some comfort he is stalking her and not Sam who is safe at home with Faith and Harry.

'You've frightened him away, Beth.' Vincent laughs. 'The poor man could be taking his evening constitution.'

'I thought he looked familiar.'

'You're shaking. Who was that man?'

'A case of mistaken identity, that's all.'

'Look at the sparkling stars above, on our way back the moon will emerge from behind clouds to light our way.'

'How do you know that?'

'The moon and I have a long-standing relationship.'

'Friends in high places, Mr Stirling.'

Vincent laughs and kisses her hand.

Stepping onto the terrace, Beth loses herself in the rousing warm glow of lanterns suspended from the lean-to, the soothing piano music coming from inside the restaurant, and the mouth-watering aroma of garlic and fried food.

'Shall we dine indoors or here on the terrace?' Vincent asks.

'Let's stay outside, it's closer to the sea.'

'I couldn't agree more, it's always too busy inside anyway.' Vincent leaves the table to order a bottle of wine. Beth looks to the seashore, straining her eyes to see if Ramin is still around. She'd recognised him earlier, in the dusky light, but now that night has fallen, only shadows wander in the distance. Refusing to let him spoil her evening, she resolves not to think of him again, at least not for several days.

Vincent returns to the table with the wine and two glasses. He tells Beth he has ordered the freshest seafood in Port Adelaide. He pours the drinks and raises his glass to toast his charming companion and their ongoing friendship.

'I like the idea of being your friend, but I'm not always charming.'

'You looked lovely this afternoon when you rose from your bed with your red hair falling around your shoulders. I didn't mention it then, but now, the soft light gives licence to daring comments.'

'I welcome kind words in any shade of light.'

Vincent smiles and gazes at Beth. 'Thank you for finding my friend Eric, at least now he and Lydia are at peace.'

'Thank you for helping, I doubt I'd have traipsed deep into the bush had I been alone. I'm sorry you've lost a close friend and colleague. Everyone who knew him appreciated his cheery nature and zest for life.'

'Did you ever meet him?'

'I'd never met him, but in a way I feel like I knew him. I tailed Eric and Anna to restaurants, music halls, theatres and hotels. I was enthralled by their whirlwind romance, they had an amazing rapport. Watching them reminded me of what I was missing in my life. I let my observations last longer than necessary because I loved witnessing their passionate connection. I often wondered if Lydia had noticed my guilty pleasures. I don't think she did. When I finally gave her my written report I felt such a loss, for Lydia, myself and for the happy couple.'

'He was always devoted to Lydia.'

'He loved Anna more though, didn't he? Their passionate relationship was all consuming. I often wonder why he didn't leave Lydia earlier and save Anna from being beaten up.'

'Divided loyalties, I guess.'

A gentle breeze blows. The moon bobs out from beneath the clouds and casts a silver path across the water. They dine on salad, fish and lobster with potato chips followed by a delicious dessert that Vincent calls *migliaccio*, an Italian pudding and the most popular sweet on the menu. The main ingredient is an Italian cheese called *ricotta* which the chef makes himself. Beth takes a bite of the moist, creamy gateau and savours the subtle hint of lemon. After dinner, Vincent orders a nightcap.

Content the lanterns cast a dim light, Beth watches him sit back in his chair, his eyes closed as he listens to *Chopin's Nocturne* being performed inside the restaurant. Not far away, gentle waves wash to shore with a rustling refrain. Sensing Beth's gaze he opens his eyes and turns to her. 'What a wonderful evening, let's toast to the good things in life.'

Beth clinks the rim of her glass on his. Sipping her cognac she feels the mellow liquid warm her throat.

'Would you like to meet Chef Marius Manassero?'

'I'd love to.'

Vincent takes Beth's hand as they enter the large dining room.

'Heavenly music.'

'Martina the pianist is the chef's daughter. Her older brother plays violin, but he's in Italy at present.'

Hearing her name, Martina looks up and nods in greeting while, amazingly, she keeps playing. Vincent smiles and throws a familiar wink, Beth feels a jab of envy, how could a young woman that beautiful be so talented?

A plump man dressed in a white double-breasted jacket and a tall chef's hat, approaches them. Chef Manassero is of Italian heritage and speaks in an animated fashion, his hands as expressive as a mime artist. A proud father, he is a man who professes to love the good things in life: family, friends, food, music, love and the sea. They chat for a long while. Before leaving, Vincent books a table for the following evening.

They amble along the seafront as if carried by a wave.

'The chef calls you Vincenzo.'

'He and my mother were born in Florence. They'd always called me Vincenzo, especially when they'd chat in the lingo.'

'Vincenzo,' says Beth, savouring the sound. 'It's a joyous name.'

'It was my Italian grandfather's name.'

'Vincenzo Stirling, the joining of two lines of descent in a name.'

Midway, they stop to gaze at the sea, waves lapping the shore, moonbeams sketched across the glinting water. Vincent wraps his arms around her, held tightly she feels his heart beating against hers. He takes her chin in his hands, caresses her face, her forehead. His fingertips trail over her lips and along her neck. Delicious sensations sweep through her body, her breath quickens. He pauses to weigh her reaction and observes her eyes are closed. He kisses her on the lips, gently yet determinedly. She kisses him back, his lips taste of spicy cognac. They continue on their way, hand in hand, emotions running high, stopping every so often to embrace. Arriving at the house they breathe in the sweet citrusy scent of freesias, the fragrance accentuated by the moist night air. Vincent clasps the key from under the mat and unlocks the door. Once inside they stand completely still for a brief moment, their gaze fixed on one another. They kiss deeply before moving down the hall to Beth's room where they undress and fall into bed together.

Beth opens her eyes to the morning sun poking through the wide gap in the curtains. Beside her, Vincent is sleeping soundly, his black hair dishevelled, his well-defined lips parted. Pulling on her dressing gown, she moves through the double doors leading to the east-facing veranda. Inhaling the fresh tang of salt air, she watches two rainbow lorikeets gathering nectar from the blooming red grevilleas.

'Come back to bed.'

'Every window in your home offers amazing scenery,' she says, returning to the room.

'You're the most breathtaking view in this house,' he grins.

Beth runs back to bed and hugs him wildly. 'I love being in my lover's arms.'

'I can see that and it's very alluring.'

'You're too attractive.' She rakes her fingers through the small patch of fine hair on his chest, acknowledging that she is captivated by his good looks and tender love-making.

'I could say the same thing about you.'

'Recently, an experienced, older person advised me to be lively and frivolous and to live a full life.'

Vincent draws her into his arms. 'Wise and breathtaking advice,' he murmurs.

They spend the morning strolling along the docks and all around town. Vincent shares snippets of his life growing up in Port Adelaide. He points out the school he'd attended and the homes where his school friends once lived. After lunch, they take the train to Semaphore beach and follow a colonnade of tall pine trees lining the foreshore, pine needles soughing in the breeze. They move onto the beach just in time to spot a pod of dolphins not far from the shore. They watch in awe as the dolphins leap in and out of the water like ballet dancers flying across a stage. Sitting on the sand, their shoes discarded, they enjoy the spectacle before ambling along the beach. When they find an isolated spot they cavort about ankle deep in the shallows, only running madly back to shore when an upsurging wave threatens to soak them. Later, a gusty wind flares up reminding them their clothing is wet to the point of discomfort. They move off, carrying their shoes, their feet sinking into soft white sand.

'Try slipping your shoes on whilst standing on one leg,' Vincent dares, successfully pulling off the dare himself.

'Now see if you can tie the laces, clever boots!'

'Easy,' he says, his right leg raised and his fingers tying the first knot in his laces just before he loses balance, totters and tumbles in the sand.

Laughing, Beth flumps beside him and hugs him.

Footwear donned, they hasten along on the compact sand edging the shore until they come to the jetties and stop briefly to observe the heightening waves sloshing against the pylons. Windswept and cold, they brush sand from their rumpled clothing before stepping into a warm teahouse with a cosy oak-panelled room and tall windows overlooking the piers. While chatting and drinking cups of coffee, they observe the men and boys fishing from the pier. A gathering of shrewd pelicans is standing by hoping the men cleaning their catch will throw them a fish head or two. The sun is setting on the horizon when they leave the teahouse arm in arm and walk the two mile stretch back to Port Adelaide, the air wet and salty, the views from the Jervois Bridge stunning.

'Why have we only made love in my room and not yours?' asks Beth.

'A lady never visits a gentleman's bedchamber.'

She jogs him playfully in the shoulder. 'Thank you for trying to protect my virtue, but it's a little late for that.'

'Tonight we'll sleep in mine.'

~

Sunday afternoon, dressed in a pale blue dress and matching hat, Beth has packed her belongings and is ready to return home. Vincent is lying on his back, his hands behind his head. She draws the curtains wide open and warm western sunshine pours in. 'Come on Rip Van Winkle, rise and shine.'

'I wish we could stay here for the week,' Vincent says, slipping out of bed and gathering his clothes.

'Me too, but we both have to return to our other lives.'

Sitting on the edge of the bed, Beth watches him dress, her eyes trailing over his broad shoulders, his slender legs. During their love making, she'd mostly seen him in a moonlit room with her fingers, her lips, her body, but now she sees him in the full light of day and is not displeased. She even likes his slight paunch, unavoidable for one who loves good food and wine.

'You're ogling me, Beth.'

'I haven't seen a man dress in ...'

'If you don't take your eyes off me I'll start charging for the show,' he smiles, buttoning up his shirt. 'My fees are exorbitant.'

'Such humility, Mr Stirling.'

'Let's lie naked on an isolated beach and ogle each other when the weather warms up.'

'I would love that and I shall dream of it every night.'

'Since you can't take your eyes off me, will you join me here next weekend? I'll let you watch me dress as often as you like.' He gives an impish smile.

'In that case, it's a tentative yes. I enjoy your company, Vincent,' she says, an understatement as every nerve in her body is tingling. 'But I have to check if Aunt Faith can mind Sam.'

'Bring him along; he'd enjoy playing on the beach. We three could go for a splash in the sea.'

'Maybe, in time, I don't want to confuse him,' says Beth, picking up his fob watch from the side table and commenting on its quality.

'My father gave it to me for my twentieth birthday.'

Beth flips the watch open, closes it and reopens it again, as if she cannot believe the hour. But there's something else that interests her. Inside there's an inscription: To my darling son, Vincent Stirling, 1884. A disturbing thought springs to mind – Eric Emerson's possessions could have been planted in the hollow. She'd been too impatient to have the case closed, perhaps too eager to impress Vincent.

'You look like you've seen a ghost. What's on your mind, Beth?'

Vincent's watch suddenly heavy in her hand, she shares her

recent revelations about Jack Spencer. 'Eric could have planted his possessions and identity papers in the hollow. Eric's handyman, Nolan Lloyd, told me he'd seen Eric arguing with a man who fits Jack's description. Eric might have killed Angus as well, so he and Anna could make a new life for themselves.'

'No, Beth, don't do this,' he says, a hint of tension in his voice. 'Eric is buried, he's at peace and so is Lydia.'

'Why are you so certain it was Eric's body?'

'Lydia, the constabulary and the medical examiner have all confirmed it was Eric. Not to mention the fact that Eric is not a violent man. May I have my watch back?'

'Sit still, Vincent. I'll thread the chain through a button hole in your vest.'

'That's too high.'

'Oh, it's the button hole below.' Beth says, rethreading the chain. 'Who's the main beneficiary of Eric's will?' She scrutinises his countenance for clues, but he remains poker-faced.

'I knew that was coming, you must be aware of the right to privacy of my clients.'

'And if a client is deceased?'

'He or she is still protected by the law.'

'Nod or shake your head. Anna Hopping has inherited Eric's assets.'

'Give up, Beth. You know I wouldn't divulge confidential information about my clients. Let me take you to lunch instead.

TUESDAY, 11TH SEPTEMBER

Charlotte answers the door and ushers Beth inside where she is met by a jumble of fragrances. Flowers in vases, some already drooping, are perched on every available platform. Charlotte sneezes into the crook of her arm.

'Bless you.'

'Too many flowers. Messy now, dropping the petals *partout*,' says Charlotte, sweeping them up. 'Mrs Emerson is in the study.'

Taking long strides, Charlotte moves along the hall like a person without a second to spare. Right behind her, Beth is almost running. They find Lydia sitting at the window, Eric's belongings on the table. Charlotte prances out of the room and goes about her business.

'A policeman from the medical examiner's office delivered Eric's possessions this morning. I'm not sure what to do with them,' says Lydia, not wasting any time with greetings. 'How on earth he managed to crawl to the hollow is beyond me. If only I'd known he was there, he might have been saved.' She regards the array of objects, clutches the gold pocketknife and flicks it open. 'He loved his knife, never went anywhere without it. It gave him a sense of power and security.'

'May I see it?'

'Of course,' she says, passing it to Beth. 'His father gifted it to him when he passed his final legal exams. He died a year later; Eric never let his precious gift out of his sight.'

Beth reads the inscription: To my dear son Eric, from your proud father, 1881. 'Was it found on the body?'

'Yes, besides the medical examiner's report, it was used as vital evidence along with his other possessions.'

Beth recalls having seen it in the right hand drawer of Eric's desk. Eric had already been reported missing when she'd spotted the pocketknife. She'd thought it was odd at the time that he'd left a beloved object behind. Now, her stomach contracts from its presence. Someone must have taken it out of the drawer and planted it on the body. It couldn't have been Lydia or she wouldn't be flashing it about so readily.

'Where did he keep it when he was at home?'

'Right here, in his desk drawer.' Lydia points to the smaller drawer on the right hand side.

'And he only owned one pocketknife?'

'Why do you ask?'

'Curiosity.'

Lydia closes her eyes for several seconds, when she looks at Beth her gaze is uneasy, almost childlike, as if she'd felt a sudden pain or discomfort. Then, she recovers just as quickly and smiles. 'Eric is at peace now, thanks to you. You've carried out the task I assigned you with judicious competence and I would recommend you to anyone, but you need to move on now.'

'Mr Stirling has said as much. I'm often accused of seeing mysterious intrigues where they don't exist. I won't bother you again about the pocketknife.'

'You and Vincent are well suited to each other. I received a telegram from my mother yesterday, she'd seen him arm in arm with a lovely lady fitting your description.'

'We took tea together in Port Adelaide.'

'Your friendship with Vincent is most beneficial, you are positively glowing.'

'Mr Stirling is an agreeable companion.'

'He's always the gentleman. Of course I thought that of Eric, so we can never be sure, can we? But nothing ventured nothing gained,' she gives a wicked smile. 'He's very handsome.'

'I'd better be off.'

'Before you go I'd like to gift you the pocketknife, it might save your life one of these days. Your profession seems fraught with danger. You'd be wise to learn how to use it.'

'I couldn't accept …'

'It upsets me. I simply don't want it. Please accept it.'

'That's very kind of you, Lydia.'

'You don't have to rush off, why don't you join Charlotte and I for tea?'

They take tea in the kitchen, an informal practice Lydia has embraced since Eric's disappearance. There are two coconut cakes and an apple tart with cream. Beth and Lydia cut the cakes into generous helpings while Charlotte prepares a pot of tea. Sipping tea, Beth listens intently to Charlotte's stories about France and her daunting journey across the Indian Ocean to the colony. When Lydia leaves the room to fetch the mail and a newspaper delivered at the door, Beth takes the opportunity to ask Charlotte if anyone had entered Eric's study following his disappearance. Lydia had received many visitors, but only one person, besides Charlotte, had access to Eric's study. Vincent Stirling had once called in to see if he could find an important document to do with one of Eric's former clients, not long after Beth had inspected the study. Charlotte had accompanied him to the room and left him to his own devices. Beth wonders if he'd taken the pocketknife.

Her head reeling, her stomach almost bursting from overindulgence, Beth bids her hostesses a good day. She hadn't planned on crossing the road and exploring the mysterious trail, but that's where she heads, wheeling her bicycle along the rutted track. A concerning thought crosses her mind: if Vincent had planted evidence in the hollow he must be somehow involved. Perhaps he helped

Eric hide the body. However, she doubts Vincent would take such risks and put his livelihood in jeopardy. She heaves a deep sigh and focusses on pleasant sounds: chirping birds, flapping of wings and creaking branches. Further on, another sound takes her attention, a dog is barking furiously in the distance, or perhaps more than one dog. Impatient to know what lies at the end of the road she lengthens her strides. The streams of water have long dried up, but the deep channels forged by heavy rain are hidden beneath thick layers of soft grey dust. The dust reveals fresh wagon wheel tracks, perhaps there is a farm further down the road. She fumbles in her pocket for her newly acquired pocketknife. Hopes she'll never have to use it.

Two miles on, wheel imprints turn left onto a wide track. Slashed grass and shrubs are piled up either side of the track, suggesting there's a working homestead at the end of it. The sound of barking dogs and a male voice telling them to shut up forces her to leap into the bush for cover. She leans her bicycle against a tree and continues moving in the brush until she comes to a tumbledown rough-hewn timber farmhouse, its rusty iron roof collapsed on one side, the rotted window frames without glass panes. Surrounding the house, native bushland has reclaimed its territory and towers over the stunted orchards. There's a wagon out front, the horse looks healthy and young. The corrugated metal sheds are heavily rusted but functional. As she moves closer, her presence sets off the dogs. The deafening tirade sends her scuttling back into the bush.

Hall emerges from the shack. 'Shut up, bloody shut up!'

A deeper voice resonates from inside the house. 'What the hell's goin' on?'

'Bloody kangaroos keep setting the buggers off!' Hall bellows, before re-entering the shack.

To get a better view of the dog sheds Beth moves through the bush facing the front entrance to the buildings and climbs onto a fallen tree trunk. From her elevated vantage point she observes two very sturdy sheds reinforced with wire over the frame and a solid wire door. Carl is in the larger shed. Several smaller dogs are huddled together in the other one. Any attempt to free the dogs would alert the two men inside and she'd end up in a cage, or worse. Wondering what the men are doing in the house she circles around within the bush to the back of the house, taking care not to set the dogs off again. There's a back door, half off its hinges, a cluster of spider webs suggest it hasn't been opened in years. She crouches at the window and listens. The men's voices are subdued by either a cleaver or axe chopping up putrid meat, probably for the dogs. Their dialogue reveals it's kangaroo meat. She hopes the meat isn't as rotten as it smells as it could harm the dogs. Apportioning the meat, Hall suggests they keep the tail for themselves. Attracted by the blood, frenzied blowflies are buzzing all around them. The men laugh raucously as they try to chop the flies in half and miss.

'Someone found that body in the hollow last week, we gotta skedaddle,' says Hall.

'How'd ya know that?'

'Everyone in town's talkin' bout it. We'll peddle the small dogs tonight, and keep the big bloke.'

'What about the wagon?'

'That too, and the 'orse. Goin' west, mate. '

Their conversation is eclipsed by raucous laughter again as Hall's mate has sliced a cockroach in half with his cleaver.

'I'll finish up 'ere, you get some firewood,' Hall says, as he fills two buckets with meat. 'We'll scoff kangaroo tail for tea, bloody tender, mate.'

Hall moves outside to feed the dogs while his mate looks for kindle and dry logs. Beth recognizes Carl's incessant whinging for dinner, a piercing sound, loud enough to make birds fall from their trees. 'Bellyache all ya like, ya won't get a scotch fillet round 'ere, mate.'

The tall man drops his pile of kindle. 'Andy, come look, there's a bloody bike in the bush!'

'Bring it 'ere, will ya!'

Beth takes a deep breath, prepares her mind and body for a swift escape. Her first instinct is to grab her bicycle from that man's bloodied hands, but she needs a head start. She scampers through the thick scrub behind the shack, snapping branches and crushing ferns. There's a narrow track veering left, she follows it. She keeps running, her throat dry, heart pumping, sweat pouring down her face and down her back. Not far behind her, two angry voices echo through the bush, threatening to kill her. Cockatoos squawk, an afternoon breeze flares up. Running for her life along the ever widening trail, she keeps up the pace. Soon, there is only one voice behind her. The man with the angry voice would be familiar with the track. He'd know where it leads. Her lungs are almost bursting when she comes to the clearing. She knows where she is. The gaping hollow is now a stack of crumbling wood. She stops to catch her breath, listens. Silence. The man has stopped yelling. He must be getting close. He wants to creep up on her. Grab her unawares. It's time to hide. Moving through the bush she spots a giant eucalypt with low lying branches. She climbs half way up and looks down. Her stomach lurches. The thought of not being able to descend crosses her mind but she keeps climbing until the branches are too spindly to hold her weight. Perched on the crown of the tree she has a clear view of the forest all around her. In the distance, smoke is billowing from a clearing, probably Hall frying his rotten meat. His tall flunky would not give up so easily. She hopes the branch holding her doesn't snap. Then she sees him, striding along the track. He turns into the clearing, looks around. Her heart is pounding. Her shaking hands clutch the branches. Something is crawling over her, ants. She feels their mild sting, holds on tight. A wallaby hops through the bush. The tall man arms himself with a solid branch. On seeing the animal he curses and lobs the branch into the scrub. Minutes later, he turns onto the track again. Numb from cold and fear Beth tries desperately to still the shaking. Her resolve strengthened by thoughts of Sam, she descends, stopping every so often to restore her balance. When her feet touch the ground, she stretches her aching body, curbs a groan. Her spirits lifted, she knows exactly where she is now, remembers walking from the clearing with Vincent and ascending the escarpment. Moving gingerly through the bush, she stays parallel to the track. Her fingers feel for the knife in her pocket. She'd use it if she had to. The sun is high in the trees when she hears his boots clomping along the track. Hidden in the bush, she parts some branches to get a better view of the tall, wiry man. Her pursuer is returning to the shack, he has given up. After a long moment, she takes a deep breath and moves out of the bush. He is far ahead, running now. When he is out of sight she hurries along the track, openly. In the dusky light she ascends the escarpment, her bruised hands clutching plants and jutting rocks as she hoists herself onto the ledge. She moves cautiously along the open stony trail and is soon tramping through the thick bush that leads to the main road. The mandarin peels, now dried, are still scattered on the ground where she and Vincent had rested the previous week. Her spirits soaring she hurries on. The rattling of wheels jolting along the road drives her back into hiding. She finds herself on all fours crawling across the ground until she is concealed by a thick shrub and feels safe enough to survey the road. Andrew Hall and his mate are leaving, she captures a glimpse of their wagon as they pass by; alongside their scant possessions the dogs are secured with chains, and so is her bicycle.

By the glow of the full moon she moves down the main road, there is just enough light to guide her along. Worn out, she takes her time. She passes Lydia's home and keeps walking until she comes to the small town along the way. She thinks to summon a cab but the roads are empty. If only she had her bicycle, Norwood Police Station is at least two miles away. She plods on.

Constable Skinner bids Beth a good evening as she enters the station. Wondering what is good about it she stands at the front counter and informs him she has discovered a farm on crown land where two dog snatchers are squatting. She states Andrew Hall's name and gives a detailed description of his accomplice. Having noticed her hoarse voice the constable gives her a glass of water. Her thirst quenched, her voice restored, she provides the location of the abandoned farm and the details of her confrontation and subsequent escape from the two men. The policeman jots down some hurried notes as she speaks.

'What were you doing wandering about in the bush, alone?'

'Because there's only one of me,' Beth smirks, but the constable is unamused. 'I'm simply here to help you find two dog snatchers and to report the theft of my bicycle.'

'Did you see the two men steal your bicycle?'

'As I've already explained, I was threatened and had to run for my life.' She has to fight back the tears when she mentions her bicycle. Strangely, she doesn't feel complete without it, it's as though she has lost an arm or a leg.

'You said you left your bicycle in the bush. If we concerned ourselves with lost property we'd never have the time to investigate serious crime.'

'I left my bicycle behind because two men were determined to kill me.'

'I'm glad you weren't injured, Mrs Durrani. Thank you for the information regarding Mr Hall and his accomplice, I have noted the address and your details, we'll look into it first thing in the morning.'

'And my stolen bicycle?'

'An investigator of your standing should be able to find it herself,' he mutters, finishing off his notes.

'Is there any chance of getting a lift home, it's only a mile or so from here in Kensington Road.'

'I'm afraid not. I'm presently the only one manning the station. Mind how you go, at least that road is well-lit.'

WEDNESDAY, 12TH SEPTEMBER

Viewed from the kitchen window, the egg-yolk-yellow sun rising in the east promises a glorious spring day ahead. Despite having slept well, Beth's perilous escape the previous day has left her aching, swollen and grazed yet grateful to be alive. Besides the loss of her bicycle, there's something else that doesn't sit right in her mind.

'A penny for your thoughts,' says Harry, handing her a cuppa.

'It's just a mild case of befuddlement.'

'Loose ends?'

'How'd you guess?'

'I always felt uneasy following an investigation, especially after a complex case. What's wrong?'

'I'm not convinced the man in the hollow was Eric. I don't know whether to leave things be or to keep digging. What would you do, Harry?'

'I would follow my gut feeling.'

'Keep digging?'

'If that's what you feel.'

'It is, I can't stand not knowing,' Beth says, before draining her cup and telling Harry he makes a great pot of tea.

'Follow the facts, follow your instincts.'

Beth doesn't mention her concerns about Vincent's involvement; a part of her thinks he is not. The thought crosses her mind she could be thinking with her heart and not with her head.

Harry fixes his eyes on her, wondering if he should speak out of turn. 'You could have been hurt last night or have perished in the bush. Never forget the golden rule, always inform the team ...'

'I will next time, I promise.'

'By the way, I've made some enquiries about Angus Hopping. He was stabbed with a kitchen knife. The police will never disclose that detail to the newspapers nor to Hopping's relatives.' He taps the side of his nose, 'Mum's the word.'

'A kitchen knife?'

'That makes it personal, doesn't it? Thugs usually carry pocket-knives.'

'Talking about thugs, if Aunt Faith is able to mind Sam this morning, I'd like to look around Hall's bush hideout, maybe find a clue as to his whereabouts. I'm determined to get my bicycle back. Could you give me a lift?'

'Of course I can. Don't get your hopes up, your bicycle could be sold by now, it's worth a few quid.'

'Or stashed at his mother's place.'

'We'll go after breakfast if you like. The stove's hot if you want to set the porridge going.'

Harry turns left onto the track leading to the farmhouse and parks in the clearing. Hall's wagon is gone, the fireplace doused, the doors to the sheds left wide open and creaking in the breeze. The dogs are gone. The place seems abandoned, but Harry draws his pistol in case. He insists on entering the shack alone. Minutes later, he emerges to confirm the men have gone and there's no sign the con-stabulary had been there either.

'So much for looking into it first thing in the morning,' Beth says.

Together they survey the rooms, what's left of them. The squalid kitchen makes them heave. Used as a butcher's bench, the kitchen table is daubed in reddish-brown blood. Beneath the table a swarm of blowflies are feeding on decaying kangaroo meat and discarded offal.

'They're pigs, the two of them,' observes Beth, slapping a handkerchief over her nose.

'Pigs are cleaner.' Wishing he'd thought to bring a pair of gloves, Harry delves through what looks like the most recent pile of rubbish stacked in a corner of the room. Besides broken whisky bottles, bones, cans and food scraps, he comes across a discarded shirt. Rummaging through the pockets he fishes out a folded newspaper clipping. Having forgotten his spectacles he asks Beth to read the fine print. She would rather not touch the paper soiled with tobacco ash and blood, but it proves useful. 'It's an advertisement for tickets on a steamer to Fremantle and beyond. It's leaving Saturday 22nd September, they might have booked a seat or a cabin, the time's blotched out by muck.'

'That's easy to find out.'

'I wonder where they're staying in the meantime.'

'I'll check on Mrs Hall's home in a day or two,' Harry answers.

~

Later that day, Beth is playing catch with Sam when she spots Ramin standing at the front gate, his hands in his pockets and simply looking. She tells Sam to go inside and stay with Harry while she talks to Ramin. Beth moves towards him, looks him in the eye and asks if he'd like to join her family for tea, an opportunity to come to terms with their differences. He declines her invitation. She wishes him a good day, yet he doesn't budge. The two of them stand facing each other, neither one of them giving in.

Whilst admiring his tenacity, his stubbornness fills her with fury. There seems no room for compromise now. She tells him she has notified the constabulary and they are keeping an eye on her home, he simply must stop stalking her and her family.

'I stop when you will give Sam to me. I am giving you chance to hand him over. You must explain to him about his family in Afghanistan.'

'He is my son, I will never give him up. Go home, Ramin.'

'He will sail with me. We leave soon.'

The determination in his eyes isn't as intimidating as she'd once thought. He's a sad person who thinks Sam will make him happy again. Watching him move away she wonders if his rigid world view could ever be stretched to include other notions. After all, Arif was well travelled and tolerant of other world views without forfeiting the principles he held dear.

THURSDAY, 13TH SEPTEMBER

Vincent's head is bowed over his work when Beth enters his office. He greets her warmly and her suspicions almost melt at the sight of him.

'You look upset, Beth. Please take a seat.'

'I'll stand, thank you. I'm not staying long. I've just come let you know I went to see Mr O'Halloran last week to tell him the case is closed, and not to threaten me again.'

'Courageous,' he smiles. 'I'd have informed him by mail.'

'When I was waiting in the clerk's office for O'Halloran's return, I noticed a photograph of a salesman, Mr Jack Spencer, wearing a suit with anchor buttons, just like the one I found in Eric's front garden.'

Vincent takes a moment to answer. 'I'm sure Mr Spencer's not the only person in Adelaide to sport a garment with anchor buttons.'

'He disappeared about the same time as Eric.'

'How do you know that?'

'O'Halloran's clerk told me, he also gave me Mr Spencer's address. According to the young man residing in Mr Spencer's home he'd disappeared months ago.'

'It could be a coincidence.'

'Jack Spencer's about the same age as Eric, same height, and similar colouring. I believe the man in the hollow wasn't Eric, it was Jack Spencer.' Intense emotion turning her hazel eyes golden, Beth studies Vincent's expression of bemusement rather than surprise.

'You've done a marvellous job of finding Eric's body, the case is closed now. Why are you doing this?'

'I think Eric is still alive and I think you know where he is.'

'That's preposterous.' His smiling eyes make him look as though he is about to laugh and thinks better of it. 'Are you going to the police with this?'

'Should I?'

'It's up to the constabulary to investigate now.'

'I won't be sharing my suspicions with the police, as you know I don't have a good rapport with them, they'd probably lock me up for wasting their time after what happened yesterday.'

'I'd bail you out,' he smiles, and observing Beth's flushed face, he adds, 'what happened yesterday?'

'I reported the hideout of a pair of dog snatchers who stole my bicycle.' She moves on without elaborating, asks Vincent to name the main beneficiary of Eric's inheritance, a part of her wanting to know if Vincent would tell her.

'You know I'm bound by confidentiality, Beth.'

'I could ask Lydia directly.'

'That's your prerogative, at least it's legal.'

'I'm guessing Anna inherited his assets. In court you'd remain stony-faced, but we are emotionally involved, I can read your face, Vincent.' Beth lies.

'Well it hasn't helped me at all trying to read your face, I'm totally bewildered.'

'Have you known all along?'

'For heaven's sake, Beth, known what?'

'Please don't play games with me. Is Eric still alive?'

Vincent gets to his feet and approaches Beth, but she moves away from him, raises her hands, palms out, maintaining her distance. 'I know what you did, Vincent. You took Eric's pocketknife from his study and threw it into the hollow.' Beth's voice is louder than she'd intended. 'The man in the hollow was Jack Spencer.'

'Look, the name sounds vaguely familiar, I'll make some enquiries.'

'I'm going home now, Vincent. Think about everything we've discussed, when we meet next time you'll tell me the truth.'

'There's nothing to think about, we haven't discussed anything. I've never lied to you, as for the pocketknife I don't know what you're talking about.'

Beth leaves the room without a backward glance. Vincent is either telling the truth or he's a brilliant actor. As she moves back onto the street, she is already berating herself for her impulsive and unwise behaviour. It'd be a miracle if he wants to see her again.

FRIDAY, 14TH SEPTEMBER

Holding his woollen waistcoat to her face she feels nostalgic for the early days of their marriage when he was a considerate, loving man. Only seventeen, she was a naïve girl when they married, perhaps impressed by his sailor suit she believed their passionate love would last forever. Everything changed when Sophie was born. He didn't understand a baby needs her mother's full attention. Surly at first, he became increasingly angry and aggressive. Over time, his violence escalated, the first, second and third slap stunned her, then it became routine. A slap became a punch, usually levelled strategically in places where the bruises wouldn't show. It's easier to remember the Angus he became rather than the younger Angus, easier to hate him than to love him. Now, Anna wants all his possessions out of the house, his clothes, his shoes, even his favourite tea cup. Having pulled his belongings out of the wardrobe she stacks them neatly on the bed ready for collection.

Beth alights from the cab and pays the driver. At the same time, a man pulls up his horse and cart outside of Anna's home. Carrying a bunch of flowers he leaps from the cart, approaches the door, knocks and enters. Standing on the other side of the road Beth is wondering if the man is Eric when a tap on the shoulder makes her jump into the air.

'Sorry luv, I didn't mean to startle you. Is Mrs Hopping a friend of yours?' asks an elderly woman.

'Yes, I'm on my way to visit her but I see she has a guest and I'm waiting for him to leave.'

'He was there yesterday as well. Her husband's only recently been laid to rest, didn't take her long, did it?' she guffaws.

'He's probably a family member.'

'Well, he seems like a very nice young man.'

'I think I'll visit my friend now, I'm sure she wouldn't mind me intruding.'

Audrey answers the door which is opened just wide enough to see her face.

'Is everything all right, Audrey?'

'We're sorry, we can't talk to you today,' she says, on the point of tears. 'Anna isn't well at all.'

'Is there anything I can do?'

'Please go.'

'It's all right, Ma. Let her in,' comes a voice from within.

The door swings open. Beth moves into the house. The competing scent of roses and vanilla cake hits her nostrils, red roses winning by an easy margin. Her face pale, Beth looks at their male guest expecting to see a ghost. At close range, this man is younger than Eric, chubby-faced, thick hair, boyish.

'Name's Charlie, Angus' cousin.'

Beth offers her hand, introduces herself, the young man has a firm handshake.

'He's come to collect Angus' stuff.'

Charlie drains his teacup and declares he'd better get on with it. He moves into Anna's bedroom, leaves the door wide open, and starts filling his bags. When he emerges from the room he thanks Anna, and sets off hauling two bags strung over his shoulders.

'He's got a young family to support.'

'Were they close, he and Angus I mean?'

'No, Charlie and his wife are staunch members of the temperance movement. Charlie tried to save Angus once and got a black eye for his efforts. He's avoided him ever since.' Anna chuckles.

'There's a lot to be said for giving up the booze.'

'I visited Eric's gravestone for the first time yesterday. I had a long chat with him, thanked him for saving us from poverty.'

'How so?'

'I've inherited Eric's estate.' She smiles broadly. 'We'll never go hungry again.'

'That's wonderful news.'

'I loved Eric with all my heart, but he should've taken us away from here before I was beaten up. We had plenty of opportunities when Angus was away. He kept going on about his finances or lack of. We could have started somewhere new, worked hard.'

'What will you do now?'

'We'll stay here. I'll engage a builder to add an extra room for this little one,' she cradles her round belly. 'Now the house is in my name I get to vote as a property owner, I might even join the suffragettes.'

'There's nothing stopping you now.'

'I've already booked Sophie into school; she's such a clever girl.'

'She'll grow up in a very different world from ours. Perhaps we'll all get the right to vote by the end of the year.'

'I really do hope so. Would you like some cake, Charlie's wife baked it for us?'

Beth watches Anna slice the cake with a steak knife, no doubt her newly acquired wealth will enable her to purchase a silver knife and server. With that thought, an alarming detail springs to Beth's mind.

Anna serves Beth tea and cake. 'Are you all right, Mrs Durrani?'

'I feel a little light-headed.' Beth drinks a cup of tea in one go.

Anna refills her cup.

'I think I was overcome by thirst,' says Beth.

'I forget to drink sometimes.'

'Has the constabulary contacted you again about Angus?'

'A few days ago, they delivered a report. In short, Angus was killed by persons or person unknown.'

'Did they indicate what kind of knife was used in the robbery, Mrs Hopping?'

'No, the report was very brief, the weapon referred to as a knife. In any case, it was a relief to be spared the gory details. Do you mind if we chat on first name basis?'

'Yes, please call me Beth.'

For the next hour, they chat about Anna's plans for the house, for Sophie and for her unborn second child. Later in the afternoon, Anna goes to her room for an afternoon nap and Audrey and Beth move outside in the warm sunshine where Sophie is sitting on a tattered blanket playing with her dolls. When a little girl appears from the house next door Sophie is invited over to play.

Taking advantage of their isolation, Beth lowers her voice to a murmur. 'Something occurred to me as I was watching Anna slice the cake. During my last visit, you told me Angus was killed with a steak knife.'

'It was in all the papers.'

'The type of knife was not revealed in the newspapers, nor was it revealed in the police report you and Anna received. Only the medical examiner and the constabulary are aware of that detail.'

'Perhaps I was just guessing.'

'I know you did it, Audrey.'

Audrey looks up, an expression of determination on her face, but also a sense of relief, there's no use denying it, Angus was a monster and she has no regrets. 'For years I've witnessed his cruelty, especially towards Anna. What sort of man beats up a woman in the family way?' Audrey's eyes are wet, her quiet confession un-stoppable. 'Report me to the constabulary. I'm not sorry I did it. If Anna and Sophie can live in peace, it's worth it.' Almost choking on emotion, she pauses to take a deep breath. 'They can hang me if they want because the world's a better place without that poor excuse for a man.'

'I'd do the same for my son. Whether I'd have the nerve to do it is another thing. Will you tell me what happened?'

Audrey invites Beth inside the house where she can recount the events in private. She stops at Anna's room and opens the door a crack, and observing Anna is sound asleep she gently closes it. They move to the kitchen and are seated. Audrey takes her time to gather her thoughts before speaking, her voice subdued. 'Anna was still in hospital. I gave Sophie a weak brew of laudanum so she'd fall into a deep sleep. Then I dressed as a man, armed myself with a sharp kitchen knife and made my way to Ethel's Dance Hall. I knew he was there, everyone in the street knows he haunts that place when there's money jingling in his pockets. I waited outside in the shadows. As it happened, he got into a fight and was thrown out earlier than usual. I watched him stumble out. Inebriated, he could barely walk. I followed him, watched him flop like a flea-ridden cur against a tree trunk. The street was dark and empty. I thought it's now or never, I had to save my family from that man. I summoned the years of hate and fury and ran at him. I stabbed him in the neck twice, maybe three times.' She pauses, the memory overwhelming, the words making it real. 'There was nobody around. I stripped his clothes off him, and his shoes, and hid them under my coat before hurrying home. I washed the knife with soap and put it in the cutlery drawer. It took me hours to wash his bloodied clothes. I went to bed late. Next morning two policemen came to the door, they told me Angus was dead. I howled, not with sadness but relief. Sophie was in my arms, the two of us holding each other so tight. The policemen gave their condolences and left soon after.'

'Will you tell Anna?'

'Not yet, maybe later, maybe never.'

Beth fears Audrey's innate honesty could be her downfall, an astute policeman would read the guilt in her countenance should she be formally interviewed.

'Don't ever tell anyone about the kitchen knife. It hasn't been revealed to the public. You'd give yourself away if you mentioned it.'

'How do you know about it?'

'It's my job to be a snooping busybody.' Beth smiles briefly and assumes a serious expression. 'If ever you are called to the constabulary, you must respond with a bowed head, loud sobbing and a handkerchief over your mouth. In any case, the police are looking for a man.'

'I'll be very careful, thank you.'

'I wish you and your family well, Audrey. I assure you I will not tell the constabulary and you mustn't either. Your family need you.'

Nausea twirling in her belly, Beth leaves the house. Her irrepressible curiosity got the better of her. Truth is a burden at times and she'll have to carry it for years. Sweet Audrey murdered her son-in-law with a kitchen knife, the one she'd normally use to slice a side of lamb or a sausage, banal cutlery turned killer weapon. Audrey saved her daughter and granddaughter from a miserable life of violence and poverty and she doesn't deserve to hang for it. Yearning for her bicycle and the thrill of speed, Beth walks briskly down the road in search of a hansom cab.

~

Sam, Faith and Harry are already seated in the dining room when Beth arrives home. Steamy baked lamb, pumpkin, potatoes and cabbage are ready for serving.

'All from the garden.' Faith boasts.

'We didn't grow the meat.' Sam laughs.

'No, Sam, we're not farming livestock yet.' Beth giggles, giving him a kiss on the forehead.

When they have finished eating, Faith shares some unsettling news. Ramin had returned to their front gate that morning calling for Sam's attention.

'I tailed him for a while, but he picked up speed and I couldn't for the life of me keep up with that young bloke,' says Harry, shaking his head.

'He'd outrun a horse,' says Beth, recalling the time she tried to follow him.

'What does Ramin want, Mama?'

'He wants to take you away to a faraway place in Afghanistan, where your papa and I once lived.'

'I want to stay here.'

'Of course you do. We won't let him take you away. Your place is here with us,' Beth says, tousling his curly hair.

'Will he hurt us?'

'No, he doesn't want to hurt us, and he would never hurt you, he's your uncle.'

Samuel tucked into bed and fast asleep, the team sit in the drawing room, their habitual sherry before them. Beth shares her speculations about Jack Spencer.

Harry's response clears things up. A friend from the constabulary has informed him that Jack Spencer has been in prison for the past six months and will reside there for the next twelve years. He'd robbed an old couple of their furniture and when confronted by the husband he assaulted him.

'So the body is undoubtedly Eric's. I've been following the wrong path all along. It could easily have been an accident after all.'

'You found the missing person, in this case missing body, job well done. Now you can move on. You've got enough on your plate with Ramin trying to kidnap young Samuel.'

Outwardly, Beth agrees with Harry but she still has doubts, a vague inkling that something doesn't add up. 'I have some good news to share; Anna is the main beneficiary of Eric's estate.'

'Good for her, she'd need it given her circumstances,' Faith responds.

'I have a philosophical question, Harry.'

'Oh dear.'

'Have you ever had a case where you'd identified the murderer and didn't report him because you knew he was simply defending himself or others?'

Harry considers Beth's question before answering with a categorical yes.

'What about a mother defending her child?'

'Audrey confessed, did she?'

'How ...'

'Anna and her two mothers had a compelling motive. Anna was ill so it was either Audrey or Charlotte. Charlotte was at the theatre with Lydia the night Angus was killed. That just leaves Audrey,' says Harry, looking pleased with himself.

'How did you work it out, Beth?' Faith asks.

'In conversation, Audrey mentioned Angus was killed with a steak knife. As we know, the police haven't released that detail. Only the murderer would know that.'

'Justice served,' is Faith's terse reply but her expression is one of astonishment.

'I assured Audrey I wouldn't report her to the constabulary.'

'As a private investigator you're not obliged to report her,' says Faith.

'Speaking of which, are you certain you don't want to report your brother-in-law for stalking?'

'I'm sure Ramin will give up and return home eventually.'

'Let's hope he does.'

Faith raises her glass to toast the conclusion of the case of the missing lawyer.

'No doubt the first of many missing persons cases coming our way in the future.' Harry grins.

The three of them chink glasses and sip their sherry.

'Now the case is closed we should see Mr Stirling's handsome face on our doorstep more often.' Faith fixes her hazel eyes on Beth's.

'We'll leave Mr Stirling out of our conversations for now, if you don't mind, Aunt Faith.'

Harry and Faith give each other a bemused glance and Beth remains taciturn, unwilling to discuss her unwarranted antagonism towards Vincent.

SATURDAY, 15TH SEPTEMBER

Harry hasn't told anyone his true intentions. He tells them he is off to visit the shooting range with his friends. There's a tournament coming up in a few weeks and he plans to be up to scratch. After breakfast, he climbs into his wagon and sets off along Kensington Road to visit Mrs Hall. He pulls up outside her home. The gate is wide open. A runaway pumpkin vine peppered with bee-attracting yellow flowers has commandeered the front yard. Trying to avoid a bee sting, Harry treads carefully between the meandering vines. He approaches the front door and knocks firmly. A hefty dog is barking within. In his vest pocket is a paper bag containing dog biscuits, should a hasty departure be necessary.

Mrs Hall answers the door. Harry tips his hat and turns on the charm. 'It's good to see you again, Mrs Hall.'

'I asked Andy if he knows a Mr Tingcombe and he don't remember you at all.' Her mocking smile is at once threatening and ridiculous as most of her teeth are missing. 'Sweetie don't like liars, do ya Sweetie?'

The dog responds by curling its lips back and baring a full set of perfect teeth.

Harry does all he can to appear unfazed, she is the first person to remember his fictitious name. He'd have to use a more complicated bogus identity in future, one he'd remember. 'I'm extremely disappointed. Andrew and I have known each other for years. He knows me as Uncle Ting; perhaps that's why he couldn't remember my actual name.'

'His memory box isn't what it used to be, he drinks too much. Anyways, Andy's leavin' Adelaide for good. He give me some money and said he'd write. I won't hold me breath though. If it's a dog ya want, you won't get one here.'

'I'm not after a dog, Mrs Hall.'

She stares at him with those pale watery eyes, wary.

'Andrew informed me he has a bicycle he'd like to sell. I'm here to purchase it. You'll offer me a good price because I happen to know the bicycle was stolen from a police constable. You wouldn't want him turning up here with a few colleagues to rummage through your lovely home, would you?'

If smoke were a sign of intense thinking there'd be billowing clouds coming from that woman's ears. Harry waits.

'You don't look like no bicycle rider to me.'

'It's for my niece.'

'Rightio, a fiver then.'

'Three quid.'

'Four.'

'Three quid, and that's more than the usual asking price.'

Pursing her lips, she holds out her scrawny palm.

The money safely in her clutched hand she shuts the door and clicks the bolt. Harry waits on the doorstep, wondering if she'd keep the money and not follow through with the deal. Five minutes later, the door swings open to reveal a shiny black bicycle. Harry takes hold of the handlebars and pulls it outside.

'It's takin' too much space in me 'ouse anyways,' says Mrs Hall before ducking back inside and closing the door.

Harry wheels the bicycle to his wagon, examines it for damage, besides a few scratches it's in perfect condition. He heaves it into the back of his wagon and smiles all the way home.

~

Beth is shopping on Main Street when she catches sight of Vincent strolling along, dressed in a dapper suit, a top hat and carrying a leather case. Without thinking, she follows him down the street, watches him come across a friend and stop for a chat. She feigns window shopping as the two men converse. When Vincent moves off so does she. He purchases a paper from the newsstand on the corner. Beth stops near him, reading the headlines.

'Beth, I thought that might be your lovely red hair tucked beneath a pretty hat.'

'Nice to see you, Vincent.'

There's an awkward silence, both of them recalling their recent interaction.

'How are you?'

'I'm well. I've been visiting my friend Ayishah, she owns a herbal shop. I've bought vanilla essence and several fragrant oils. Lavender helps me sleep.'

'You've been trying some samplers no doubt, they smell wonderful. I must visit her shop one of these days.'

'I'd like you to meet my good friend, she's a fascinating person. She's travelling to India in a few days to stay with her family; perhaps we should visit her when she returns.'

'I'd love to.'

Looking into his dark expressive eyes, Beth apologises for doubting him. She admits she was wrong about the victim being Jack Spencer, as he was serving a prison term before and during the time Eric disappeared.

'I knew the name sounded familiar, I should have remembered him. He'd assaulted an old man during a burglary and got ...'

'Twelve years in the lock up.'

Vincent nods.

'Are you angry with me?'

'I wasn't angry, Beth, I was baffled.'

'You're a stickler for protocol, I should have trusted you.'

'It's your job to be suspicious.'

'Anyway, case closed. I'm convinced the victim was Eric Emerson.'

He takes Beth's hands in his. 'I'm going to Port Adelaide tomorrow; would you care to join me? Perhaps we could rekindle our friendship.'

Beth looks into his smiling eyes and would love to break the rules of propriety and fall into his arms and kiss him passionately. Instead, she pecks him on the cheek and tells him she has some unfinished business to attend to.

'Is it in regards to the Eric Emerson case?'

'Yes, it is.' There's a constant unease tugging at her and it won't let go until she discovers the cause. She hopes Nolan Lloyd might have the answer.

'So case not closed?'

'Not quite.'

'It's not dangerous, I hope.'

Beth smiles and shakes her head. 'I need to tie up a few loose ends.'

'Is there anything I can do?'

'You could buy me a coffee,' she smiles, fixing her eyes on his. 'I can't wait to hold you again.'

'I'm thinking the same thing,' he says, offering his arm.

SUNDAY, 16TH SEPTEMBER

Harry is tight-lipped about how he managed to retrieve Beth's bicycle but he has useful connections in the constabulary and Beth doesn't insist on more details. He has his ways and she appreciates him, for his expertise and his gift for making her aunt joyful, although at times a little immoderate. Thrilled to be riding again, she looks smart in her new royal blue bloomers with matching jacket and gaiters, purchased from *La Bicyclette Boutique* in town specialising in women's cycling garb. Now, with a spare costume in her wardrobe, she no longer sees herself as a bird with clipped wings when her costume is in the wash.

Hoping to meet a healthier Nolan Lloyd in hospital, Beth is pumping hard at the bicycle peddles as she zips down Kensington Road, a box of chocolates shuffling about in the basket attached to the handlebars. With a bit of luck, a sugar surge should activate Mr Lloyd's mind, and coax him into blurting out the details he's hiding about the Emerson household. Half an hour later, the towering chimneys perched on the hospital roof come into view. She props her bike against the wall facing the front office and the friendly office clerks are happy to keep an eye on it. She grasps the chocolates and bounds up the stairs to room sixteen. The door is wide open, she taps gently before entering. Mr Lloyd's bed is empty. The two patients who were sound asleep during her last visit are wide awake this time. Mr Lloyd was discharged and gone home they tell her, he's moving up north to live on his brother's farm. They give her Nolan's address. Before leaving, she offers them the chocolates. They bellow their appreciation as she dashes out of the room and takes the stairs two by two. She thanks the office staff and retrieves her bicycle. Outside, she mounts and rides off in the hope Nolan Lloyd hasn't left town.

Nolan is loading his dray with his scant possessions when he notices a cyclist turning onto the footpath leading to the flat he is vacating. Recognising her instantly, he asks where his chocolates are before bursting into laughter.

'I gave them to your mates in room sixteen.'

'Good on ya, they need 'em more than me.'

'They told me where to find you. You look well.'

'Still above ground,' he grins. 'I'm off to my brother's farm in the Barossa Valley, lookin' forward to breathin' good country air. There's a vacant cottage on his land and I'll help him with the farm chores and the like.'

'That sounds perfect for a man who loves the outdoors,' says Beth, thinking his weathered face looks as dry as toast.

'What can I do for you?'

'I'd like to know if you remember anything else about Mr and Mrs Emerson.' Beth suspects he's holding something back and this is her last chance to get it out of him. 'Please, Mr Lloyd, I need your help.'

'They fought a lot, nothin' violent, no blood spilled and the like, but they was sick and tired of each other, that's for sure.'

'Last time we met you told me you were sacked. Do you remember which of the two let you go?'

He takes his time to answer as if troubled by the question.

'Mrs Emerson.'

'You seem like a very reliable fellow. Why would she let you go?'

'I seen things I shouldn't 'ave. I saw Mrs Emerson and her cook …' he leaves his sentence short, fumbles for his handkerchief and dabs his brow. 'I'm not pleased with myself, but I couldn't for the life of me look away. I'm leavin' town so I can be frank with ya.'

'Then please elaborate, Mr Lloyd.'

'I seen Mrs Emerson and her cook being intimate like a man and a woman, they was always kissin' passionately and touchin' each other. That's why Mr and Mrs Emerson was fightin' all the time, she fancied her cook more than him.'

'So Mrs Emerson let you go for spying on her and her lover?'

'I promised I wouldn't tell nobody but she still insisted I go, she called me a peeping tom. At least she gave me a reference so I could find work elsewhere. Then I got sick, sometimes life just don't go the way you want.'

'That's true, Mr Lloyd, sometimes we have little control over our destiny. I wish you a good life in the Barossa Valley, it's a lovely spot, I remember passing that way more than ten years ago.'

'And plenty of vino,' he grins.

'Would you be prepared to give evidence in court if called upon?'

'Buckley's chance of that happenin'. I won't be wastin' my life hangin' round a courthouse. I want nothin' more to do with Mrs Emerson.'

'I understand, Mr Lloyd. You've been more than helpful. We'll never speak of this again, I wish you well.'

Beth turns to walk away and remembers she has one final question.

'Did Mrs Emerson pay your hospital bills?'

He looks sheepish. 'I would of kept me trap shut, but she insisted.'

Beth slows down to a halt outside of Lydia's home, her tired legs almost giving away under her when she dismounts. Puffed, she wheels her bicycle to the front porch and leans it against the handrail. She rings the bell, hears the ringing reverberating all through the house, and waits. About to ring again, she notices the drapes in the front room are drawn open and the sun is pouring in. A moving shadow suggests someone is inside. Beth won't leave until she has spoken with Lydia. She plonks on the chair out front and gazes at a flock of rosellas heading for the flowering red bottlebrushes across the road. Ten minutes later, she rings the bell so loud she fears it could resound in her ears for eternity. Perhaps the person she thought she'd seen was simply the outline of wavering foliage reflecting on the windows. Comfortably seated, she mulls over the case. If only Nolan Lloyd had told her about Lydia's relationship with Charlotte when she'd first talked with him. And what about Irene, the dotty lady who'd gone to work on the wrong day, what does she have to do with Eric's death? According to her sister, Irene had repeated the word 'chair'. Lounge chair, sofa chair, dining chair, invalid chair. Eric's father was an invalid. Beth has a sudden desire to inspect Lydia's shed, perhaps there's a chair or chairs of interest within.

On her feet again, she moves to the side of the house. Straight ahead, there's a stone outbuilding with wide double doors painted bright red. Gingerly, Beth opens one of the doors. The building is large enough to house a family. Large windows on every wall provide ample light to see into every corner. Beth's thoughts turn to the times she'd enjoyed rummaging through her aunt's shed when it was full of discarded clothing, furniture and other curiosities – all of it sold now. This shed is grander though. It's an orderly space, strange for an untidy person like Eric; perhaps Nolan Lloyd tidied it up. Along the back wall, there's a thick timber bench with various tools spread across it. On the right hand side, heavy garden tools lean against the wall. A raincoat and a wide-brimmed hat hang from a coat stand. In the centre, there's a timber wheelbarrow, bright red in colour and spotlessly clean. Garden implements, watering cans, a pair of gumboots and several ceramic pots are arranged in a row on neat shelves. Beth clutches the arms of the wheelbarrow and pushes it to the side. Behind it, there's something covered in a blanket. She removes the cover and finds a solid timber invalid chair with two large iron wheels and two smaller ones in front, there's a decorative top rail, an elaborate wicker back, and armrests, recently polished by the looks of it. Pulling it out of the corner, she wheels it to and fro, it moves easily. Immersed in her thoughts she doesn't notice the footfalls coming towards the shed.

'What on earth are you doing here?' Lydia's face is flushed, and her brows drawn together.

'I thought you were out.'

'Are you in the habit of poking around people's sheds when they are out?'

'I rang the doorbell several times, I thought you might be in the shed.'

'I was working in the back garden.'

Observing Lydia's hands and pale blue day dress are immaculately clean, Beth doubts she was gardening.

'You seem fascinated by the invalid chair.'

'It's beautifully crafted and sturdy.'

'It belonged to Papa during his final years.'

'I noticed it's been well-maintained. Has it been used recently?'

Lydia crosses her arms and assumes a rigid stance. 'We keep it polished to preserve the memory of my father.'

Feeling vaguely vulnerable in Lydia's company, Beth's instinct is to leave immediately, but her desire to know what happened to Eric is a stronger compulsion.

'Why are you here, Beth?'

'I would like a word with you, if it's presently convenient.'

Lydia's face softens to almost friendly. 'I'm about to enjoy a glass of Charlotte's homemade ginger beer, would you like to join me?'

Beth gives an enthusiastic nod; having cycled all over town that morning, she is thirsty.

'Let's stay outside on the back porch – it's so pleasant in the sunshine.'

Beth is invited to sit at a round table with a colourful mosaic finish while Lydia disappears into the house to fetch their drinks. Beth's eyes trail across the backyard, the grass turned green and tall from recent rain, large black and orange butterflies bobbing about the blooming flower beds.

Lydia emerges from the house within minutes and sets down the glasses.

'Where's Charlotte today?'

'She's visiting Anna.'

'Anna Hopping?'

'You don't have to pretend you don't know. Charlotte has told me all about her struggling past.' Lydia raises her glass to her lips and sips. 'Drink up. You look a little peaky, no doubt from the exertion of cycling.'

Beth's mouth is as dry as chalk, but her glass sits untouched. Her head aches, the clanging doorbell is still ringing in her ears.

'Charlotte resides in my home now, I have plenty of room and Mrs Zambetti's boarding fees are exorbitant.'

'That sounds like a very convenient arrangement.'

'As you probably know, Eric bequeathed his insurance payout to Anna so she's financially secure.'

'I didn't know that, not through want of trying.' Beth lies.

'I wasn't cognisant either until a few days ago. Very unfair, considering I'd paid the hefty premiums.'

'You must feel very angry about that.'

Lydia takes a sip from her glass before speaking. 'It's a merry-go-round isn't it? My husband's lover is my cook's daughter. Anna is with child, probably Eric's.'

'Not to mention your intimate relationship with Charlotte.'

'Charlotte is my closest friend and confidante.'

'I visited Mr Nolan Lloyd this morning. He told me he'd seen you and Charlotte being intimate, like a man and a woman.'

Lydia glares at Beth. 'That's utter nonsense. No wonder Eric let him go. The man is a liar and a voyeur.'

'He told me you dismissed him.'

'Eric, me, the man in the moon, what does it matter?'

'He'd been spying on you and Charlotte. That's why you let him go.'

For a long moment, Lydia looks down and fiddles with the rings on her fingers. Then she raises her eyes and gives a resigned sigh. 'How much will your silence cost?'

'Do you think everyone can be bought, Lydia?'

'As a matter of fact, I do. Most people anyway.'

Lydia drains her glass, fixes her dark blue eyes on Beth and gives a weak smile. 'You haven't touched your ginger beer.'

Beth takes her glass, draws it to her mouth, feigns a sip, just enough to wet her lips. She feels dizzy, and wonders if it's something in the drink or simply dehydration.

'The plum blossoms are a delightful deep pink this year.'

Beth nods, studies the plum trees, barely visible beneath the climbing wisteria clinging to its flimsy branches like coiled snakes.

'Do you think I am trying to poison you, Beth?'

'I'm not sure.'

'I do not wish to harm you.' To prove her point, she clutches Beth's glass, pours some of the contents into her own empty glass and drinks. 'Now do you believe me?'

Beth does not reply, she lifts her glass to her dry lips and quaffs the remaining contents. Revitalised, she fixes her glare on Lydia. 'I know you tossed the pocketknife into the hollow. You didn't know I'd seen it in the drawer that one time you left me in Eric's office alone.'

Lydia regards Beth, dismay written all over her face. Beth has wedged in the final few pieces of the jigsaw puzzle. Bully for her.

'I can't prove anything, you know that, Lydia. I should have known better. I've taken a few wrong turns. But I think I've worked it out now.'

Her thin lips stretch into a gloating smile. 'Please enlighten me.'

'What I believe, Lydia, is this. While you were away in Port Adelaide Charlotte killed Eric, then she transported him into the bush in the invalid chair as far as the escarpment where she pushed him off the cliff. But Eric wasn't dead, he managed to crawl down the track as far as the clearing where he entered a tree hollow and died. Later, you discovered the pocketknife in his office drawer. You or Charlotte threw it into the hollow. You hired me to find Eric, dropped hints about his love of bushwalking, knew I'd assume he'd come to a bad end in the bush and eventually find him.'

'Touché.' Lydia is clapping her hands. 'I hadn't expected Mr Lloyd to tattle though. I paid handsomely for his silence. I didn't count on you persuading him to admit he's a voyeur.'

'You have no reason to fear Mr Lloyd; he's in very poor health and leaving Adelaide as we speak.'

Relieved, Lydia closes her eyes briefly. 'Charlotte is the love of my life. She consoled me when Eric was gallivanting around with Anna, she consoles me now. At first Eric didn't mind, he found it amusing, even titillating, but when he rekindled his relationship with Anna he changed. He wanted to divorce me and start a new life with Anna. He withdrew his assets from the bank and I thought he'd leave soon after. But he wanted more. He demanded I give him more than half of my substantial wealth. If I refused he threatened to report me to the constabulary and sell the scandalous story to the newspapers. I offered him enough to buy a home, start a business, and start a new life, but that wasn't enough. I wasn't going to be left a pauper.'

'So you and Charlotte planned to murder him.'

'There was no plan.'

'When did you discover Eric's body in the hollow?'

'About a week after the incident we dared to walk into the bush. He's body was gone, we believed he'd survived. We were terrified until we went for a longer walk and came across the tree hollow. As you know, we waited until the body decomposed before commissioning you to investigate.'

'What happened exactly on that fateful day? I imagine Charlotte has filled in the blanks.'

'Eric was seated at his bay window when he noticed Charlotte picking roses from his garden. They were for me, my welcome home bouquet. Eric hurried outside to confront Charlotte. He warned her if he caught her stealing his roses again she'd be dismissed. She told him in no uncertain terms that the house and gardens belonged to me. Furious, he clutched her shoulders and started yelling at her. Charlotte retaliated with a swift punch in the chest. She thought she'd winded him and he'd be up and about soon after. But he didn't get up. Eric was dead, or so she thought. She hurried to the shed, grabbed the invalid chair and hoisted him into it.'

'Where was Irene Howard at the time?'

'Irene was eating her lunch. The rumbling chair being wheeled into the house drew her out of the kitchen. She was very upset to see Eric slumped in the chair. Sweet Irene, she was one of the few people who enjoyed his silly jokes.' Lydia pauses to swallow a bitter taste rising in her throat. 'Charlotte accompanied Irene back to the kitchen, telling her that Eric had fainted from exhaustion and needed to rest. Irene was told to help herself to a tot of brandy to calm her nerves. Charlotte wheeled Eric into his study and left him there; she took his key from his lunch table and locked the door behind her. Then she returned to the kitchen and reassured Irene that Eric was sleeping soundly on his daybed. They drank brandy before leaving the house for the little village up the road where Charlotte put Irene in a cab and did some shopping. When she returned to the house she proceeded to wheel the chair into the bush and, well, you know the rest.'

'It must have been difficult pushing the chair along that bush track.'

'Despite being a woman of great strength Charlotte was exhausted when she returned at dusk. Yet, she mustered the energy to return the invalid chair to the shed, cook dinner, pop a note under the study door, and leave at her usual hour, taking the key with her. '

'So the study was locked when you returned home from Port Adelaide.'

'Yes, I didn't find out about Eric's fate until Charlotte turned up for work on Monday morning. With a few omissions, everything I told you was true: I had returned home and looked for Eric; I had looked through his study window as the room was locked; and yes, I did not sleep a wink that night. That's why I was a plausible victim when relating my plight to the policemen. When they thought I was out of earshot, one of them remarked, 'Mr Emerson's done a bunk and left the lady in the lurch.' His comment was sadly lacking in empathy yet proof they believed Eric had left me.'

'So Charlotte tidied the cutlery?'

'Yes, I was going to disarrange it but we decided it was solid proof he'd left the house calmly.'

'Keeping the door locked was a clever ploy suggesting he'd left the house with the intention of returning at a later date. Was there a spare key?'

'No, we used Eric's key.'

'Eric was keeping the door locked as his withdrawn savings were hidden inside.'

'Yes, I found the bundle of cash and locked it in the safe.'

'A perfect crime,' says Beth, 'the result of good luck and opportunity rather than astute planning.'

'You have risen to the challenge. I anticipated you'd find him but you have exceeded all my expectations.'

'Charlotte killed him and you covered it up.'

'If he'd just gone away with Anna Hopping he'd still be alive today, but he simply couldn't forgo a lavish lifestyle.'

'It worked out well for you.'

'Not entirely, I miss Eric. We had been together for eight years.'

'So you've forgiven Charlotte.'

'There's nothing to forgive, she didn't mean to kill him. Charlotte was defending herself.'

'What will you do now?'

'It's been a difficult year, Eric's indiscretions, reporters, police tramping through my home and garden. I'm glad it's over. I'm going to France in a few weeks. I've booked passages for myself and Charlotte. Parisians are so much more open-minded than the parochial population in Adelaide. We're going to live openly, the way we like. Be ourselves.'

'How long will you be away?'

'Months, maybe years. Mr Stirling will manage my finances and my home whilst I'm away.'

'Does he know about your relationship with Charlotte?'

'My personal life is none of his business.'

Lydia gazes at Beth, perhaps wondering what she'd do with the incriminating information she has. Beth has never seen Lydia look so vulnerable; there is uneasiness in her countenance, her life as she knows it could disappear like steam from a boiling kettle – her planned voyage across the oceans in peril. Perhaps she wishes she'd poisoned Beth after all. But Lydia weeps, as if the murder, the deceit, and the lies, are pouring out in tears, cleansing her memory, cleansing her past of everything damaging.

Taken aback, Beth waits for her to regain her composure.

Lydia clutches a handkerchief from her sleeve and wipes her nose. Silent for a long while, her vulnerability diminishes, strong will again taking control. Summoning back her steely demeanour, she tucks her handkerchief into her sleeve and glares at Beth before speaking. 'You have no proof.'

'Correct.'

'I'm friends with Inspector Taylor. Eric and I were often invited to dinner parties at his home. I assure you the constabulary think you're a laughing stock, a dog-catcher masquerading as an investigator.'

Beth does all she can to hold back her rage. 'That doesn't surprise me at all, Lydia. If I reported you they'd tell me to let men get on with their jobs.'

'The felons, thieves and thugs in Adelaide are safe as long as they're in charge.' Lydia laughs nervously.

'Fortunately for you, I don't work for the constabulary, never will, solely because I am a woman. I really don't find anything amusing about that.'

Lydia fixes her gaze on Beth. 'It is utterly unfair.'

Beth gets to her feet, stands tall and takes her leave. The irony does not escape her; three women will avoid the hangman's noose because a female investigator is not and never will be permitted to join the constabulary. She cannot arrest them. She cannot report them. She would never be taken seriously. Besides Faith and Harry, she will never say a word to anyone, not even to Vincent. The constabulary owes her, they are wrong to deny her the right to enter their ranks, whereas, she owes them nothing; she is under no obligation to report miscreants, she is free to reveal what she sees fit. And she will not reveal this. Thinking about the law, she decides it's a fickle dogma, never black or white; rather it is painted in more colours than she'd ever imagined.

FRIDAY, 21ST SEPTEMBER

The three sleuths are comfortably installed in the drawing room sipping sherry, the fire noticeably out, the spring weather perfect without its assistance. Beth is eager to share the details of her menacing interaction with Lydia but she keeps it to herself for the moment, at least until they have Carl back in their clutches. She starts the meeting by placing her recently acquired pocketknife on the table. 'Lydia gave it to me, it was Eric's and she never wants to see it again. It's worth a pretty penny, the handle is pure gold. I was going to keep it for self-defence, but I think we should save it for the pawnbroker should we find ourselves in dire financial circumstances again.'

'A wise decision, use your hat pins instead.' Faith grins.

Beth agrees and asks her partners if they'd like the good news or the bad news first. Good news triumphs.

'The good news is we're in the black again. Mrs Emerson has paid our fees and expenses with a generous thirty-five pound bonus for any damage caused to our clothing and property.'

They raise their glasses to toast a successful outcome and financial security, at least for the moment.

'The bad news is Mr Burkett has given us two weeks to find Carl. After that deadline, he's going to purchase another dog, perhaps one less prone to running away. Have you discovered any more details about Hall's travel arrangements tomorrow evening, Harry?'

'Hall and his mate are booked in cabin number six, third class shared accommodation. Carl would be locked in, probably wearing a muzzle. We'll break into the cabin, grab Carl and run for it. It won't be easy, they could be armed.'

'That's a plan?' Faith asks. 'What if they're in the cabin?'

'We'll cross that bridge when we get to it. They'd probably be on deck like everyone else.'

'We trust your experience will come to the fore, Harry. Weather permitting, Tillie, Sam and I are going to Semaphore beach tomorrow,' says Beth.

'There's a lovely teahouse on the port, suitably named the Wharf Teahouse,' says Faith. 'Harry and I will meet you there around five.'

'I have some good news to impart,' says Harry. 'Would you like to read about it in the newspapers tomorrow morning or would you like to hear it *tout de suite*?' He sits back in his chair and takes a sip of his sherry.

'Stop teasing, Harry, tell us your news,' Faith insists.

Smiling, he throws his arms in the air in surrender. 'Three generations of O'Halloran men have been arrested. Police searched their premises this afternoon, and significant, undisputable evidence was collected against them. An Adelaide lawyer, who asked to remain anonymous, had secretly carved his name beneath the furniture he'd purchased before it was stolen. An undercover policeman working in their factory traced the furniture as it was restored and delivered to a new client. Jack Spencer has also given evidence against them in exchange for a reduced sentence.'

'Was Vincent Stirling the lawyer?' Beth asks.

'Sorry I couldn't inform you of his involvement earlier, but …'

'I understand you gave your word, Harry. It's funny because I remember Vincent telling me O'Halloran's days in business were numbered. I thought at the time it was a strange comment.'

'The poor bloke was dying to let the cat out of the bag, but he couldn't.'

SATURDAY, 22ND SEPTEMBER

The sea is calm with knee-high waves coasting gently to the shore. Seagulls shriek beneath a clear blue sky. In the distance, fishing boats are anchored near the jetties, their white sails glowing in the sun. Beth, Tillie and Sam are enjoying the white sands of Semaphore Beach along with several other families, mostly mothers and young children. Wearing wide-brimmed hats and sitting on a picnic blanket, Beth and Tillie chat while Sam is playing in the sand with his bucket and spade. Several boisterous children join him to build castles and moats and engage in imaginary battles between knights and dragons.

'Edward and I went to the town hall last night, the concert was amazing but we had to sit miles apart in case the headmistress turned up,' says Tillie.

'It must be awkward working in the same school.'

'We have to steer clear of each other. I dare not even glance at him, unlike the headmistress who openly enjoys his company – one law for her and another for the rest of us.'

'Lucky for you she's well past her prime.'

'Edward only has eyes for me,' Tillie giggles, miming a violin virtuoso.

'Of course he does. I'm meeting Aunt Faith and Harry at the Wharf Teahouse around five. We intend getting Carl back. We think Andrew Hall is taking him to Fremantle on the steamer leaving tonight. The reward is a whopping twenty-five pounds.'

'Sounds lucrative, yet dangerous.'

'I appreciate your taking Sam home, just in case there's violence.'

'I'm looking forward to his company.'

They sit in silence watching the girls and boys play. An older boy arrives throwing a ball into the air and catching it. Soon after, assembled in a wide circle, chirpy children are playing catch and throw. Beth wonders why the older boy would play with little ones; he's at least twelve, maybe older. Skinny and ragged, if he's an orphan he'll request a fee for entertaining the children.

Guided by the older boy, the circle of children becomes a line in preparation for a race. At his command, the children run along the beach, the older boy out front. Watching the race, the mothers cheer their children on, happy to see them participating. Beth notices the older boy dropping the ball and taking Sam's hand, perhaps to help him along. Several of the youngest children stop racing and wearily return to their mothers. Only the tall boy and Sam are still running. Edgy, Beth leaps to her feet, Sam is too far away and with a total stranger. She hurries off, her legs are strong from cycling but her skirts are heavy and her boots are full of sand. Barely clad and barefoot, the boy is sprinting. Further on, she is shouting Sam's name and waving her arm in the air beckoning the boy to stop. The boy scoops Sam up and holding him on his right hip he dashes along the beach at great speed. He ascends the steps two at a time and leaps onto the kerb where a one-horse cart holding two men is waiting. Sam is lifted into the cart and the boy is paid the agreed fee before he darts off. Beth picks up her pace. Panting, breathless, her hat fallen from her head, she reaches the steps. A deep voice urges the horse on, the cart creaks and clanks as it jerks forward, just yards away now, surely the driver will respond to her gesturing him to stop. But it picks up speed and passes her just as her boots step onto the kerb. Sam is positioned between the two men now. Running after the cab, falling more and more behind, Beth watches it roll down the street, turn left and disappear. If only she could fly.

Sam looks out the window at the stone buildings rushing by. The cart turns into a side street and continues until it crosses the Jervois Bridge and travels onwards to Port Adelaide.

'Why didn't you wait for Mama?'

'She will come to us later.'

'When?'

'Soon.'

'What's your name?'

'Ramin Durrani. I am the brother of your father. You can call me Uncle Ramin.'

'Mama told me not to talk to you.'

'I am your uncle, you can talk to me.'

Fifteen minutes later, Ramin and Sam climb out. Ramin pays the driver and waits for the cart to disappear before entering a squat building with a thick timber door. Ramin knocks three times before a tall man with a bushy black beard answers and ushers them inside. Books and children's toys are spread across a table for Sam to occupy himself while they wait. Ramin tells Sam they are going on a voyage to visit his grandparents in Afghanistan.

'Do you have our tickets?'

'Yes.' He shows Sam his ticket.

Sam has never seen a steamer ticket before, he studies it. 'My name isn't Arif Durrani, that's Papa's name.'

'You can read?'

Sam nods.

'Our name is a secret.'

'Why?'

'You ask too many questions.'

'Is Mama coming?'

'Soon.' Ramin is certain Beth will pursue her son and return to Afghanistan with him. His bearded friend hands Sam a glass of milk and a pastry slathered in honey. The men's kindness puts him at ease, but he doesn't understand what they are saying to each other. When he enquires he is told he will soon learn their language.

'Is *soon* your favourite word, Uncle Ramin?'

Ramin laughs heartily and tousles Sam's hair. 'You are just like your papa.'

Her heart pounding, Beth hurries back to the beach. Tillie has gathered their belongings and is waiting on the side of the road. Handing Beth her hat she'd collected along the beach, she suggests they report the kidnapping to the police. Beth insists they keep the police out of it.

'My good friend, Vincent Stirling, lives in Port Adelaide; he'll help us look for Sam. We'll leave our belongings at his home. If he's not there I know where he keeps his key. When Aunt Faith and Harry get here they'll help us. We'll find him. We have to.'

'Got any ideas?'

'I'm hoping Ramin will board the steamer bound for Fremantle tonight.'

'Ramin?'

'He's Arif's brother. Sam's uncle.'

'Why didn't you mention him before?'

'He wants to take Sam to Afghanistan, I'll tell you about it later. If we alert the police their presence would make Ramin run and we'd never find him. Or worse, he might do something reckless. We have to be discreet.'

'I hope you know what you're doing, Beth.'

They board the train for Port Adelaide just two miles away and hurry to Vincent's home, a short walk from the station. He cannot believe his eyes when he finds two sobbing women on his doorstep. He ushers them inside and insists they accept a glass of his best brandy and take a few minutes to relax. Beth shares her story, how Ramin has been stalking her for the past two months and now he has her son.

The three of them spend hours scouring the main streets, tearooms, restaurants and parks. Exhausted and despondent, they take tea in the Wharf Teahouse. With just a short time to spare before Faith and Harry are to meet them at the wharf, they sip their drinks in silence. Beth does all she can to dispel fears that Ramin and Sam may have travelled back to Adelaide and could be hiding elsewhere. 'He will sail with me. We leave soon', he had said, more than once. She hopes it's the steamer sailing out tonight.

Docked in Port Adelaide, the chimneys and rigging well-defined in the golden glow of late afternoon, an impressive steamer will soon set sail for Fremantle and then onwards to Colombo. Excited passengers are jostling each other as they hurriedly make their way to the ship. The limited space on the bustling wharf is taken up with well-wishers, sightseers, horses, bicycles and cheery porters pushing luggage barrows.

The minute she lays eyes on her niece's despairing faces, Vincent beside them and Sam nowhere to be seen, Faith knows something is wrong. She, Beth and Tillie form an empowering hug. 'We'll find him,' they chant in unison until the hope becomes a surety.

The group put their heads together to come up with a plan to free Samuel. It is decided that Faith and Tillie remain in the wagon, the elevation allowing them to see over the crowd. Vincent and Beth will go first with a plausible reason for going on board. Harry will follow them flashing his police badge, albeit invalid, at the boarding officer. Their first call will be shared cabin number six, in the third class. As soon as they find Carl he'd be given a feed of Harry's biscuits before being put to work. His hunger satisfied, he'd have an item of Sam's clothing held under his nose and told to find Sam, the child Carl had met several times in the past.

With a clear strategy in place, Beth and Vincent approach the gangplank where a man in uniform is checking tickets and advising passengers to ask the officer on deck for directions to their cabins.

Beth explains her dilemma, she had been hoping to say goodbye to her son before he sailed with his uncle but she had been delayed on the way. Told she has thirty minutes before the gangplank is lowered she is allowed to go on board. Just behind them, Harry flashes his police identity and is permitted to embark. With no time to waste, they stride up the gangplank and descend the steps to third class cabins which are marked in red numbers. Most of the passengers are outside on deck waving to their friends and families. They come to cabin number six and knock to check Hall isn't within. Beth uses her hat pin to unlock the door. Carl leaps to his feet and looks up, his big brown eyes moist with confusion and woe. The muzzle on his face is far too tight, it's no wonder he isn't making any noise. Beth removes it and gives him some dog biscuits, then she holds Sam's coat under his nose. 'Come on Carl, find Sam for me and I'll take you home.' Carl's tail is wagging madly, a familiar face, his freedom restored.

Holding onto the leash, Harry is pulled along so fast he can barely control it. Carl leads them out to the bow where there are fewer people. Ramin is leaning against the rail, his eyes on the fiery red sunset glimmering over the calm water. Sam is seated in a deck chair, eating an apple. His tail wagging, Carl goes straight to Sam, licks his hand and gobbles what's left of his apple.

'Mama!'

Ramin wheels around, but as Carl begins snarling at him he stands stock-still.

Beth takes Sam in her arms then quickly passes him to Vincent. 'Take him to my sister and aunt, I'll be down soon.'

'Come with us, Beth, there isn't much time.'

'Please, Vincent. I just want a word with Ramin.'

Carrying Sam, Vincent moves away.

Beth looks into Ramin's sad eyes. 'Go home, Ramin. Your mother needs you, your family needs you. If you try to take Sam again, I'll report you to the police.'

'I come with you to say goodbye, then I go home.'

'You've passed a stolen afternoon with your nephew, that's all you're getting.'

Beth and Harry leave without looking back. Anxious to disembark, Carl gallops like a stallion with Harry barely able to stay on his feet. Beth moves along the deck, memories of her last sea voyage on her mind. Andrew Hall catches sight of her as she is about to disembark. He and his mate rush to their cabin to discover Carl is gone. Guessing it was the red-headed woman, Hall arms himself with a loaded pistol. Telling his mate to wait in the cabin he hurries off to retrieve what belongs to him.

With little time before the final boarding call, Hall elbows his way through the crowd, his fury rising with every step. Then he sees Carl tethered to Harry's wagon. Beth is laughing with her family gathered around her, probably at his expense. Just as Hall joins the group, Carl starts growling. Holding Sam in her arms, Beth tightens her grip. The pistol in Hall's hand is pointed directly at Sam. He warns Harry to untether the dog and give him the leash or he'll shoot. Just as Hall pulls back the hammer, Ramin leaps in front of Beth, his arms reaching out either side of him. Harry quickly unravels the leash. Freed, the dog runs headlong into Hall's legs setting off the gun, the loud blast subdued by the ship's roaring horn. Carl scampers away, his leash dragging along behind him. There's a call to passengers to board the steamer. People are shouting their farewells, waving their hats and handkerchiefs in the air, totally oblivious to the calamity going on in their midst. In shock, Hall drops the pistol. A final warning to passengers to board the ship puts him back on track. He dashes away, making it by seconds before the gangplank is removed. Harry picks up the pistol and places it in his wagon under his seat.

Ramin's hand presses his shirt, it's wet with blood. He looks dazed.

'Oh Lord, he's been shot.' Vincent catches Ramin before he falls.

'Let's get him in the wagon, we'll take him home,' says Beth urgently, 'and we'll stop at Doctor Eva's on the way; she'll help us.'

Harry and Vincent lift Ramin into the wagon. Beth and Faith sit one on each side of him. Tillie and Sam climb onto the front seat next to Harry. The wagon is overloaded; they'd have to take the eight-mile ride home with great caution, especially at night when it's difficult to avoid the potholes in the road.

Vincent offers to travel with them but Beth tells him they have the situation under control. Before going home he wishes them well and promises to make contact soon.

Moonlit, the steamer moves out to sea. The crowd disperses, cabs and buggies roll away and the street clears, the only signs of the crowd and brouhaha are food scraps, fallen hats and the odd hand-kerchief. Soon the street orphans will be out tramping the streets on the lookout for a fallen coin or two.

'Is Uncle Ramin all right, Mama?'

'He'll be all right, my darling boy. We'll take him home with us and help him,' says Beth, kissing Sam's sweet face.

Five minutes away from home, they stop by Eva's house. Her medical bag in hand, she climbs into the already crowded wagon and returns with them.

When they reach the house a room on the lower floor is prepared for Ramin. Eva cleans his wound, inspects the injury and finds the bullet had gouged an inch trench in his shoulder. The impact had knocked him back against the wagon and stunned him. There is no sign of the bullet though; it must have bounced off sideways. After giving him a strong dose of laudanum she washes the area with alcohol and sutures it together. Then, with Harry's help she applies a thick bandage. The prognosis is good provided sepsis doesn't set in. She promises to return within a day or two to check on him and to replace the bandages. Harry gives Eva a lift home.

Unable to sleep, Faith, Harry, Beth and Tillie sit in the kitchen for hours sipping hot cocoa and discussing the events of the night. Sam has fallen asleep in Beth's arms. She wants to hold onto him forever, to keep him safe forever.

SUNDAY, 23RD SEPTEMBER

The following morning, Beth wakes up beside Sam. He wraps his arms around her neck and asks after Uncle Ramin.

'He's asleep.' Beth looks into her son's green eyes and asks the question that has haunted her mind since he was abducted. 'Was Uncle Ramin kind to you?'

'Yes, he gave me lollies and cakes and toys to play with.' Then in his unique tongue he recounts everything Ramin had told him about Afghanistan. He smiles when he says he would like to learn how to ride a horse and swim in a river. But he wasn't happy about Ramin changing his name to Arif, his father's name.

'Yes, your name is Samuel and you belong here. When you're a grown man you can make your own decisions.'

'Can we see him, Mama?'

Beth gets out of bed, slips on her dressing gown and tells Sam to do the same. They move along the hall and down the stairs. Beth follows Sam who skips along to Ramin's room. Lying supine, Ramin is sleeping soundly. Beth lays her hand on his brow, he isn't feverish. Using a teaspoon she dribbles some water between his lips, he swallows without waking. She remembers those nursing rituals when Arif lay in bed ill for weeks on end. Sam offers to take over but he misses and dribbles water down the patient's chin, he giggles and tries again. When the water touches Ramin's lips he moans, his eyes twitch and he settles again.

'He's awake, Mama.'

'He's still asleep but he seems to be responding a little. That's a good sign.' Beth smiles. 'Well done, Doctor Samuel.'

'He said he would teach me how to make a kite.'

'I'm sure he will when he's better.'

'Will we try to find Carl?'

'We'll look for him when we get time. Go to breakfast, darling boy. Auntie Tillie's already downstairs tell her I'll be down soon.'

Gazing at Ramin, a man still mourning the brother he'd idolised, Beth tries to consider him as a family guest come to visit them. In a way she admires him for tracking her down, not out of malice but driven by the love of his family, the core of his existence. When he tried to stop her from leaving Afghanistan he was equally driven by loyalty.

'You silly man, you should be at home helping your mother,' says Beth, placing a damp cloth on his brow.

He mutters a few words in his first language and dozes off again.

Ramin's presence calls to mind Beth's final weeks living in the Durrani household, although surrounded by Arif's family she felt lonely. Everyone was fussing over her simply because she was carrying Arif's child. She would often dream of crossing the Khyber Pass and travelling home to Australia. Sometimes she imagined she could smell the eucalypts. But a life sustained by dreams was not fulfilling, she desired real freedom for herself and her child. She had to leave. The ideal opportunity came on Mina's wedding day. Arif's widowed sister was marrying for the second time. It was a grand affair with more than fifty guests. Closing her eyes, Beth's mind is taken back to the day of the wedding.

~

Everyone except Gabina (too busy entertaining Roshina) was assigned a chore. Beth worked in the kitchen with Nazdana and

Nazreen. Ramin, his father and several farmhands set up the tables and the dance areas in the large courtyard. The celebrations began at midday. Following a sumptuous lunch, music, laughter, animated chatter and dancing carried the day. The zerbaghali drums were beating, and several relatives took it in turns to play the rubab, a lute-like instrument. Just before the speeches began, Beth told her mother-in-law she wished to rest. As she hurried to her room, she felt Ramin's eyes on her and knew he was following her. She locked the door, listened for his clonking boots moving down the hall and clutched a bag containing her scant possessions and money. Arif had told her to take her favourite horse. She threw on a coat, riding boots and a hat and leaned out the window to check if anyone was about. The coast was clear; she climbed out, landed on her feet, and scuttled across the space between the house and the stable. This would be her last chance, if caught the money would be appropriated from her. Her pulse pounding she hurried inside the barn where her horse was stabled. Stroking his face, she told him he was going on a journey. Thankfully, the beating drums concealed his neighing response. She lifted a saddle from the timber rail and thrust it on his back, waited a minute or two until her body recovered from the heavy weight of it. She felt her baby move, the bump of a foot kicking, a small tug, her child's message all was well. The saddle fastened, she stroked the horse's nose. A reliable colt, he'd take her to Jalalabad. She fastened her bag to the saddle and mounted. The crack of a stock whip made her jump. Ramin flicked the whip in the air, then against the stable door, and again in the air as he approached her. He demanded she dismount and return to the wedding party. She knew he would not hurt her, she was carrying Arif's child. She told him to get out of the way, she was leaving. His bluff exposed, he dropped the whip and rushed towards her, reaching out as if preparing to pull her off the horse. Kicking the side of the horse, she rushed past him. He tried to grab the bridle but her booted foot jutted out and struck him hard. Fifty yards on, she halted and looked back. Ramin was lying on the ground, not moving, blood oozing from a head wound. As she was wondering whether or not to help him two employees turned up. One of them dashed off to inform Ramin's father and one stayed with Ramin. They would not pursue her, nor would they make a scene or do anything to ruin Mina's wedding day. Without another thought, she galloped away.

Beth travelled at speed until she reached Jalalabad late in the afternoon. She hurried to Michael's home. Calmed, given a cup of tea, she recounted the details of her escape. He advised rest and promised he'd make some enquiries about Ramin's injuries. Beth stayed several days in Michael's large home. One of Ramin's employees came to the house to ask after her, Michael told him she had left Jalalabad for India. When Michael asked after Ramin he was met with silence.

Michael arranged for Beth to travel with a troop of British soldiers across the Khyber Pass as far as Peshawar. One of the soldiers accompanied her to Mr and Mrs Halligan's home where she received a warm welcome. Several days later, she boarded a train for Karachi and stayed with Ayishah's family until she felt strong enough to face the sea journey home. Whilst there, in the privacy of her bedroom, she studied her reflection in a full-length mirror, her breasts and belly large and rounded. She'd never imagined her body could stretch with such amazing elasticity to accommodate a small life growing within her – she wondered if she'd make it home in time. Ayishah's family urged her to stay with them until the birth, but she was eager to return to Adelaide. They insisted on purchasing a first-class ticket for her. From Karachi, she boarded a steamer for Colombo and onward to Fremantle and Port Adelaide.

The Indian Ocean offered smooth sailing to Fremantle, where many passengers disembarked and were replaced with new passengers for Port Adelaide. Two gentle days went by before they encountered rough weather. Beth was in her cabin, soothed by the gentle rocking of the ship when the storm struck and caught the crew and passengers by surprise. She looked out the porthole in dismay as the sea turned black and white-rimmed waves were pounding the decks. When a huge wave struck the ship it shook so hard passengers were thrown to the floor and furniture scuttled across the dining room. Beth clung to her bed as the ship tilted to the side, threatening to capsize any minute. Ill from fear and seasickness, she threw up. Another wave struck and the ship tilted further to the side. Her head reeled; she threw up again and again until there was nothing left in her stomach. The pounding waves lasted for days. Crew members regularly knocked on cabin doors to ascertain the occupants were coping. Helpless, feeling the ship bend and twist to the sea's will, lying on her bed, Beth got through the worst times by speaking to her baby, telling him to be calm, they would soon be home. The storm took its toll on the ship's crew and passengers, especially at night when the howling wind kept everyone awake. The briny air did little to quash the overwhelming odour of vomit in almost every corner of the ship. Morale was low amongst everyone on board; many feared the creaking steamer would fall apart if the storm lasted much longer. Some sixty knots from Port Adelaide the storm abated. Needing a service, the weather-beaten steamer tottered into the dock mid-morning. Weakened by dread, illness and fatigue, the passengers disembarked with the help of the crew. On land, some passengers were kneeling on the earth as if they'd been shipwrecked and had swum ashore. Some were praying. There were people everywhere, hugging each other, laughing or crying or both. Policemen were helping disorientated people regain control of their land legs. Several injured were taken to Adelaide Hospital. They wanted to take Beth to the hospital but she insisted on making her way home. That was when a liquid ran down her legs and she could not stand upright any longer. Falling, she thought she was being sucked into the ground. Assisted by two nurses, themselves looking mighty ill, she was again on her feet. How Samuel knew he was home and could venture into the outside world was beyond her.

The repeated sound of her name turned her attention to an older woman running towards her with arms outstretched. Beth blacked out before being helped into a cab and taken home. Aunt Faith summoned a midwife. Hours later, a baby's cry resounded through the house.

MONDAY, 24TH SEPTEMBER

His eyes wide open, he regards the clean bandage wrapped around his shoulder, lifts his head and looks about the unfamiliar room. Then it comes to him, that night in Port Adelaide, he was on board the steamer with Samuel. It was all going so well until Beth turned up. Ramin vaguely recalls the chaos of that night, an angry man with a pistol, a dog running off, and the deafening ship's horn. He assumes he is in a hospital under police guard. Stifling a groan he sits up, waits for the giddiness to subside then places his feet on the floor. Clutching the bedhead he stands upright. Conscious his hands are shaking he waits for several minutes until his balance is restored. The door is closed, possibly locked. He manages two short steps before tumbling.

A short time later, Beth finds him lying on the floor, his bandages bloodstained. She helps him back into bed. His first words are a request for his rucksack.

Beth glares at him. 'A jolly good morning to you as well.'

'My rucksack.'

'Yes, we have it, and the leather purse within.'

He sits back, relieved. It contains the means for his return home. 'What is this place?'

'My family's home, we're caring for you. As soon as you're well enough to travel you'll be on the first ship to Fremantle and beyond.'

'I am well.' He tries to sit up too quickly and moans as pain shoots across his shoulder.

'You're not strong enough to travel yet.'

Appalled by her brother-in-law's rudeness, she gives him a piece of her mind but finds he has dozed off half way through her tirade.

TUESDAY, 23RD OCTOBER

Faith is reading the paper when Beth enters the kitchen. Harry has already set the cast iron stove alight; she throws in enough wood to keep the kettle hot and sets about making a pot of porridge.

'Ramin and Sam had an early breakfast of bread and fruit. They're making kites. It might be windy enough to fly them today,' says Beth.

Immersed in her newspaper, Faith nods her head without having heard a word. 'Martha Needle, a South Australian citizen who'd moved to Melbourne, was hanged yesterday in Old Melbourne Gaol.'

'What did she do?'

'She poisoned five people, including her three children, and attempted to poison another man with arsenic. The strange thing is, she collected a fortune in insurance payouts but spent most of it on an elaborate family grave which she visited regularly.'

'Lydia and Charlotte are saints compared to Martha Needle.'

Faith looks up from her newspaper. 'They were both fond of Eric Emerson but I guess they couldn't see any other way out. If what Lydia told you is true, and we've only got her word for it, the man wanted everything: his lover, his freedom and Lydia's wealth.'

'She seemed genuine.'

'Some people are adept liars.'

'The porridge is just about ready. If you could tear yourself away from the gruesome news and grab some bowls ...'

Faith lays her newspaper down. 'Do you trust him?'

'Who?'

'Ramin.'

'Of course I do, he's very fond of Sam.'

'Why do you lock Sam's door at night then?'

'Just to put my mind at rest.'

Before they start making kites, Ramin tells Sam all about the history of kite running in Afghanistan, and how it is an ancient pastime that involves mid-air duels between opponents. He draws pictures of two rivals flying kites and explains how one of them must cut loose the string of his competitor to win. Normally, powdered glass is applied to the string to make it sharp enough to snip a competitor's string, but they will not be using the powder today. Sam asks what happens to the kite that is cut loose and is told that it belongs to whoever catches it.

'Did Papa make kites?'

'Arif taught me how to make them when I was your age. My brother taught me many things.'

A pile of lightweight bamboo sticks, sheets of flimsy paper, scissors and string are spread across the veranda table. Heeding Ramin's instructions, Sam cuts his paper into a diamond shape, three feet wide. Then he ties a bamboo stick to each corner. Tying the string to the kite is the most difficult step but Sam persists, and after several attempts, he succeeds. Their handiwork finished, they use black paint to design an eagle on each of their kites.

'Will we fly our kites today?'

'Later if the wind ...'

'Flares up,' Sam completes Ramin's sentence, his overplayed mimed explanation more like a volcano erupting than the wind flaring up.

'Yes, flare up.'

'Are you going to stay with us, Uncle Ramin?'

'I will soon go home to my country. Do you wish to come with me?'

Sam shakes his head. 'Why don't you stay here?'

'My family need me.'

'I'm your family.'

'I cannot live in two places at the same time,' Ramin smiles.

By late afternoon, the wind is brisk enough to launch their kites. Faith, Harry and Beth are assembled on the veranda cheering them on.

'Put your back to the wind,' Ramin says, standing behind Sam, guiding his every move. 'Point the nose of the kite upwards.'

'Eagles don't have noses,' Sam laughs out loud. 'They have beaks!'

Ramin tells Sam to pull on the string so the kite flies higher. Sam screams with delight as the kite climbs into the sky, the wind keeping it buoyant. More like a big brother than an uncle, Ramin is running along with Sam, their arms raised, their hands grasping the string, their kites soaring and hovering hundreds of feet into the air like a pair of broad-winged birds.

'What if the birds take us high in the sky and drop us into the clouds?' Sam laughs and Ramin laughs back until his eyes are filled with tears.

WEDNESDAY, 7TH NOVEMBER

The tide is at its peak, the sea is calm. An imposing steamer is docked in Port Adelaide, her two thick chimneys billowing black smoke. Several sprightly sailors are rolling the last of the teak barrels containing provisions up the gangplank. Jaunty porters are pushing barrows loaded with trunks. Preparations almost ready, the steamer will soon set sail for Fremantle, then north to Colombo and onwards.

Amongst the crowd of well-wishers, dressed in their Sunday best, Beth, Sam, Faith and Harry are seeing Ramin off.

'Write to me,' says Ramin, shaking Sam's hand.

'When I'm grown up I might come and see you,' Sam responds.

The ship's horn roars a final call to board. Ramin bids everyone farewell. Without holding onto the rails, he strides up the gangplank and steps onto the steamer, his rucksack strung over his shoulders containing pictures and postcards of life in Adelaide and photographs of Sam. The thought of his mother's face when she sees those photographs makes him smile.

Standing on deck, Ramin scans the noisy crowd trying to catch a last glimpse of Sam. Then he spots him perched on Harry's shoulders. He doesn't know if Sam can see him, but he waves anyway. The gangplank is lowered to the docks, and the ropes are unfurled from the mooring bollards and cast aside. Clouds of black smoke surge from the chimneys as the ship sets sail.

'Will Uncle Ramin come back, Mama?'

'You and Ramin will write lots of letters to one another.' Beth gently rubs Sam's tears from his eyes. 'Would you like an apple pie?'

Sam bobs his head. 'Mmm.'

They move off strolling along the brick path towards the smaller jetties where fishermen stand immobile for hours, poised to catch a big one. Beth is surprised to see Paddy the Pieman's red cart still in service, but now it is his son who runs the business. A kitchen on wheels with a smoking stove pipe chimney, there's an assortment of pies to choose from. They purchase apple pies and eat them sitting on the docks observing a school of stingrays moving gracefully through the water. Two barefoot boys wearing shorts down to the knees and neat oversized shirts approach them, their golden hair gleaming in the sunshine. Harry opens a bag of lollies and Sam offers some to the boys. The older boy has a dog on a leash. Sam asks them if the dog bites. The boys chuckle and tell him the dog is as gentle as a kitten. The large black dog with the slobbering jaws rolls over onto his back and enjoys a tickle. 'What's his name?' asks Sam, patting his soft fur.

'Carl,' responds the older boy who goes on to recount the story about how they found him sleeping in the sand hills. Carl was weak and hungry and they had to use their billy cart to haul him home. They knew his name was Carl because his collar and leash were still attached to his neck. Their mother, who had no intention of letting them keep him, placed an advertisement in the local *Gazette*. Not one person responded. By then, they'd formed a bond with Carl and decided to keep him. It all comes together in Beth's mind: rescuing Sam, Ramin shot and Carl storming off into the night, his leash trailing behind him. By the time she and Harry looked for him all over Port Adelaide, it was too late. They'd missed out on the reward, but today Carl is happier in the company of adventurous children.

TUESDAY, 11TH DECEMBER

Beth is munching a slice of toast and marmalade when Faith enters the kitchen and hands her a letter from Anna Hopping.

'I wonder how she's going.' Beth wipes her sticky fingers on her apron before opening the letter and as Faith is hovering over her she reads it aloud.

> Dear Beth,
> I am writing to thank you for all your assistance during our difficult times. I thought you would like to hear some good news. I gave birth to a healthy baby girl three weeks ago. Her name is Erica. Mama can't stop looking at her and Sophie is thrilled to have a little sister.
> I have joined the Suffrage League and made some lovely new friends. They think I am a particularly special member as I have lived a hard life and understand the life, views and needs of the poor. Who knows I may enter parliament one of these days! Or perhaps my daughters will. Surely, by the 1920s parliament will comprise at least fifty percent women.
> We are living well, we feel very secure. As a widow, I am permitted to have my own bank account, so I don't have to hide money beneath the floorboards anymore.
> I wish you and your family a wonderful Christmas and year ahead. You are always welcome to visit us any time, perhaps accompanied by your son who might enjoy Sophie's company.

Yours very sincerely,
Anna Hopping

PS. My friends have assured me my voice matters and I believe it does. My letter has been edited by one of my educated friends in the Women's League, and she has very kindly offered to tutor me each week. I am hoping within a year or so to submit articles to the local newspaper on matters that concern women and children. In other words, I wish to make a difference for those less fortunate than myself.

'Good Lord, Beth, you're crying. What's wrong?'

'I felt guilty at the time suggesting she join the suffragettes, totally disregarding her dire circumstances. It seems she wanted to all along, like so many women probably do. Maybe I wielded a small influence on her ambitions.'

'Of course you did.' Faith wraps her arms around her niece.

WEDNESDAY, 19TH DECEMBER

A supporter of women's suffrage and a member of the Women's Suffrage League, Robert Caldwell has during his term as a Member of the South Australian House of Assembly presented three unsuccessful female Suffrage Bills to the South Australian Parliament. His tenacity was rewarded on 18th December 1894 when he and thirty other parliamentarians supported the final passing of the Bill to enfranchise women in South Australia, with no restrictions by age or marital status. South Australian women became the first in the world to achieve the right to vote and enter politics as members of parliament.

Beaming a wide smile, Faith enters the office waving the newspaper. 'We must celebrate tonight, all women, not just rate payers have the right to vote in elections.'

'Let me see it,' Beth snaps the newspaper and reads aloud:

The South Australian Parliament has passed the Constitutional Amendment Act following a decade-long struggle to include women in the electoral process. The Bill giving women in South Australia the right to vote and the right to stand for Parliament, subject to the same qualifications and the same manner as men, will be signed into law in February 1895 when the Act is approved by Queen Victoria.

Beth cheers and hugs Faith tightly. 'So Mary's work is done.'

'Mary Lee's work is never done. Being in her seventies won't slow her down either; she's an advocate for so many projects: education, housing for the poor, female unionism, you name it.'

'Long live Mary Lee!' Beth proclaims, her fists held aloft as if in the midst of a suffragette rally.

A gentle tap turns their heads to the door where a tall, suited silhouette is outlined on the frosted glass. 'A gentleman caller.' Faith chuckles. 'I'll let him in.'

'Good morning ladies and congratulations on the excellent news, a giant step closer to true democracy.'

'How nice to see you again, Mr Stirling' says Faith. 'I was just about to leave to prepare morning tea, please join us.'

'I'd be delighted, thank you, Mrs Ellsworth.'

Vincent offers a colourful array of flowers and a bottle of champagne. 'For the spirited suffragettes in the household,' he smiles.

'How very kind, I'll put the flowers in a vase,' says Faith.

Vincent and Beth raise their hands to cover their ears as Faith leaves the room slamming the door behind her.

'That's a very robust door, I must say.' Vincent grins.

'Thank you for the gifts.'

'My pleasure. You look beautiful, good news becomes you.'

'Good news makes the world beautiful. After all these years it's finally happened.'

'Because women like you are fighting for their rights.'

'There are thousands of women who'd love to join us but they don't have a voice.'

'There's the next battle. Talking of which, have you heard from your brother-in-law?'

'Yes, we've received a telegram from Ramin, his mother is thrilled to have received the photographs of Sam. I guess his journey wasn't in vain.' Beth gazes into Vincent's eyes, 'I shouldn't have judged you for not sharing confidential information, I understand now.'

'May I ask what sparked your epiphany moment?'

'I know who killed Angus Hopping and Eric Emerson, but I've given my word I wouldn't tell anyone outside our agency.'

Vincent's eyes are wide open. 'I won't even hazard a guess. That would only cause a moral and legal dilemma.'

Beth looks out the window at a perfect blue sky. 'I'm not sure if all murder victims deserve justice, or pity for that matter.'

'What about the perpetrator? Do you believe all murderers deserve punishment?'

'It depends on the circumstances. It must be very difficult abiding by the confines of the law for every case you come across.'

'The law is black and white but those who can afford a competent lawyer can justify and take advantage of the grey undertones. Legal loopholes are like holes in a roof, you patch one up and another one opens. On the other hand, without law and order, there's chaos and anarchy, so we do our best with the rules we have.' Vincent stops talking and fishes for a note from his pocket. 'Before I forget, here's the ten pounds I owe you from our wager.'

'The legislation doesn't come into law until next year so perhaps we're both right. No winners, no losers.'

'It passed through parliament yesterday. I really must insist you accept your prize.'

'Would you have accepted the winnings from me if you'd have won?'

'Without a doubt. A bet is a bet.'

'Thank you. I'll quit gambling while I'm ahead.' Beth slips the note under her blotting paper pad. 'Have I told you how I admire you for helping the constabulary put O'Halloran and his cronies behind bars?'

'More than once.'

Clacking crockery followed by a teaspoon tapping the silver teapot announces tea is served.

'In anticipation the Bill would pass, I decorated some celebratory cakes with purple icing.'

'Purple icing sounds delightful.' He smiles. 'To be honest, I wasn't as optimistic as you. When Ebenezer Ward introduced a proposal giving women the right to enter parliament I thought that would stymie the Female Suffrage Bill, as did he. It's an extraordinary outcome, his subterfuge backfired and now he's a laughing stock.'

'And we ended up getting more than we bargained for.'

They move out of the office and meet Faith and Harry on the veranda where morning tea is served. Vincent asks after Sam and is told he's out shopping with Tillie.

'This is a perfect breezy spot, sheltered from the stifling heat, Mrs Ellsworth.'

'We'll probably enjoy Christmas lunch here. Beth's sister Tillie, my brother Skipp and his friend Florence are joining us this year. And our dear friend Ayishah is coming as well.'

'Would you care to join us for Christmas?' Beth asks Vincent, without thinking. 'Of course, you may have other plans.'

Vincent gazes at Beth, a twinkle in his eyes. 'I'd love to join you, thank you. I couldn't imagine a better place than right here with you and your family.'

'We'll have a wonderful time,' says Faith, gazing at the jacaranda tree spilling purple flowers all around its base, a reminder of the eternal cycle of change.

ACKNOWLEDGEMENTS

Denise George, author of *Mary Lee, the life and times of a turbulent anarchist and her battle for women's rights*. Denise's fascinating research gives an in-depth biography of Mary Lee, an advocate for social justice and a significant leader in the South Australian suffrage movement.

Many thanks to Lynk Manuscript Assessment Service for your invaluable expertise, feedback and encouragement.

All my love to Philippe Dumaine and Maureen O'Keeffe for reading my early drafts, and spotting some silly errors! Your wise comments are always appreciated.